ARKHAM HORROR

It is the height of the Roaring Twenties – a fresh enthusiasm for the arts, science, and exploration of the past have opened doors to a wider world, and beyond…

And yet, a dark shadow grows over the town of Arkham. Alien entities known as Ancient Ones lurk in the emptiness beyond space and time, writhing at the thresholds between worlds.

Occult rituals must be stopped and alien creatures destroyed before the Ancient Ones make our world their ruined dominion.

Only a handful of brave souls with inquisitive minds and the will to act stand against the horrors threatening to tear this world apart.

Will they prevail?

Also available in Arkham Horror

In the Coils of the Labyrinth by David Annandale

Mask of Silver by Rosemary Jones
The Deadly Grimoire by Rosemary Jones

Litany of Dreams by Ari Marmell

The Ravening Deep by Tim Pratt

Wrath of N'kai by Josh Reynolds
Shadows of Pnath by Josh Reynolds

The Last Ritual by S A Sidor
Cult of the Spider Queen by S A Sidor
Lair of the Crystal Fang by S A Sidor

The Devourer Below edited by Charlotte Llewelyn-Wells
Secrets in Scarlet edited by Charlotte Llewelyn-Wells

Dark Origins: The Collected Novellas Vol 1
Grim Investigations: The Collected Novellas Vol 2

ARKHAM HORROR™

The
BOOTLEGGER'S
DANCE

ROSEMARY JONES

ACONYTE

First published by Aconyte Books in 2023

ISBN 978 1 83908 251 1

Ebook ISBN 978 1 83908 252 8

Cover art by Daniel Strange

Distributed in North America by Simon & Schuster Inc, New York, USA

Printed in the United States of America

9 8 7 6 5 4 3 2 1

ACONYTE BOOKS

An imprint of Asmodee Entertainment Ltd

Mercury House, Shipstones Business Centre

North Gate, Nottingham NG7 7FN, UK

aconytebooks.com // twitter.com/aconytebooks

PROLOGUE

A dying man gifted me this blank book so I could write my thoughts, but my thoughts are birds, winging wildly toward the sky, hounds baying below them. My mind is a cemetery full of hideous sounds created by the hungry trees surrounding me. Then I hear your voice and the birds of my thoughts return to my head. I want to ask you, before I forget again, what is your name?

My name changed frequently in my life, almost every time I crossed a border or entered a new city. Many days I forget what I call myself. Then I remember a name and write it in this journal which ties me to a better world.

My name is Paul.

Forgive me. Such a terrible way to introduce myself. My words may frighten you. Do not be afraid. Please do not be afraid. One of us must be without fear. Let me start again.

My name is... but I have written down my name, at least the one that I remember.

So let me begin with a proper beginning, the beginning to the stories we whisper in the dark to comfort children. Let me start again with a sentence to hold back the night terrors. Let me speak it out loud and drown out the baying of the hounds and the whispering of the trees.

"Once upon a time, something happened. If it had not happened, it would not be told."

Let us start there. I remember so little, but I know in my bones how to start a story, even a story as strange as mine. All my life, I have listened to stories. I have taught myself languages by listening to stories.

A creaking graybeard recited "if it had not happened" every night when we were all packed together in a boxcar rolling across a vast steppe, packed as tight as fleas on a well-fed dog. The men on the outer edges of the crowd fell asleep and did not wake. We rolled their frozen bodies out the doors in the morning.

But the rest of us sat shoulder to shoulder so the old man stayed warm in the middle as the train clacked on and winter settled over all of us. His tales quieted the fear. His stories kept us alive.

I have lost so much out of my head, but I remember his tales of the wonderful twins with stars on their foreheads.

I have not seen stars in such a long time. When I first looked up here, I saw only darkness, a night without stars. So I kept my eyes on the ground. Until I heard the howling of the hounds, their terrible baying, and then I ran.

I am still running. I run through cities. I run through time. This something happened to me, but it must be told to you.

CHAPTER ONE

"Isn't it beautiful, Raquel?" my aunt exclaimed as she ushered me out of her Rolls Royce and pointed me to her latest business. The long two-story white building occupied nearly the entire length of the street. The sign high overhead proclaimed in large letters the name of the Diamond Dog. Posters plastered on either side of the double doors promised dances with live entertainment.

Snow swirled through the air while the clouds above looked like a bruise, but the glow of lights outlining the marquee made the whole street seem warmer and welcoming. The rest of the town, from what I'd seen when we'd driven across it, looked like it once modeled for an old-fashioned Currier and Ives print. With snow gilding the rooftops, and even along the edges of the well-shoveled walks, it appeared like a scene from a Christmas card.

My aunt tipped her head back to smile at the lights brightening the gloom of the December afternoon.

"Kingsport," said Aunt Nova with a look of pride that I had come to know in recent weeks, "never had a place like this. It's all the best inside. Wait until you see the ballroom.

And–" she pointed to a small door further away, "–we built the radio studio right there. We broadcast one show every day at noon and then live from the dance floor four evenings a week."

"But if they can hear the music at home for free," I said, following my aunt through the double doors and into the Diamond Dog, "why would anyone pay to come to dance here?"

Nova laughed. "It's because they hear our broadcast that they're wild to come to the Diamond Dog. Why, the phone rings off the hook during every broadcast with people asking if they can come the next week to the show." She pointed out the box office inside the lobby, a glass and brass kiosk where couples could buy tickets that allowed them an evening of frolics inside. Prices were posted on a fancy printed card resting on an easel. I noticed tickets for Friday and Saturday nights were slightly higher than Wednesday and Thursday. All promised tickets included dancing until midnight and a light refreshment during the evening.

Seeing the direction of my gaze, my aunt explained, "We have a buffet supper around 10 PM for the dancers. Just sandwiches and soup, along with coffee, tea, and other beverages."

"No liquor?" I said. Supper clubs in Boston, especially private clubs that required tickets or membership, were notoriously false fronts for the sale of illegal booze.

"No liquor," promised Nova as she walked me through the lobby. "I run a dry house in Kingsport. Not that the police completely believe that. We've had a few raids and they've looked mighty embarrassed to come up with nothing but a kettle of fish chowder and coffee on the stove."

On another easel, a separate printed poster showed pictures of the house band, extolling the keyboard virtuoso Billy Oliver and the chanteuse Harlean Kirk. Across the bottom of this lobby card, printed in red ink with letters as large and flamboyant as those spelling out the performers' names, the poster proudly proclaimed: "As Heard on the Radio."

We crossed the lobby and entered the ballroom itself. The room ran the length of the building, with a gleaming wooden floor, small tables ringing the outer edge, and a stage for the band built along the side closest to the radio studio. I'd been to public ballrooms in Boston as well as many college dances; the dance floor appeared as fine as any of those, with a very pleasant spring underfoot and beautifully polished to a honey glow.

The red velvet curtains swathing the back wall, the crystal chandeliers gleaming overhead, and the white and gold walls decorated in the art deco style showed that Aunt Nova had spared no expense in her creation of the Diamond Dog. The only question was how she could afford so luxurious a place as the owner of a small cafe known for its chowder and its apple pie.

Music swelled through the room, a welcome distraction from the niggling questions raised by even a brief walk through the Diamond Dog. I told my conscience to hush its nagging and turned toward the band.

On the stage the band was practicing, a mix of men and women playing together with exuberant style.

Oh, the music! I could not only hear the notes ricochet off the white plaster walls, but the tune shook the very floor until I felt it throughout my body. Since my illness earlier in the summer, I avoided symphonies, concerts, and even the college's tea dances. In short, I tried to never be in the same space as someone performing on the piano. The Black man on the piano played with brilliant technique as the singer beside him belted out "It's All Your Fault," one of my favorite Eubie Blake songs.

"My poor heart is aching, it's almost breaking. And it's all your fault," the song concluded with a crash of emphasis from the piano.

Aunt Nova walked across the room and said to the pianist, "Billy, I'm not sure about that one. Isn't it a bit old?"

The young man spun around on the piano stool and bounced to his feet. "Hello, Miss Malone. Why, no song ever sounds old, not when Billy Oliver plays it. I make everything sound like it was composed this morning! And everyone can dance to it."

"Oh, leave it in the program," said the singer, a slender woman who topped the dapper Billy by nearly a foot. She was a platinum blonde, with a figure so long and lean that she'd look elegant in anything that she wore. She draped one arm across the shoulders of the piano player. "I love a good heartbreak song. I heard Miss Sophie Tucker sing it once and never forgot the performance. I asked Billy to add it to tonight's list," she added.

"Harlean sings it better than Miss Tucker," declared Billy, "and everyone will love it."

"What does the rest of the band think?" said Aunt Nova

with a nod toward the woman playing the saxophone and the man behind the drum set.

"It swings," said the saxophonist. "The people listening to the broadcast will recognize it."

The drummer just gave a crash of cymbals and a nod.

Aunt Nova nodded. "I hired you to play the music so I should trust you to pick the songs."

"It will be a spectacular evening or I'm not Billy Oliver," said the piano player, reaching behind his back to give a glissando of the keys with more of a bop at the end than I'd ever heard in any concert or dance hall. The sound made my fingers itch to try it. "Who is the pretty lady? Is she here to help the radio boys with their broadcast?"

My aunt turned to me with a smile. "Come over here, Raquel, and let me introduce you to the band."

Billy Oliver hopped down from the stage, to be followed more slowly by the two women, while the drummer stayed enthroned behind his drums. From our very first encounter at the Diamond Dog that day through all the years that I sought him out wherever he was playing, I never saw Billy move slowly or even stand still for more than a minute, whether on stage or off it. When he played, all his sizzling energy poured out of him and into the piano until his audience could practically dance on the music streaming through the air. His technique dazzled me. I doubt the world will ever know another virtuoso like Billy at the piano.

"Billy Oliver," he said with a twinkle, "which you may have guessed. This is Harlean Kirk and Ginger Devine. Up there on the drums is my pal Cozy."

"We call him Cozy because he likes to be comfortable and warm. This time of year, he hardly ever ventures out beyond that drum set," said Ginger, shaking my hand. "His real name is Charles Lane, and he comes from Georgia. The New England winter has been a terrible shock to his system." The drummer gave an impatient double tap on the top of the snare drum. "He's not much of a talker either. So I do the talking for both of us."

"We call her Ginger," said Harlean, "because she is spicy hot on the saxophone."

Ginger laughed at this comment and gave Harlean a little wink. Then she said to me, "Is Billy right? Are you here to help with the broadcast?"

"No," I said. "I'm Nova's niece, Raquel Gutierrez. Why did you think I was with the radio station?"

"Because of the headset, of course," said Ginger with a nod to the gadget sitting on top of my head.

I really had forgotten that I was wearing it. Or rather, I wanted to forget I was wearing it as all eyes turned to the strange contraption. Like a home radio headset, there was a metal disk covering my left ear that amplified conversations picked up by the microphone. The earpiece was held in place with a hair band going right across my head. The round microphone swung like a pendant across my chest.

Another wire snaked into the purse over my arm which held the battery pack.

This latest model was designed for a lady, according to the salesman who looped the wires around my head and neck. He said it looked like jewelry with art deco trim covering the microphone and earpiece. "Please note this battery fits in any handbag," the man bragged as he fought to squeeze it into a new leather purse that my aunt purchased for me. My own handbags were far too small for the battery.

We purchased the listening device in New York after several doctors said it was the only solution. The thing was hideously expensive, but Aunt Nova paid for it without complaint. Everyone told me how lucky I was to have an aunt willing to give me such a marvel.

I hated it.

The hearing aid did amplify sound in my left ear, which was the better of my two ears at this point. I could hear certain people better with the hearing aid turned on than off. But the device also buzzed in my ear and created a jumble of noise which was more distracting than not hearing anything. I often reached into the purse and turned off the battery just to give myself some peace.

But I couldn't tell Aunt Nova how I felt.

Her kindness, her generosity, and her sheer enthusiasm for the hideous device made it impossible to do what I wished to do: tear it off my head and stomp it under my feet.

So I wore it. And tried to forget I was wearing the hearing aid even as the headset rubbed my ear, the microphone pulled on my neck, and the battery banged awkwardly against my hip no matter how carefully I moved.

"No, this isn't for the radio," I said and hoped to avoid further explanations. I still hadn't come to terms with the fact that a simple bout of fever left me with a significant loss of hearing in both ears, a loss the doctors predicted would only become worse. Because what was more useless than a piano teacher who couldn't hear?

"It's a hearing aid," Aunt Nova boomed. A big woman with a big voice, I could hear her with or without the device. She draped an arm around my shoulders and gave an affectionate squeeze. "The very latest technology."

This was greeted with an awkward silence as everyone stared at me.

"I could hear you even without it," I said to the musicians. "When you were playing. I felt it in my body. I've never seen anyone handle a piano like that."

Billy Oliver's face split into a wide grin while the two women groaned. "Now you're in for it," said Ginger with a shake of her head.

"I was born to play," Billy replied. "From the time I was a little baby, my hands were dancing across the keyboards. I am on this earth to make music."

"I would love to hear more," I said, and I meant it.

"You are a beautiful lady with a rare appreciation for my musical genius," said Billy with a smile so sweet that his boast was obviously meant to make people laugh. "I would be happy to play for you." Billy hopped back on the stage and seated himself at the piano.

I chuckled at his comments as he intended. I loved music in all forms and flavors and was intrigued by how Billy played. However, I knew I wasn't beautiful. The fashion in 1926 was for tall flat-chested women like Harlean or little sprites like the movie star Betsy Baxter. As a tall woman myself, I easily matched Harlean for height, but all similarities ended there. I was broad across the shoulders, and curved in all other places, just like my Aunt Nova and my own mother. What would have looked magnificent when they were young women in the nineties definitely did not suit the current fashions. Instead of trying to look like a flapper, binding my chest and bobbing my hair like one of my college students, I draped myself in sensible sweater sets and tweed skirts. I looked like what I used to be: a piano teacher, although hopefully a young and stylish college-educated teacher, not one of those old ladies in lavender and lace.

Cozy gave a tap of the drums. Billy set off with his hands flying up and down the keys of the piano. For nearly an hour, he played through a medley of songs, the latest jazz pieces and old standards made new by his improvisations. Harlean and Ginger danced on the floor to his music, pulling Nova and me into an impromptu circle. Other employees came out from the kitchen and radio station next door with a whooping shout: "Go, Billy, go!"

He just grinned and waved. The music swelled through the room. The songs shook my worries out of my head. All the anger and frustration, all the sorrow, flowed away as people grabbed my hand and swung me through the dance. They shouted their names at me, welcoming me to the Diamond Dog.

Then Billy started a boogie-woogie version of "Jingle Bells" with everyone hollering the lyrics at him as they swayed across the floor. I dropped panting into a chair beside Aunt Nova, who'd wisely left the dance floor earlier to sit on the side of the room and sip a cup of coffee.

"I never liked that song before," I said to her. As a child, the verses always disturbed me. So jolly but also so sinister, with the line about "Misfortune was his lot." However, the rest of my family adored the song and I could play it in my sleep. I certainly never played "Jingle Bells" like Billy did, and his jazz rendition made my toes tap against the floor.

Nova smiled at the raucous group gathered near the stage. "Billy can make any song into a party," she said. "Some nights he takes challenges from the floor, to see if they stump him with a tune that can't be danced to. Never have, so far. I went all the way to Chicago to recruit him for the Diamond Dog. I'm glad I did."

"He is amazing," I started to say, but the sound of barking distracted me. It sounded like a large hound in considerable distress, so I looked around the room trying to spot it. I couldn't see any dogs. I tapped the earphone of the hearing device with one finger, followed by a similar tap on the microphone. I doubted either gesture did anything for good or ill, but it made me feel better to fiddle with it, as if I controlled the device and it did not control my ability to hear the world around me. A second glance around the room confirmed no dogs, but the howls grew louder. Certain sounds, amplified by the hearing device, could mimic other things as I had found to my confusion while staying in New York. Once I believed that I heard the singing of a canary. It turned out to be a poorly oiled hinge in the hotel dining room. A fact I discovered after questioning the waiter several times and causing looks of amusement or pity throughout the dining room.

Still, this did sound like a hound baying. The deep cry started very low and very far away. When I shifted in my seat, I could swear I heard wind whistling through trees and the call of the hound grew closer. Perhaps the animal was penned up outside and echoes of its barking were sounding in the ballroom.

Just as I turned to Aunt Nova to ask her if she had a pet, the door at the far end of the hall flew open. A tall man dressed in an impeccable suit came striding in, followed by a policeman in uniform.

The music came to a crashing halt. Everyone stared at the intruders.

The newcomer pushed his glasses higher on his nose and then proclaimed with a shaking of his finger, "Do you see? I told you that they were holding illegal dances here." He pointed at Aunt Nova with her coffee cup half raised to her mouth. "And serving alcohol. Do your duty! Arrest that bootlegger."

INTERLUDE

Let me try another beginning. This one I learned from a man in the trenches of a war that I wish I could forget. Why so much of my life is lost while the memories of mud drenched in blood remain, I don't know.

"In olden times, there once was a very poor man who had no coat." My fellow soldier in the trench began his story just so.

Where I am now, I wandered for a long, long time without a coat. Before I became lost in the terrible place, I had a coat, nothing rich or fancy, just a plain black coat like a tramp might wear on a summer day. There was a reason for wearing the coat. Somebody handed it to me and asked me to wear it, but I do not remember why.

But then the hounds pursued me. I barely escaped their sharp teeth and claws. They rent my coat from my shoulders, tearing it with their bloody mouths. I ran away through a forest of trees without leaves, bare branches stretching over my head and a misty starless sky above those hungry trees.

The hounds bayed behind me, horrible mournful cries

full of every sorrow in the world and every promise to destroy me. I found a track circling under the trees and ran down it. Eventually the cries grew farther and farther away. I stayed on the muddy path going deeper into the forest despite my terror of the trees.

Have I said yet that the trees here bite? They snatch at you with long twiggy fingers and try to pull you into their open trunks, all lined with teeth and oozing green sap. Twice I narrowly missed being ground up to nothing by their ravenous mouths. I learned to stay on the path and never try to leave it. If you leave the path, the trees will eat you.

Finally, I dropped to the ground in exhaustion and woke up in an alley, surrounded by brick buildings and ashcans. In my ears was the cheerful whistle of a tune, a tune I knew but could not name. A big dog panted in my face.

I screamed, expecting the dog to tear my throat out. Bone-weary with fright, I could not run anymore. I lacked the strength to thrust the beast away. I simply lay upon the cold ground and waited to die.

"Duke, Duke," called a man's voice. "Let the poor man alone. Hey, buddy, don't worry. He's a good dog, my Duke."

The dog sat down in front of me, beating its stubby tail upon the ground. A roughly dressed man held out his hand to me, pulling me into a sitting position.

"You look half frozen," he said as I fumbled through the languages echoing in my head until I realized he was speaking English. An American by his accent, I decided.

My own English came back to me with a stuttering, hesitant "Thank you" to him.

"My name's Pete," he said with the casual friendly handshake that Americans loved so much. I worked for a time in Hollywood and all the men, and many of the women, would grab my hand just so.

I never felt so happy to be touched by another human being. This man could have kicked me or hit me and I would have wept with joy. For his touch meant that this moment was real and not a dream.

"My name is Paul," I told him as words and memories flooded back into my head now I was out of the hungry forest.

"What are you doing sleeping outside with no coat?" Pete asked as he sank down on his heels to look me in the eyes. "This is too cold a night to be sleeping rough like that. The Mission is open, Paul, if you need a bed. Nobody is going to turn you away on Christmas Eve in Arkham."

I struggled to my feet. The kind dog owner held my arm until I was steady.

"Say," he said, "don't I know you? Weren't you in Arkham a while back? Been years, but you look familiar."

I shivered and shook my head. I didn't know him, although I doubt that I would have recognized anyone, no matter how many times we had met. Memories of a forest trying to eat me overwhelmed my mind. I could barely remember my own name, much less the names and faces of others.

The air was cold, far colder than I expected. In my head it was early June and the air, even at night, should have been warm and slightly humid. But as I looked around the alley, I could see signs of snow and frost along the edges.

Large icicles dripped from the building gutter overhead. I recognized nothing. I was certain that I'd never seen this dreary place. A trio of ashcans were lined up beside a door opposite us. The dog abandoned us to sniff around these.

Pete laughed. "Duke's treasure hunting tonight. You wouldn't believe what people throw out, and just before Christmas too. You'd think with the stock market crashing they'd want to save stuff. But maybe they figure 1930 will be a better year."

Distracted by the dog, I missed part of his speech, but something sounded wrong. The last year I remembered was 1923 and everyone in Hollywood gossiping about the wealth to be found on the stock market. I rubbed my head wondering if I'd hit it or if Pete was the one confused.

Pete swung a large rucksack and a guitar off his shoulder. Carefully propping the guitar against the wall, he opened the rucksack and stuck a hand inside. "Here, Duke must have found this for you."

To my amazement, he thrust a leather jacket into my hands.

"Go on, take it," he said. "You need a coat."

With trembling hands, I took the jacket from him and pulled it over my dirty shirt. The warmth embraced me.

"Now," said Pete, humming a little under his breath as he pulled the neck of the rucksack closed, "I'll walk you to the Mission. It's not far."

I nodded, willing to follow this man anywhere, as long as it took me away from my nightmares.

"Oh, what sport," sang Pete as he strode ahead of me, whistling to his dog.

The song nagged at me. I started to ask him the name of the tune as I pulled on the coat.

But when I walked out of the alley, I stood again under the terrible trees with their grasping branches. I heard the howling of the hounds, more eerie than the wind. Pete and his dog Duke had vanished. I was alone.

So I ran.

CHAPTER TWO

When the man in the suit began shouting about arresting Aunt Nova, everyone stood completely still, staring at him. Though I could swear my microphone still picked up a faint echo of someone singing "Jingle Bells." It sounded nothing like the raucous way that Billy had been playing the tune, rather a simpler rendition of the melody in a pleasant baritone. I decided the dratted thing had picked up the song from someone out on the street. I put my hand into my purse and switched off the hearing aid.

I truly didn't need it to hear Aunt Nova reply in her booming voice, "Now, Chilton Brewster, you know that there's no liquor here. In fact, if you find one drop in any cup in this establishment, I will pay $10,000 toward your next campaign."

Again, I wondered how my aunt could speak so causally about spending thousands of dollars. Then I stifled my doubts about the legality of Nova's fortune. If she said that there was nothing wrong, I decided to believe her. The alternative was – well, I didn't know the alternative, which was why I persuaded Nova to let me spend Christmas in Kingsport.

"Furthermore, it's not illegal for my employees to rehearse for the dance tonight," Aunt Nova said to the policeman accompanying Brewster.

Brewster strode forward. With his slicked back hair, stiff clean collar, and neatly knotted tie, he appeared a wealthy businessman. His perfectly trimmed goatee and his round glasses gave him something of the look of Dr John Romulus Brinkley, the famed radio doctor.

"Nova Malone," said Brewster. "You may have gotten away with your tricks in Innsmouth, but Kingsport is a different type of town. We don't need you or your sinful dance hall here."

"The only sin is in the eye of the beholder, and this is a ballroom for the enjoyment of anyone who wishes to dance. Don't pretend it's some low-class saloon," said my aunt. She turned again to the policeman. "Well, Mac, are you arresting me for listening to my band rehearse on a Wednesday afternoon?"

"No, Miss Malone," said the man with a baleful stare at his companion. "Mr Brewster and I were just walking down the street when we heard the music. It sounded mighty fine, Billy."

Billy Oliver gave the policeman a wave from the piano stool.

Mac continued, "I told Mr Brewster that there's nothing in the ordinances about people playing music during the day. Figured you were practicing or making a broadcast. Fact is that you could even hold afternoon dances as long as the activity does not interfere with the other businesses on the street."

"Ah," said my aunt with a gleam in her eye. "A Wednesday afternoon dance might be popular in some quarters. We could serve tea and cucumber sandwiches to go with it." The last part she spoke with a fair imitation of a Boston Brahmin drawl, a direct tease, I realized, about Brewster calling her place a low-class dance hall.

"Now, Miss Nova," said the policeman, "you would have to get the agreement of the other shop owners and businesses up and down the street first. They might not like it."

"Or they might consider it a good way to bring business into Kingsport on a slow December day," countered Nova. "It's certainly something to consider."

"When I'm mayor–" interrupted Brewster, apparently realizing that the conversation was running away from him. Certainly, all attention was on Aunt Nova.

"When you're mayor, governor, or senator, you can try to change the law," said Nova. "But until then, you're a citizen like all the rest of us. Even then, you may find the position isn't as powerful as you believe. When you hear the piano playing in the Diamond Dog, you needn't come busting through the door with a policeman in tow. You're welcome to dance whenever you want. I hope you enjoy the broadcasts just as much from the comfort of your home."

"I find your broadcasts disturb the peace of our beautiful city," said Brewster. "When I am in charge, we will clean up, clean out, and keep it clean. Why, just today the Talking

Machine and Radio Men's Association sent a proposal to Congress to better regulate the airwaves."

"When they make a law, I'll run my business according to the law. I always do," replied Nova without hesitation. "You need to find a new slogan and a new topic to beat to death in those editorials you read to Kingsport every morning. Radio stations broadcast what the people want to hear. You cannot stop it any more than you can shut down the movie theaters or put folks back into horse-drawn buggies. This is America, Chilton, and Americans do love their contraptions. It's 1926 and nobody is willing to live like it is 1896. Movie theaters, automobiles, radio, and airplanes. It's all here to stay, no matter how strange you find it."

Brewster started to sputter, then he looked around the room. The looks he was getting back weren't hostile – mine was probably slightly bemused as I had no idea who he was then – but the faces weren't friendly either. So his own expression shifted, just smoothed out to a pleasant smile and slight tilt of his head.

"Miss Malone," he said to my aunt in tones which were meant to carry to everyone in the room. Certainly I could hear him almost perfectly. "We welcome new investment in Kingsport. But we cherish the atmosphere of our town as well. If you'd only come to us before you began this venture, we could all have found a way to make it more harmonious."

"I went to the mayor," replied my aunt. "I paid the fees and filled out the paperwork. I did the safety upgrades requested in your letters to the city council. You can inspect the new hose yourself since you are here."

Nova gestured at the red velvet curtain draped across the back wall. One of the men grabbed the edge and pulled it aside to display a coil of hose attached to an oversized spigot. "That's a regulation fire hose," said Nova, "connected to the town's water supply. If any fire breaks out in the hall due to it being electrified for the radio station, we can put it out before the fire station even sounds their bell. You'll note the extra extinguishers hanging on the wall as well. There are additional extinguishers in the station itself and upstairs in my apartment. I had the fire chief himself in the building to oversee the installation of all our safety measures. He told me that this is now the safest building in Kingsport."

The policeman strolled over to the wall to inspect the hose and extinguishers. "Chief was very envious of these," he said, gesturing at the copper extinguishers. "He said you had the very latest, some chemical I can't pronounce."

"Methyl bromide," said Nova. As I'd recently discovered, my aunt loved scientific discoveries and new ways of doing things. She made a habit of searching such stories out in the newspapers and magazines as well as purchasing such items as often as possible. "It's much more effective than the older combinations. I gave a few to the fire station. Even donated extinguishers to the school as well as a considerable sum toward the school's new roof."

"Your donation to the school was most appreciated," Brewster said. He didn't seem like a man inclined to stay silent for long. "The education of the young is one of the most important duties of any civic organization. Our children are our greatest resource to build a better future."

Nova stopped him from launching into a longer speech. "Happy to help the kiddies. As I said just a few minutes ago, everyone is welcome to dance at the Diamond Dog. Further, any good citizen of Kingsport can come to the radio station and contribute to our broadcasts. Mrs Jacob read her favorite ginger snap recipe on the radio just a few days ago. I understand it was popular with our listeners. There's nothing more wholesome than cookies." She chuckled at Brewster's grimace. "Bring your favorite Christmas cookie recipe to the station tomorrow and we'll put you on the air too, Chilton."

He started to frown and then with a strange quirk of his face smoothed all expression away. "I prefer to speak elsewhere," he said, but so blandly that it took all the sting out of the statement.

"Your friend Elmo's station doesn't have half the strength of mine," said Nova. "Nor half the listeners. Although I do enjoy hearing you read the headlines every morning. You must subscribe to an awful lot of newspapers."

"New York and Boston," Chilton Brewster replied almost automatically. Then he puffed himself up a bit more and his voice was again pitched to reach the back corners of the room so I could hear every word perfectly even with my hearing aid switched off. "A man should be well informed. It's my civic duty to share news of the wider world so Kingsport's good citizens are aware of the dangers outside our town." Then he looked around the room again and spoke directly to the policeman. "Mac, don't you have work to do? Let's be going. I want to talk to you about the new streetlights."

"Yes, Mr Brewster," said Mac with something that was almost but not quite a roll of his eyes.

The two left. The room broke out into such a buzz of conversation that I lost track of all the comments. When one or two people were speaking in a room, I could follow conversations as well as before my fever. Perhaps I missed a word or two, but it was usually easy to fill it in from the rest of the conversation, which is what I've done in writing my story here. I always had a knack for observation too. While not as good at lip reading as I would become, I often guessed correctly what a person was saying even when they weren't speaking directly to me.

This trick served me well as a teacher, interrupting whispered conversations at the back of the room with a telling phrase or two. My college students had called me clairvoyant. As I'd only been a handful of years older than them, it was a reputation that I cultivated to help preserve order in my classroom.

Now I had no students. Once the dean learned of my increasing deafness, my contract was terminated. If Aunt Nova had not answered my letters, I would have been forced to return home to Denver. I hated the thought of having to admit the failure of my grand dreams of becoming a concert pianist. I was sure it would ruin the Christmas celebrations for my entire family. They would be so concentrated on comforting me that there would be no joy in such a reunion. Or so I told myself. The truth was that my family had weathered a greater sorrow, but my own disappointment would sour any homecoming for me. I was barely used to the hearing aid and I dreaded exclamations from strangers. I was certain that it would be much worse to endure the same from people I loved.

I felt a tap on my hand. I looked up at Aunt Nova leaning across the table. "Lost in your thoughts?" she said with a shrewd but kind look. As we made the round of doctors, Nova often broke through my increasing moments of despair with small gestures and pleasant distractions. Shopping was her favorite hobby. She was particularly keen on jewelry and gadgets.

While in New York, we spent considerable time at Tiffany's and almost as much time in tiny walk-up offices where inventors demonstrated everything from electric bread slicers to a strange wristwatch that displayed minuscule maps printed on scrolls. The latter, claimed the inventor, would keep drivers from ever becoming lost. Nova had been intrigued with the invention until it turned out the only maps printed so far showed roads in England.

"Come and meet the rest of the Diamond Dog's crew properly. You can't dance and talk at the same time," my aunt said to me, pulling me out of my chair. "You'll like this lot. They're sure to cheer you up."

I smiled at her. Reaching into my handbag, I switched the hearing aid back on and followed her across the room.

"Let's see," said Nova. "You've met the band. Here's Reggie. He's the genius behind the radio station."

A lanky man in his early forties shook my hand. His hair, despite attempts to grease it into place, stood up in odd spikes around his head, giving him the look of a slightly puzzled porcupine. I recognized the mess created by dragging a headset on and off.

"Nice to meet you," said Reggie, shaking my hand. "Reggie Stubblefield. I'm the station's chief engineer. I keep all the equipment running so people hear sound instead of static."

"And I'm the voice of WKP," said a gentleman with a rich baritone standing next to him. An inch or two shorter and much more solidly built than Reggie, the bearded gentleman introduced himself as Johnny Carlucci. "Giovanni Carlucci, of course," he said. "But we're calling me Johnny Carl on the air."

"My dean insisted I call myself Miss Malone when teaching," I replied, "and not Miss Gutierrez."

"In my father's day they objected to Malone," said Nova, overhearing us. "I'm a bit surprised your Boston college didn't object to the Irish as well. Stuffy place. You're well rid of it."

I knew she meant to be kind, but the loss of my job still stung. The college, while small, held an outsized reputation with Boston's patrons of music. I hoped when I took the position to earn a place in the faculty concerts and, possibly, even be taken to New York to perform. All those dreams were dust and ashes, although only Nova knew that yet. As reluctant as I was to write home and tell the disastrous news to my parents, even worse would be disappointing my younger sister. Clara planned to come back east and take her studies at a similarly prestigious school. I spent many days discussing this with Aunt Nova. I feared my misadventures would end Clara's academic career before it began.

My father reluctantly agreed to my own plans of teaching at a Boston college while making his usual concerned predictions of disaster. There was no man on earth that I trusted or loved more than my father. However, his tendency to wrap all his children in cotton wool, especially after the death of my youngest brother at age eleven, sent us all out into the world aching for adventure.

My older brothers sidestepped banking careers, much to my father's dismay, to join the Navy during the Great War. David seemed intent upon climbing the ladder to admiral. My brother Luis had been bitten by the flying bug and was currently working as a consulting engineer for a company impressed by his passion for propellers.

After far too many family discussions around the dinner table, my father finally agreed that Boston was a reasonably safe city for his eldest daughter to pursue her musical ambitions. "At least she is not interested in Hollywood," he said to my mother.

Clara also scorned the movies, being intent on a career in literature. She wanted to pen intriguing mysteries for the magazines and experiment in theater, being an admirer of the writer Eleanor Nash. Clara talked of the latest trends in modern dance and how those could be incorporated into the type of performance that she longed to see. All of which, she was convinced, could only be truly experienced in New York.

To overcome our father's sure objections, we planned for her to start college in Boston while sharing lodgings with me. Then, with some distance between us and Papa, she could move to New York in pursuit of her literary adventures. However, if I didn't have a position in Boston, her dreams might well be at an end too.

I hadn't had the heart to write Clara. I didn't want to spoil anyone's Christmas with my troubles, even though my aunt kept assuring me that we would find a way to bring about Clara's college career.

Nova clapped her hands, interrupting my gloomy thoughts.

"It's the first of December," she said. "Which means we have twenty-three days until our biggest dance yet. With Christmas Eve falling on a Friday, I plan to make it a true humdinger of a party. Have the special invitations been sent?"

"Yes, Miss Malone," said an older woman in a dark blue dress. She pulled a little notebook and a pencil from one pocket. "I took them to the post office myself yesterday. The box office started selling tickets for the Christmas Eve dance today and we've already had a small rush from the regulars. Now, what shall we do next?"

Nova smiled at the woman. "Lily, you're a treasure. Raquel, come meet Lily McGee. She's the office manager for both the station and the Diamond Dog."

"I was Chilton Brewster's secretary at the bank," said Lily, shaking my hand, "until your aunt hired me away with a fancier title and a better salary."

Nova shrugged. "You deserved it. I could tell that from the first time that I met you. Besides, I need good people to keep this place humming."

"Still, I can't imagine why Mr Brewster came in here making such a fuss," said Lily. "He's been so disapproving of this project from the beginning, but it's a nice high-class business. Just what he said he wanted for Kingsport."

Nova shrugged. "Who knows why one person dislikes another? Myself, I've always thought it was a waste of time to bother about such rivalries. Now, let's decide on the decorations."

As the two fell into conversation, the crackle of my hearing aid increased to an uncomfortable pitch. Besides the two women talking in front of me, I heard a jumble of voices, like the sound of several men speaking all at once. The barking resumed, except this time it sounded more like a hound's baying. I remembered a neighbor's bloodhound sounding off with a similar mournful howl.

I moved away from the others, closer to a pair of roughly dressed men that I hadn't yet been introduced to. I was fiddling with my microphone when I swung it toward one of them. I clearly heard him say to the other, "We'll make the run tonight. It should be safe. There's almost no moon."

"Best ask Miss Malone," said the other. "She'll be hopping mad if we lose this one too." At least that's what I thought he said, although his voice was more muffled and the static of the headset continued to disturb me.

"Nah, the boys will be right where we need them," replied the first man. "Our cookie lady made sure of that."

The other made some answer, but the howling was so loud in my ears that I missed his words entirely. I twiddled the controls of the hearing aid, determined to make the thing behave or shut it off completely. According to the salesman's instructions, I was supposed to shift my body so the microphone hanging across my chest was pointing at a person speaking. I couldn't imagine anything more embarrassing than maneuvering the microphone in such a way. Nor did I want the two men to think I was trying to eavesdrop on them.

My aunt looked around for me. Seeing the men standing close beside me, her eyes narrowed and she called out, "Otis and Tim, don't you need to fetch some supplies?"

"Yes, ma'am," said one. "We're on our way."

They brushed past me without any further conversation and I promptly forgot about them due to my struggles with the hearing aid. Over the following days, I would see both men working around the Diamond Dog frequently. But they rarely interacted with the rest of the staff. Their major responsibilities were carrying in boxes of supplies or working on the truck, a large delivery van, that Nova dispatched frequently to fetch more boxes.

Disturbed by the noise generated by the headset, I left the hall entirely, searching for the dog or dogs that I heard howling. But there were clearly no hounds inside the hall. The salesman had been clear in our discussions that the range of the hearing aid was limited, but I still wondered if I was picking up more noise generated outside than he thought possible.

However, when I looked out the door leading to the street, I saw only the snow falling faster in the waning light. Kingsport still looked like a Currier and Ives picture, like the print decorating the wall of my old music studio. The dusty relic had been left behind by some other teacher with a poor taste in art. I recalled the picture's bare black trees stretching toward a sinister moon masked by wisps of clouds. I always thought it was a singularly unpleasant depiction of winter and quickly replaced it with a sunnier print by Maxfield Parrish.

The wind turned. The icy flakes of snow blew into my face. I shut the door upon the cold and went back into the ballroom to discuss decorations with Aunt Nova.

INTERLUDE

"This happened or maybe it did not." So stories began in the boiler room of the steamer as we crossed the Pacific. The stoker hailed from Cairo, and he told his tales as we shoveled coal and sweated through the voyage.

This encounter happened, maybe, after I met the man with a dog. I was wearing the leather coat, so I think it was after, except it was also before. How can I explain?

The hounds chased me. I stumbled through the woods with teeth until I saw an open space, an ocean of waves which rose and fell but did not reach the shore. All was completely still although it looked as if the water could come crashing onto the shore any second. This ocean of not waves made me giddy to look at it, but I wanted to get away from those terrible trees. So I clambered over the rocks onto the beach filled with gray grit instead of sand.

One step on the rocky shore and I fell, as you fall in a dream, with a jerk and a start. Then I was standing on a wharf. An older Black man was whistling as he loaded boxes onto his boat. I could almost name his sprightly tune. He looked over his shoulder and saw me there.

"Hello, friend," he said in an American accent. "Out late tonight?"

I struggled with the words. It felt as if I had not spoken for days but I had talked with the man who gave me my coat and that had been… well, I did not know how long ago that had been or how far I had run from the hounds.

"Good night," I said and suddenly realized in English those words could also mean goodbye. I did not want to leave. I was speaking only the truth. Now it was a good night for me. I wanted to stay. I desperately wanted to stay.

Luckily, the sailor took the meaning of my words literally and said, "It's not a bad night at all. Clear and cold, but no sign of snow yet. I mean to sail out of the harbor by midnight. Heading south. Soon it will be warm nights and sweet breezes for me and *Molly Gee*."

"Can I help you?" I said, pointing at the boxes. I meant, "Can I go with you?" but I was afraid to say that. I had tried to follow Pete out of the alley, but the hounds had found me. I had been snatched back to the terrible world of hungry trees and motionless oceans. This time, I thought, perhaps I can sail away. Some tales tell you that you can escape evil spirits by crossing water. I so wanted to escape.

"I'd appreciate your help," the man said. "I'm Leo. Captain and crew of the *Molly Gee*. She might not be the prettiest ship in the harbor but she's all mine. You're not an Innsmouth man, are you?"

I shook my head as I grabbed a box and swung it aboard the boat.

"Didn't think so," said Leo. "Innsmouth is not a friendly town. Look at them, all closed up tight. You'd never know tonight was Christmas Eve."

He pointed toward the end of the dock. I saw the dark outlines of buildings, shadows mostly against the night sky.

"I never like putting in here," he said. "There's not many who do. But it's worth my time to pick up a few commissions from the locals. Miss Malone always deals fairly with outsiders too. What with the war and all, something always needs to be taken somewhere else."

"There's a war?" I said with memories of the trenches bursting in my head. "Another one?"

"I think it's the only one," he replied. "Our boys started shipping over in June and it left even the Innsmouth skippers a bit shorthanded. Of course now that the US is in it, they say the end is coming. Maybe not by Christmas but next year for sure. Did you hear that they even established aero squadrons to beat those Germans?"

"Germany is at war again?" I shook my head. After November 11, I thought Germany was a ruined country. Were they attacked by one of those who hated them?

"Again?" said Leo without ever breaking the rhythm of picking up boxes and loading each carefully on the boat. "Oh, do you mean they've declared war on someone else? This Great War of the Kaiser seems to be stretching all around the world. But I expect it will all be over soon."

"But the war is over," I said, suddenly certain of my facts

if not of where I was. "The war ended years ago. Kaiser Wilhelm abdicated."

Leo paused his work and looked doubtfully at me. "Seems to me if Germany's Kaiser left his throne, it would be in the newspapers." He pointed at a stack of paper near the crates. He had obviously had been using them to wrap more fragile items.

I clutched at the papers. Crumpled and well-read but not old. No, every newspaper felt and smelled new. Every newspaper bore a date that was years in my past. "Policies for Allies War Conduct Settled Soon" read one headline. Another proclaimed "10 Killed, 70 Injured in Air Raids on London." I shuffled through other newspapers, reading these in disbelief. The December dates changed but the year remained the same on all of them.

"It says 1917," I said with some indignation to the man watching me with a puzzled look.

"That's because it is 1917," Leo said. "Christmas Eve. December 24."

"But I cannot be here," I said. Because on Christmas Eve in 1917, I knew I was elsewhere, at the edge of a ruined country, deep in a trench where the ground smelled like blood and death. Not on a dock in America.

Once again, I wondered if this was a nightmare. Was I dreaming of this place while in the trench as rockets exploded overhead? I do not remember my dreams from when I slept in the trenches. I remember only the terror and exhaustion as men died all around me. In those days, even this cold dock, with the smell of oil and seawater rising up through the pier, would have been a good dream.

During the war, the true nightmares happened when we were awake.

Footsteps sounded on the wooden planks, stopping my contemplation of the newspapers. A man's voice was raised in song.

"There's Cuffe," said Leo. "He'll know what to do. He's a clever chap. He writes for the magazines. Also, he is not an Innsmouth man, which makes all the difference. He comes from Kingsport."

"Hi, Leo, I found a bottle of wine. We can really celebrate Christmas before you ship off," said a rotund man with a bald head gleaming white in the moonlight. His round cheeks were nipped pink by the wind. As he stepped onto the icy dock, he teetered and flung up his arms. Leo gave a shout, hurrying to him as the other slipped and fell. Cuffe rolled as he slid, somehow landing on his back, still waving the bottle of wine above his head.

Leo stopped and chuckled. "Lucky you've had a drink or two already. But you'll feel the fall in the morning, Cuffe," said the sailor.

"Not me! But you're cruel to leave me lying here," cried the other with a mocking grin, pulling the bottle away from Leo's outstretched hand. Then he broke into song: "He laughed as there I sprawling lie."

As Leo and his friend sang the next line of the song together, they vanished. Standing on the edge of the shore with the unmoving waves, I looked at the newspaper still clutched in my hands. The date remained December 24, 1917. "Soldiers Send Xmas Greetings Back Home" said one headline on the front page.

But I lost my home long ago. I drifted around the world. Now I am sending a message to you. I hope you are still reading this.

CHAPTER THREE

During dinner, I asked Aunt Nova about Chilton Brewster and his unforgettable entrance into the ballroom earlier in the afternoon. "An odd man," I said as I dished out a second bowl of fish chowder for myself. Nova kept a spacious apartment on the second floor. Dinner had been sent up from the Diamond Dog's kitchen for my first night in Kingsport, drawn from the supper buffet created nightly for the customers in the ballroom.

"Tomorrow we'll have something more fancy. Thelma comes and cooks for me most days, but she's off tonight," Nova had said earlier, upon surveying her neat little kitchen at the back of the apartment. "There's always chowder on the stove at the Diamond Dog. Good for the dancers when they get tired, and for the performers too."

I assured Nova that chowder was all that I wanted after being in the car all day. Sitting in her quiet apartment also made conversation much easier than a noisy diner or a restaurant. I could, without any apologies, leave the headset in my bedroom, which was a relief as well.

The soup tasted very good. But my curiosity wouldn't let me enjoy dinner.

"This Chilton Brewster," I asked again. "Who is he?"

"A banker and a busybody," said Nova, pushing her chair back a bit and resting her hands over her stomach with a satisfied sigh. The lamplight winked on her purple cat brooch. She called it her lucky piece and never went anywhere without it. Despite dining at home, my aunt wore all her diamond rings and a pair of gem-studded bracelets around one wrist. Around her other wrist was a platinum wristwatch studded with diamonds, a beautiful piece that she'd purchased in New York when we had been touring jewelry stores on Fifth Avenue. Like a magpie, Nova adored anything that sparkled, but she had a particular eye for diamonds.

"Nothing like a good chowder to set a person up for a day or evening of work," continued Nova. "We never went a week, your mother and I, without making chowder when we lived in Innsmouth."

"Brewster shouted so much when he came into the Diamond Dog," I said, refusing to be distracted by family stories. Like her sister, my aunt was very good at sidestepping direct questions. But years of practice with my mother made me persist. I wanted to know more about Brewster and continued to press Nova for answers. Actually, I wanted to ask her directly about the bootlegging allegation, but talking about Brewster seemed easier. "He appeared to be so angry about your business." I emphasized the last word a bit, hoping Nova might be inspired to talk more about what she did when not planning Christmas dances and starting radio stations. "But then Mr Brewster became so very polite and quiet."

"That's Chilton. He's the strangest man. Starts an argument like any fool, shouting and waving his arms as if such actions could persuade anyone to do anything. It's all theater as far as I can tell. The minute he begins to lose his audience, or the debate turns against him, he becomes very quiet and polite. So you're left wondering if he really meant anything that he said before," Nova concluded. "His letters are worse."

"Letters?" I asked.

Nova waved a hand to a neat stack of correspondence on the polished cherrywood desk in the corner of the room. The dining room in the apartment doubled as her office on certain days, according to Nova. On other days, she worked downstairs in the Diamond Dog and still, at least once a week, went to her Purple Cat cafe to oversee its operations.

Her desk, outfitted with a phone and neat black typewriter, was set into an alcove which the builder might have meant for a china hutch or, in pre-Prohibition days, a bar.

"From the moment I moved myself to Kingsport, Chilton Brewster has been writing to me," said Nova. "He wasn't keen on my purchase of the Diamond Dog this fall. The place began as a saloon more than seventy years ago. The owners closed up when Prohibition was passed, determined to wait it out or sell at the best price possible."

"I'm surprised they waited so long," I said. Prohibition had been the law of the land for nearly six years but had been in operation even longer in Colorado. My family had never been much for drinking, other than my parents enjoying a glass of wine with dinner, and nobody at our house cared about the politics of who was "wet" and who was "dry."

My mother frequently and vocally regretted how the debate surrounding the Volstead Act almost overshadowed the granting of the vote to women, an issue that she found far more important. The swirl of discussion around Prohibition in our house largely centered on whether or not to serve wine with dinner when having guests outside of the family. The wine came from Mr Lucianno, who purchased grapes from California. My father often praised Lucianno's red for being as good as anything from France.

"Not many have a use for such a large place," Nova said about her purchase of the Diamond Dog. "I hosted dances at the Purple Cat. I knew how popular it would be if I could find a larger space, a proper ballroom with a bandstand. Also, I wanted to expand the radio station. We have a 50-watt transmitter at the Purple Cat and you could hear it all right a few miles away, especially at night, but we couldn't do much more. I saw at once this building had the ideal setup for a bigger station."

Nova's Purple Cat cafe was located very near Innsmouth, the town where she and my mother had grown up. The sisters once owned one or two buildings in Innsmouth, the legacy of their sea captain father. Nova long ago bought out my mother, who used her share of the inheritance to invest in my father's bank. My mother never spoke about why she left Innsmouth and never expressed any interest in returning to the town. I had never seen the place but understood it to have fallen on hard times. Nova's comments about Innsmouth were almost as vague as my mother's, except she had been living there until her recent move to Kingsport. From one or two comments dropped when we were in New York, I had the feeling that Nova wanted to avoid the place.

Still not answering my questions about Brewster, Nova instead chattered about her plans to expand her radio station in Kingsport. "This building has a nice flat roof for our antenna, and we upgraded the transmitter too. A Western Electric 1,000-watt!" I must have looked properly baffled because Nova laughed and said, "Let's just say I've had my eye on the Diamond Dog for some time. It's perfect for my plans. But I was only able to buy the building in October and Brewster wasn't happy. He wanted to run the one and only radio station in Kingsport, but he broadcasts barely two hours each morning with a 250-watt transmitter run out of his friend Elmo's house. Kingsport might hear him but very few others can. I told Brewster he could have his morning broadcast. I never go on before noon here. Although who wants to listen to a banker read headlines, I don't know. He also gives a little editorial about ways to clean up the town, practicing for his political career, and some rather decent advice related to his savings and loan business – how to calculate the cost of a mortgage and such things. So some of his broadcasts are useful. I'm thinking of adding more like that to our station. Amazing how many folks don't understand business and should."

When we talked, Nova was always happy to share her thoughts about everything from air travel to the robbery of the Bradley home headlined in the newspapers while we were in New York. But when I asked questions about her more immediate past, she was quick to turn our discussion to innocent memories of times shared with my mother when they were children.

As a banker's daughter, I couldn't automatically disapprove of Brewster or easily dismiss his reservations about Nova. Given my family's own attitude toward Nova's wealth as well as the accusations shouted downstairs, I wondered if the allegations of bootlegging might have finally driven Nova from Innsmouth. She'd been remarkably quiet about where she was and what she was doing earlier in the fall.

We had our suspicions in the family about Nova's nearly inexplicable wealth. It was one of those questions that my mother was so good at avoiding, but nobody who read newspapers could be unaware that bootlegging existed everywhere. It could be as innocent as a neighbor making a few bottles of wine for friends every year, or as dire as the stories coming from New York and Chicago about the gangs there. I doubted Nova bothered with brewing "Sugar Moon" or the other hootch generated from homemade stills. But she was definitely a woman of means, and it was hard to imagine how she could have achieved so much through completely legitimate business enterprises.

Still, I liked her enormously. Illness might have forced me to request her assistance, but I was glad to spend time with my aunt. It had been a lucky day when I wrote to her using the address reluctantly supplied by my mother when I moved to Boston.

My mother had given me my aunt's information with many warnings that I was only to contact her sister if I could not wait for help from Denver. Aunt Nova was only hours away from Boston while it could take days for my parents to make the journey from Denver.

"But only if you absolutely must," repeated my mother, pressing the folded piece of paper into my hand. My father pretended that he did not hear our conversation. While my mother often spoke of her sister fondly, she would quickly follow such statements with a sorrowful shake of the head and a reminder that Aunt Nova was not a good example for us children. This speech drove my brothers and sister wild with curiosity but both parents would then retreat into diplomatic silence when peppered with our questions. My father relied heavily on, "You must ask your mother about her sister." My mother simply said, "Not now, dears, I'm busy."

"You must write," whispered my sister Clara to me the night I received Aunt Nova's address from our mother. "It may be your only chance to meet the fabled Nova Malone."

Aunt Nova was famous in our family for the Christmas gifts which arrived each December, shipped from the most expensive department store in Boston. Other peoples' aunts might send socks or similar sensible items, but our aunt sent the most marvelously impractical gifts.

Christmas packages from Nova brought such things as a wind-up tin train that blew real smoke out of its funnel if you lit a string – although we were only allowed to wind it up and run it through the house without the smoke and sparks. My mother pronounced the train's string a fire hazard after my father lit it and ran the clockwork toy under our Christmas tree. Only one or two branches were scorched, but the train never belched smoke again.

Other gifts included musical instruments such as drums and trumpets (again my mother sighed but allowed us to keep them); porcelain dolls with beautiful brunette curls and long-lashed brown eyes which closed when the doll's head was tipped just so ("Where did Nova find those?" exclaimed my father, who had been dismayed by all the blonde and blue-eyed dolls that we exclaimed over in the toy shop); and for my baby brother when he was seven, the most fierce and terrible pirate costume complete with a plumed hat and a shiny metal cutlass that could actually slice an apple in half ("Oh no!" exclaimed both our parents, but my brother Benny slept with his sword until the day he died).

Our older brothers almost died with envy when they saw the pirate costume. However, that particular Christmas, David and Luis were already enlisted men and recipients of generous checks from Nova, along with a letter from her to use the money for whatever needs that they had as sailors. The pirate costume did much to comfort Benny following the departure of his older brothers in their Navy uniforms.

For my mother, a second letter from Nova similarly consoled her as her two oldest boys, both under the age of twenty, departed for a war which had claimed so many men and ships. "She will always help," she whispered to my father as they sat with hands clasped and made brave smiles at my boasting brothers. "Nova may be a bad woman at times, but she never forgets those that she loves."

Aunt Nova might have had a checkered past, at least according to whispers between my parents and frustratingly vague comments to us children. But her gifts remained magical and highly anticipated. Even as we grew older, Nova's gifts continued to be both thoughtful and delightfully impractical, as well as notably more expensive in the last six years since Prohibition started. I owned a sterling silver desk set, marked as coming from Tiffany's, and Clara received a dresser set, also in silver, from the same store. Upon my graduation from college, Nova sent a string of pearls with a congratulatory note of such warmth and pride that I kept her letter tucked in my jewel box too.

When illness derailed all my plans, I wrote to Nova rather than my parents. It seemed easier to admit to a slightly mythical figure all that had gone wrong in my life rather than deal with the very real fear and grief of my family.

And Nova had come up with a fantastical solution in the form of a very expensive hearing aid. Only it wasn't the solution that I wanted. It wasn't a return to my life as it was before I fell ill.

A now familiar twinge of guilt drove me to smile and ask my aunt, "How can I help with this Christmas Eve dance?"

Nova looked very pleased but asked in a slightly troubled voice, "So you're sure you want to stay through Christmas? What will you tell your parents?"

I reached across the table and squeezed her hand in the same manner she had used to reassure me so many times in the past weeks. "I'll tell the truth. I'm delighted to spend Christmas in Kingsport with my marvelous Aunt Nova and learn a little more about my mother's family. Perhaps we can go see your old home in Innsmouth."

What I would leave out of the letter was all my doubts and fears about my future. There would be time enough in the new year to write about what came next.

Aunt Nova patted my hand and then pushed back from the table. "No trips to Innsmouth," she said. "It's a bad time of year to visit. Besides, we'll be too busy in Kingsport. I'm heading downstairs to check on the crowd."

From the vibrations under my feet, it felt like the band was in full swing. "I think I'll read for a bit," I said, "and then go to bed."

"Whatever you like," said Nova, rinsing off the dishes and piling them in the kitchen sink. "Thelma will cook breakfast and deal with these. I keep threatening her with a dishwasher, but she has taken a strong dislike to every model that we have looked at. She claims they don't clean nearly as well as she does."

"I didn't know about dishwashers for the home," I said. One of our major duties as children was to wash the dishes after the meal. When my brothers complained about the task, my mother told them that it was good to know that for every plate that they dirtied, somebody had to clean it.

"Josephine Cochrane invented a very good model for a hand-powered dishwasher," said Nova, surprising me again with her knowledge of gadgets. "But there's been a number of electrified models installed in large hotels and restaurants. I'm thinking of getting one of those for downstairs at least."

She checked the soup pot. "Maybe enough for lunch,"

Nova decided, thrusting the pot into a gleaming new Frigidaire Electric Refrigerator. I'd read magazine advertisements for such refrigerators, but never seen one in somebody's home. Back in Denver we still used an actual icebox.

Nova swept by her desk, gathering up Chilton Brewster's letters, and dropped all of them into a drawer that she locked. She pocketed the key. "Goodnight," she said.

"Goodnight," I replied. When she left the apartment, I realized that she'd never answered my questions about why Chilton Brewster was so angry with her.

INTERLUDE

When I was a boy, I lived for a little time with traveling people. I, who had no home, found a place with folk who forever moved but were always with their family. All the rest of the world treated them as strangers no matter how many times they passed on the roads through their towns. The traveling people, too, treated me as an outsider, but they were kind. "Far, far away, across the great waters," the old women would begin when they told the tales of those they had left behind.

I kept returning to the beach that wasn't a beach. I couldn't find my way back to the dock. I wanted so badly to see the real ocean again. I wandered farther and farther along the shore. Things watched me from the shadows beneath the trees, things with eyes like flames, but if I didn't look directly at them, then they didn't move toward me.

Like before, between one step and the next, I found myself walking down an ordinary street. Snow crunched under my feet. As I passed beneath a slightly open window, I heard a man singing about his longing for a Christmas like the ones he had known before. Transfixed by the sad song, I stood on the street, my heart breaking even though Christmas never meant much to me. But this song was not about the day. This singer yearned for a home.

The song ended. I heard another man's voice saying, "There it is, folks, your most requested song for Christmas Eve, 1944. Just know all around the world our boys are listening to Bing Crosby and thinking of you too."

More music came on and I realized that I was hearing a radio, although the broadcast was clearer and more distinct than any I had heard in Los Angeles. When I lived in California, radios were not common. But that was more than twenty years in the past if this really was 1944. I knew a man who liked new inventions, and he talked me into seeing a demonstration of a radio broadcast. Fred claimed such things would be common in the future. I wondered if I was dreaming about Fred's future or actually living it.

The smell of pipe tobacco drifted out onto the street.

A woman's voice from the room inside said, "Close the window, Michael, and I'll put away the dishes."

"In a minute, old girl," responded a man's voice. "One last puff and a look at the moon tonight."

"Oh, your smelly pipe," she said, but there was great warmth in her voice. "Turn off the light if you're going to open the window. Don't forget the blackout rules!"

The window slid up higher and an old man leaned out. He had a large pipe clenched between his teeth. His head was tilted to the stars. I must have made some noise because he turned his face to me.

"Oh," he said as he spotted me standing there in the

shadows of the street. Like all the others that I had met, he spoke with a crisp American accent. "You're not the patrol, are you? I turned off the light."

The minute he said it, I realized no light shone from any window or streetlamp. I could not remember ever seeing any town so dark in America and wondered where I was.

"Strange," he continued, looking up and down the street. "To see our streetlights out. I used to complain all the time about the lights shining in when I was trying to sleep. But now I hate to see Kingsport like this. Still, you can see every constellation tonight."

I looked up. The waning moon shone clear overhead.

"It looks so beautiful," I said, for I had not seen the moon and the stars in such a long time.

"Does, doesn't it?" the man replied. He knocked out the last burning bits of tobacco from his pipe. The shreds fell like small burning stars onto the snow below the window.

"Shh," said the man with a chuckle. "Don't tell the wife! She hates when I leave ash outside. Hopefully it will snow later tonight. Then we'll have a truly white Christmas tomorrow."

He dropped the pipe into a pocket and started to slide the window shut. "Merry Christmas," he called to me.

I stepped toward the window, intent on asking him for help, when a woman spoke behind me.

"You don't belong here," she said.

Startled, I turned to face her in that unlit street. I could only see her outline, a shadow visible due to the pale snow and moonlight. The tilt of the head, the line of her shoulders, and something else, a scent perhaps, told me that the dark shape standing there was a woman. But I couldn't judge her age or see her face clearly. I could hear her voice though, and it was a weary voice. The voice of one who has long ago cried out all her tears and carried her fury at loss under her heart. It was the voice of the orphan, the one without home or family, with strength and protection like broken glass glittering in her speech.

"Agent Adams," a man called from the darkness behind her. "I think we've found it." A flash of red light came from the space between the buildings.

"Coming," she yelled. Looking at me, she raised her hands to her breast and lifted a round object dangling from a chain. Something about it made me uneasy. I had never seen it before, I was certain, but still her amulet reminded me of the forest with teeth.

"It's starting to move!" screamed the man. "Oh, oh, no! That's not possible. Agent Adams!"

"I can't help you," she said to me. "Not here, not now. I am sorry but you must go." She whirled around, racing toward high-pitched screams and squeals of agony.

To my shame, I retreated from the cries. My heart hammered in my chest as terror once again crept over me. The smell of rotting vegetation wafting from the alley covered the street like a damp fog. In the darkness I could not tell where the woman was. Disoriented, I spun around, fumbling for the wall of a building or anything that would give me my bearings.

The window nearest to me opened and the pipe-smoking man leaned out. "What's happening?" he said. "I thought I heard something."

The radio inside his apartment sang out with a merry jingle of bells.

The crunch of snow under my feet became the crunch of sand on an empty beach. When I looked up, there were no stars and no moon.

CHAPTER FOUR

On Friday I watched Reggie set up the microphones for the evening's broadcast. "So many cables," I remarked to Harlean.

"It's a mess," she agreed. Dressed in trousers and a white shirt with a sweater thrown across her shoulders, Harlean waited for Reggie to finish cabling her microphone so she could sing a few test phrases into it. "I'm always having to watch where I put my feet so I don't trip over anything."

"Someday this will be wireless," Reggie told me.

"And all the instruments will be electric," proclaimed Harlean, "if Reggie has his way."

"I'm almost ready to show the world my ideas for electric amplification," Reggie said. As always, his hair stood up in spikes around his head and his own shirt was coming untucked from his exertions. "You could take parts of a phone and use those to amplify the sound. It's just a matter of wires connecting the piano to a speaker."

"I don't know if the world is ready for Billy Oliver to be any louder, Reggie," said Harlean.

Reggie mumbled something that I didn't catch and then crawled under the tiny stage with a trail of cords following him.

"The man's obsessed with microphones and amplifiers and who knows what else," said Harlean to me. "He thinks electricity makes everything better."

"It's a crazy time," I said. "I think there's new inventions every week. But I enjoyed listening to the broadcasts, even the one with Chilton Brewster."

"Mr Brewster lacks poetry," Harlean agreed, "but he does pick some interesting headlines to read."

Nova switched on her radio almost as soon as she got up. For breakfast, we sat at the dining table while Thelma served up fried eggs and hot coffee. Then, to the sounds of Thelma splashing in the kitchen, we listened to Chilton Brewster reading the day's headlines with occasional comments from a man named Elmo about the expected weather and predictions for the coming year from the Farmer's Almanac.

At noon, just in time to accompany lunch, the deep voice of Johnny filled the room. Perhaps it was family prejudice, but I enjoyed Johnny and Reggie on the radio much more. They also gave a little news, mostly culled from local newspapers rather than the New York headlines that Chilton read, along with comments on the weather and tidbits about people who lived in Kingsport. Quite a few of these stories centered on businesses in the town. Nova revealed over our sandwiches that she'd arranged for local shops to "sponsor" the program in return for being included in the broadcast.

As they talked, the two men often joked with each other and invited the listener into their stories. Then a woman named Mrs Daisy read her favorite sugar cookie recipe with accompanying exclamations and silly asides about ingredients from Johnny. The man made the statement "Two more spoonfuls of sugar would be truly as sweet as you" sound positively flirtatious but in the most endearing manner possible, rather how a younger Johnny might have teased his aunties during the holiday baking. We could almost hear Mrs Daisy blushing with delight as she responded.

After Reggie complimented Mrs Daisy again on how tasty her recipe sounded, Johnny invited everyone listening to tune back in later in the evening to hear a live broadcast of the dance at the Diamond Dog. Altogether I thought it quite a charming way to spend an hour and could see why people enjoyed the noon show.

Nova clicked off the dial and nodded with satisfaction. "We used to broadcast our dances from the Purple Cat," she said to me, "but it was much harder to pick up. Some nights they tell me that you can hear our Diamond Dog broadcasts all the way to Canada. The noon broadcast may not travel as far, but it's popular."

When I went down to the Diamond Dog later to watch them set up the stage, I asked Reggie about how far the broadcast traveled. The answer that I received was confusing.

"During the day you can't expect more than a hundred miles, and that's only in the best of circumstances for your groundwave," he said. "But at night, the skywave can bounce the signal much further."

After that, Reggie tried to explain the differences between groundwave and skywave, and how the earth's atmosphere changed how far radio signals could travel. I understood a little of it, having grown up with a pack of brothers fascinated by all the changes happening in the world. Spending time with Nova, who thought nearly every invention an invitation to a brighter future, also helped.

But Reggie's passion for radio eclipsed even Nova's love of gadgets. It became clear that all advances in listening and hearing devices intrigued Reggie. Every time his gaze drifted below my chin I could tell he was staring at my microphone swinging from its cord. Once or twice he almost reached for it but caught himself before committing any breach of etiquette. In another man, I might have found this attention annoying, but Reggie reminded me strongly of Junior, a high school friend of Luis, who could spend hours talking about airplanes. So caught up in his interest, Junior would often forget all good sense and manners, desperate to impart knowledge to whoever would listen.

Finally, Reggie said to me, gesturing at my hearing aid, "It's like your headset. If we could bounce the signals in the right way, you could be standing here but listening to conversations in Los Angeles. Not just what comes through your microphone."

"But why would I want to listen to people in Los Angeles?" I asked. The thought of voices or sounds coming from far away was vaguely disturbing. I'd caught enough distortions of ordinary noises on the microphone as it was. As much as the salesman had promised clarity from the device and renewed confidence from hearing "every word spoken," I still found the hearing aid more bedeviling than divine.

When I put it on that morning, I could have sworn I heard someone scream. But I'd rushed through the apartment to find only a bewildered Thelma and bemused Nova drinking their first cups of coffee together in companionable silence. The memory of my blunder made me blush hours later.

"I don't think I want to hear someone in California," I added to Reggie.

"Oh, it's fascinating how far sound waves can reach," Reggie replied. "On my own equipment, I've contacted other operators in England some nights. The farthest that I've gotten the signal to work is Nottingham."

"As in Robin Hood?" I asked.

"Exactly." He grinned. "It's quite a thrill when you pick up an international signal."

Johnny walked by. Seeing my confusion at his friend's last statement, he added, "Reggie's talking about his home radio, not this station. He's a ham."

Now I was absolutely baffled. I'd heard bad actors being called hams but didn't think that was what Johnny meant. I wondered if I'd heard the word incorrectly. "A ham?" I repeated with some reluctance. I hated repeating words back at people – I thought it made me sound witless – and preferred to fill in the blanks in my head rather than admit that I hadn't heard what they said. But Reggie's discussion was intriguing and I wanted to know more.

"Home radio operator or amateur radio," said Reggie. "We started a club in college. Got shut down by the war, of course. The Navy didn't want any of us broadcasting and messing up their signals."

"Or giving away their ships' positions to the enemy," Johnny drawled.

That I understood. We'd all worried about the ships and the men sailing on them during the war. Anything which kept them safe was paramount.

"Like a U-boat would have cared about anything we said," Reggie declared. "But Congress finally gave us our radio waves back. Then Miss Nova moved to town and offered to set up this station."

"Did you know my aunt before she came here?" I asked.

"No," said Reggie. "I listened to the broadcasts from the Purple Cat and liked how they handled those. Then I heard she'd bought this place and was looking for an engineer."

"Reggie's dream come true," said Johnny. "A rich lady interested in radio. Most women run farther than the sound of his voice, skywave or no skywave, when he starts on the future of broadcasting."

Reggie just grinned at Johnny, which told me that this was an old tease between the two, much like their banter on the show earlier that morning. "Like you didn't want to be on the radio as soon as Miss Nova offered you a job."

"I wanted the job," Johnny admitted. "I love the sound of my own voice. Even more than Chilton Brewster. Someday I'm going to be a great star."

"Well, you're already famous in Kingsport," said Harlean, joining our conversation. Then she told me, "Half the women who come to the dances want to see Johnny and hear him talk."

"And the other half?" said Johnny.

"They've already been out on a date with you," said Harlean. To me, she said, "If your aunt hasn't warned you, he's known as One-Time Johnny. He only asks a lady out to dinner once. When the evening is over, it's over. He never calls again."

"False claims by jealous rivals! However, I do see all my dates to their door like a perfect gentleman and never even steal a kiss," said Johnny.

"I think that's why they are all so mad at you," Harlean replied. "But it doesn't stop the others from trying to catch his attention."

Johnny just chuckled and strolled out the door. I stayed with Harlean to watch Reggie setting up the microphones and cables until he, too, disappeared back into the studio to check out something to do with the evening's broadcast. I felt a twinge of envy at his industry. He had plenty to do. Simply being an observer was an odd feeling for me. I had spent years in school and then teaching, always with plenty of plans for what would come next. Derailed by my illness, my plans were useless. Less than six months ago, if anyone asked me what I wanted to be, where I wanted to be, in five years' time, I could have answered them in precise terms. Now I simply did not know.

"What do you think about our setup at the Diamond Dog?" asked Harlean, interrupting my melancholy thoughts.

"It's fascinating," I admitted, smiling at her. As glamorous as she was – and even in her daytime clothes, she looked like a star from the silver screen – Harlean seemed genuinely kind and welcoming. I took a renewed interest in the bustle all around me. "When I was younger and played in school concerts, I always liked those moments before the concert began. The anticipation of what came next."

"That's the very best part," said Harlean. "Better even than the applause. Even when I feel like puking out my guts in the bucket behind the curtain."

"I know the feeling," I said. "You too?"

"First time that I went on the stage in *Shuffle Along*, I thought I'd die, but it was the most glorious night of my life. That's how I met Ginger and Billy, they were both on the tour."

"I didn't know there were any white singers in the cast," I said. The musical was famous for its all-Black cast, composer, and director.

Harlean shook her head at me. "I'm not white," she said. "My parents were light enough to pass in the north, but we never lied about who we were." She pointed at her platinum blonde bob. "And this is hair dye, honey."

I felt like a fool, but Harlean stopped my string of apologies.

"It's all right. You're not the first to make that particular mistake," said Harlean. "You're Nova's niece. I never met a woman who tried harder to make everyone welcome. Besides, you told Billy that his playing was magical yesterday."

"It is," I said. "I've never heard anyone as good." I meant it too. My only surprise was Billy played in such an out-of-the-way venue. The Diamond Dog was impressive, but Kingsport was no New York or Chicago. In either city, Billy's band would be in high demand.

Harlean smiled. "I think he's marvelous too. That's why

I'm here, that's why I talked Billy into taking this gig with Nova. Someday the world's going to appreciate Billy's talent. I think her idea of broadcasting the dances on the radio is the way to succeed. We'll make everyone listen to what he plays before they can judge Billy on how he looks. Reggie and Nova believe we'll be able to broadcast from coast to coast. And not too far in the future. We could become the dance band of the nation. Even if they ban us in the South. But don't say anything to Billy about my plans and dreams. I'm working on this with Nova. Billy thinks it's success enough just to play for a crowd in a place like this. I like to talk about what will happen in the future, but he wants to talk about what to perform today. Sometimes I think we understand time completely differently. But I know Billy can be a big success!"

Looking at Harlean's determined face, I was sure that she would succeed. Billy was too big a talent to only play ballrooms and nightclubs. If more people could hear him, he would become a sensation. Remembering Harlean's singing during the band's practice session, I felt she also deserved fame and fortune. Nova's radio broadcast seemed to be feeding many people's dreams, including those of Reggie, Johnny, and Harlean. I just wished I had a dream of my own to hitch to that particular star.

"Success at what, darling?" said Billy, bouncing into the room, obviously catching just the end of Harlean's speech. The man walked like he was attached to springs. He hugged Harlean and waved at me.

Harlean bent and kissed him soundly on the mouth. "Why, making everyone dance tonight! I was telling Raquel that this is going to be the best show. We shake out all our early week blues in the Wednesday dance and by Thursday, we're truly sparkling. The crowds just keep getting bigger and bigger as the week goes along."

"Of course they keep coming," said Billy. "I'm playing, and you're singing. Ginger and Cozy have us all hopping. There's nothing but joy as the gentlemen and ladies dance at the Diamond Dog. And they can hear that all the way to Arkham thanks to our radio station."

I tried not to be jealous, but I was. Just a little. Because they would perform, and I could only watch. Harlean was right. Billy would get better and better. All I could hope for was to be able to hear him play. With my hearing slipping away, I would certainly never perform again.

And I would sell my soul for a chance to change that future.

INTERLUDE

Once there was a faithful servant full of good advice and I met him today. If that is not the opening of a story, it should be.

One moment I was beneath the trees, wondering if I should walk into their mouths and end my misery, and the next I was standing outside the door of a tavern. The windows were brightly lit and cast squares of warm yellow light upon the snow. The door swung open. A group of men pushed past me, singing with their arms around each other's shoulders. I stepped inside.

It reminded me of the Bierhallen of my youth. A long bar ran down one end of the room where a giant of a bartender slung mugs upon the counter. Two equally round women gathered these mugs up on trays and moved amid the crowd of men and women seated around the tables. They plunked down the full tankards and plucked up the empties.

"Drink up, drink up," cried the bartender. "Get your whistles wet tonight because next month we're all dry!"

The crowd gave a lusty boo and drained their mugs with shouts for more.

The buzz of conversation convinced me that I was still in America, but where or when I had no idea. In all my time in this country, I had never known it to have such a beer hall. Such things were illegal unless the beer was nonalcoholic. But judging by the red faces of the patrons, and the fumes rising around me, this was beer as the Germans brewed it in the north: light golden in color with a dry hoppy smell.

A fireplace filled one end of the room. Drawn by the warmth, I slid between tables toward it. One table stood a little to the side, half tucked into the corner between the wall and the fireplace. A very soberly dressed man sat there with his feet in well-polished half boots, toes and heels lined straight and tight against each other. What little hair remained on the back of his head was thin and gray. With a high shiny forehead and deep lines under his eyes and nose, I judged him to be a man of mature years. In front of him was not a mug of beer but a small glass containing a red liquid which glimmered in the firelight. Opposite him was the only empty chair in the place.

"May I sit here?" I asked him as one of the waitresses jostled me in passing.

He raised his eyes from contemplation of his glass and nodded. When I sat down quickly to avoid another waitress with a full tray, he spoke. "When one is in service, it comes as a small gift to be served. Every Christmas Eve, I allow myself one hour after the end of dinner and before the final preparations for tomorrow for a glass of sherry in a quiet bar."

"More beer, Hans!" shouted the crowd.

The man across the table sighed. He sat very neatly,

elbows tucked into his sides and his hat balanced upon his knee. "I rather underestimated the impact of the Volstead Act. With less than a month to serve his beer, Hans has been encouraging these crowds. I understand that even though he will close tomorrow, the family intends to be open as early as they can on December 26 and stay open every possible day until January 17."

The warmth of the fire, the shouts of the crowd, and the smell of beer, enough of which had sloshed upon the floor to add both odor and stickiness to the bottom of my shoes, all threatened to overwhelm me. I struggled to talk but the old man appeared to take no notice, continuing his conversation more with his glass than with me.

"Carson Sinclair," said the old man with a tap of one finger on his chest. "I have completed so much today including wrapping the master's presents and leaving them under the tree for the children." He looked a little sad. "It seems a great pity to me when a man relies on his servants to purchase his gifts. The master would do better to spend more time with his family." He sighed and shook his head. "I speak out of turn. It must be the season. There was a time when the house was very festive, and the family used to play little jokes with hidden packages and riddles to solve on Christmas Eve to find the prize on Christmas Day. Such games and parties. As a younger man, I remember candles in all the windows and garlands. There was a feeling then, throughout the house, a feeling of joy. That's the trouble with growing old. Along with a certain creaking in the knees, one finds oneself falling into melancholy during the holidays."

"I have no such memories," I said, thinking back to long winter nights alone as a youth and as a man. "This time is simply dark and cold, and I do not think it will change."

The crowd behind me began to sing, the same song that the gentlemen leaving the tavern a little earlier had belted out. This time the singers treated the song as a round, one part of the tavern singing one line and another group picking up the next.

Carson glanced up and the look he gave me was very shrewd. Although I had said so little, I felt as if he perceived my bewilderment and sorrow.

"Take heart," he said to me as the song rose in volume. "You are still a young man. There is time, there is always time even for us who are older, to dream of a world much improved. At least the terrible war is over, and they say that it is the end of all wars if the League of Nations comes to be. If you will allow me to be a touch sentimental in this season, we must hope that even a single act of service can significantly help others. I must believe this is the truth, for the sake of the children."

He picked up his glass of sherry and saluted me with it. "Take my advice," he said. "A single step can place you on a better path, if you are willing to take it."

Once again, I stood in that terrible forest. My shoes were damp and smelled of beer. My coat gave off the tang of woodsmoke. I looked into the mouth of the tree, the gaping red ring of teeth and monstrous tongue, and I stepped away.

CHAPTER FIVE

On Monday, Nova insisted that I walk around the town. I'd stayed as close to the apartment as possible during the weekend, spending most of the time in my room and listening to the Saturday night dance on Nova's radio rather than joining in downstairs. I decided Harlean was right. Billy's performances were just as electric on air as in person.

As far as I was concerned, staying inside avoided any awkward conversations about the contraption on my head. But Nova obviously belonged to the generation who believed walking was essential for good health. Or perhaps she'd had enough of a niece brooding in her living room. "Kingsport is quaint," she said. "And far more friendly than Innsmouth. Take a stroll, enjoy the fresh air, and," in the longstanding habit of mothers and aunts, she added, "here's a list of a few supplies that we need. Nothing too much. Tell the shops to deliver to the Diamond Dog."

The sky was a deceptive blue, looking as innocent as a summer sky, but the cold definitely nipped my cheeks and nose as soon as I ventured outside. I wrapped my fluffy red scarf more tightly around my neck. The heavy wool coat that I'd brought from Colorado was barely enough for wandering the streets in a New England winter. The dratted headset was cold against my left ear, the metal earpiece feeling like ice even though I had covered my head with a knitted cap. I deeply regretted wearing it for my walk around town but lacked the courage to turn back and take it off.

Nova would have noticed if I went out without the hearing aid. She smiled so broadly, practically beaming, when I fidgeted it onto my head earlier. Nova's fascination with gadgets was actually quite endearing. I'd never known another so obsessed with contraptions. The gleaming new electric refrigerator might hold pride of place in her kitchen, but she also possessed an electric toaster, a Hoover vacuum cleaner, and, of course, a very fine radio.

A heavy truck rumbled down the street and turned the corner at the far end of the Diamond Dog. I spotted Otis behind the wheel, which meant yet another delivery to the back door. There'd been a similar, or perhaps the same, truck idling under my bedroom window much earlier that morning. When I'd glanced out the window, I'd caught a glimpse of Otis and Tim unloading heavy wooden crates and carrying the boxes into the Diamond Dog.

I told myself that those boxes contained nothing more than supplies for Nova's upcoming dance. If any crates clinked, I was too far away to hear it, even with the headset turned on.

As Nova claimed, Kingsport was charming, or at least what people expected of a small town in winter. The streets did have an unexpected way of twisting, so I found myself circling the same block twice with no idea how I'd arrived where I started. I thought the town's founders were a bit too fond of clever cul-de-sacs and wondered who designed the labyrinthine tangle of streets. However, given the age of many houses, I suspected that some of the maze was caused by the inevitable building, tearing down, and then rebuilding that cities further west had not yet been obliged to suffer through.

Since hurrying was not a necessity, I lingered on the sunny side of the streets, enjoying the leisure to work my way through Nova's list of needed items. Also, Nova had proved to be right. The more I walked, the better I felt. Many of my worries were forgotten as I allowed myself to be distracted by the holiday displays of the merchants.

Piles of merchandise gleamed in the store windows, designed to tempt the younger members of the community. At the hardware store, a shiny red bicycle and an even more brightly painted toboggan were prominently displayed. A crowd of small boys stood outside the window, chewing on candy cigarettes to impress each other with their swagger, but unable to keep their eyes from straying to the bike and the sled.

I laughed at the sight, so much like my own brothers that I felt a little homesick. Then I hurried into the nearby five-and-dime to find the notions on my aunt's list. The door gave a merry jingle when I opened it. The plump lady in a gingham dress behind the counter put down an angel doll with a porcelain head, fine feathered wings, and fluffy skirts made of silvered lace.

"That's a pretty thing," I said with a nod at the doll.

She smiled at me. "My grandmother ordered dozens of heads years ago for ladies to make up their own dolls. Somehow the box got stored away and the doll heads were never put out. I only found it a year or two ago." Looking closer at the angel, I saw it did have the black painted curls of the last century. The glazed white porcelain face sported very pink cheeks and dots of black glaze for the eyes. "Little girls don't want such dolls," said the shopkeeper. "They want bisque heads and open-and-shut eyes. But my older ladies remember these with affection. I make them up as angels and they buy the dolls as decorations."

"It's very clever," I said. I wondered briefly if my aunt would like such a decoration, but it seemed too sentimental for her. It was hard to imagine Nova playing with such a doll, even as a child. My mother, on the other hand, adored decorating the house at Christmas and rarely left any corner untouched. "I'll buy it," I decided. "Can you wrap it for shipping?"

"Of course," the shopkeeper answered. "I'm Mrs Quick, by the way. I'll put some extra cotton around the angel's head to protect it. Is there anything else you need?"

"I'm looking for hooks," I said, checking the list that I held in one gloved hand. "For putting ornaments on the tree. And tinsel."

"I have both," she said, bustling around the counter to gather up what I had asked for. "How many of each?" The first time she asked the question, I caught the sound of her voice but not the meaning of the words as she was walking away from me. She placed the angel in a box upon the shelf, shifting aside an ornamental string of bells which jangled as she moved them.

A warbling from the headset distracted me from Mrs Quick's chatter. A whining howl sounded in my ear. Then I heard a voice, a man's voice. He said clearly, "I want to ask you, before I forget, what is your name?"

I turned around but there was nobody else in the store. I glanced out the window but saw no one on the street.

"Did you just ask me my name?" I said to Mrs Quick, deciding that the voice must have been hers but was somehow distorted. I shifted my scarf to fully uncover the microphone hanging outside my coat.

"No, dear," she said. "I know who you are. You're Nova Malone's niece, Raquel."

I must have looked rather surprised because Mrs Quick smiled and added, "We've all been keeping an eye on the Diamond Dog since Nova Malone opened the ballroom and started the radio station. Everyone is interested in what's going on there. And I do like the radio program. The gentlemen on it mentioned you on Saturday's noon program."

"They did?" I said. I'd been wandering around the apartment on Saturday, chatting with Nova and Thelma, but not paying much attention to the radio program. There had been a cookie recipe for something with walnuts and raisins, and a particular quip from Johnny about the instructions which caught my attention. Then Johnny switched to mellifluous stories about various people in the town and I'd left the room on some errand or other. My name must have come up in that section of the broadcast.

"Oh yes, quite nice it was, about how you were visiting your aunt for Christmas and enjoying your stay in our town, including dancing at the Diamond Dog. I gather you're a music teacher, an actual college professor."

"I was," I said, not wanting to explain further or admit the only dancing I'd done so far was on Friday night with Johnny. We'd done a whirl around the floor during one of his breaks and then I'd excused myself to return to the apartment, sure that everyone had been staring at my hearing aid. But I did remember chatting with Johnny just before we danced, talking about how I both missed teaching and didn't. Grading people had never been my favorite thing to do. I resolved to have a talk with Johnny and Reggie when I got back to the Diamond Dog. I'd listened to their chatter about various encounters around town with some amusement, but I didn't want to be one of their broadcast anecdotes between reading the headlines and the latest cookie recipe.

I asked Mrs Quick again about the availability of ornament hooks. She eyed my microphone with polite but visible curiosity and then queried how many hooks I wanted. She also informed me that such had been her original question to me.

I didn't know how much was needed. Nova hadn't written anything besides "ornament hooks" and "tinsel" on her list.

"It's for a large tree," I said. "We're decorating it for the Diamond Dog's Christmas Eve dance."

"Ooh," she said, and I heard her excitement with no trouble at all. "I expect the decorations will be something special. And a very big tree. Miss Nova doesn't seem like the type of woman to skimp on such things."

Considering my aunt's larger-than-life personality, I had to agree. "I saw several sets of electric lights to string up on the tree," I told Mrs Quick. Nova also wanted to outline the doors of the Diamond Dog in Christmas lights, but Reggie had protested, saying none of the strings would survive the night if placed outdoors. Looking around Mrs Quick's crowded five-and-dime, I asked her if she'd ever heard of outdoor Christmas lights.

She frowned. "No. I don't think so. But what a good idea. If there were such a thing, you'd probably need to go to one of the larger cities to find it. Or the Sears Roebuck catalog."

Eventually the counter was covered with several boxes of tinsel, hooks for ornaments, a long paper garland I found in a bin, and one very well wrapped angel. I wrote out my mother's name and address. Mrs Quick promised to have the angel shipped as soon as possible. While I paid for the angel and its delivery to my home in Denver, the rest went on Nova's account. "I'll have my son deliver her items," said Mrs Quick. "He won't mind an excuse to stop at the Diamond Dog. He's very curious about the radio station."

I begged Mrs Quick for directions to the grocer, explaining how I had been turned around on the streets more than once. She giggled a little and acknowledged Kingsport was tricky for newcomers.

With her directions, I set off confidently in the direction of the grocer, determined to order the butter and eggs requested on my aunt's list.

As soon as I rounded the corner, I ran smack into a man.

We did the awkward little dance of two strangers trying to step out of each other's way. I noticed he was very tall and conservatively dressed in a brown suit. His overcoat wasn't doing much to keep him warm as it was unbuttoned and hung open on his lanky frame, as did his suit jacket.

"Are you all right, miss?" the stranger said. As an afterthought, he also tipped his hat to me, a modest fedora.

"Fine, fine," I replied, embarrassed to cause such a fuss simply trying to walk down a sidewalk. "I wasn't looking where I was going."

"Ah, Tawney, there you are!" Crossing the street was Chilton Brewster, his hand outstretched to catch the other man's hand in a quick shake. The whole move pulled Tawney a bit further off his balance, causing his overcoat and jacket to flap open.

Not wanting to attract Brewster's attention, I ducked around the other man and hurried away.

As I twisted around Tawney, I spotted an odd leather strap and bulge beneath his suit jacket. While I'd never seen such a thing in person, I had seen something similar at the movies. As I hurried to my next destination, I could not shake the feeling that the man was wearing a holstered gun under his coat.

INTERLUDE

"*Es war einmal...*" the grandmothers began the stories. The Grossmutter who whispered into the ears of the Grimm brothers told of nightmares, queens who danced in red-hot shoes and bad sisters rolled down hills in barrels studded with nails.

As a boy, I improved my German by reading a tattered copy of *Kinder- und Hausmärchen*, so old and stained that it practically disintegrated in my hands. I stole it off a junkman's barrow along with a pair of shoes that did not leak.

The shoes pinched my feet and it made my eyes ache to read the fading type under the light of the streetlamps, but eventually the book kept me warm. I burned it one night in a barrel with some other tramps. It was Christmas Eve, I remember, and we passed a bottle of schnapps back and forth which scorched the throat but kept us singing until dawn. I did not freeze to death, although the schnapps on an empty and hungry stomach made me think freezing might have been preferable.

I am never cold here under the trees, but I shiver as I pass beneath their whispering branches. I wish for the warmth of a fire and a friendly hand extending a bottle of schnapps to a starving boy.

Then I see a flame, a blue flame that sputters and then flares in front of my eyes. Between one step on the path and the next, I stood in a laboratory.

I entered, if it can be called entering, near a shelf of dishes and jars, all filled with liquids smelling of brine. I looked into one of the jars and an eyeball peered back at me. In another time and another place, I might have been horrified. But I had stared too often into the hungry mouths of the trees to be frightened of body parts preserved in jars.

I heard voices arguing just past the shelves, so I ignored the eyeball and peeped past the specimens into the room.

At one end of a long table, some type of experiment seemed to be bubbling away in beakers and test tubes suspended over the blue flames of Bunsen burners. I once worked cleaning a laboratory belonging to a chemical factory. It had similar setups which meant nothing more to me than something fragile to be avoided when I mopped the floor, emptied out the trash from bins, and tried, often unsuccessfully, to clean stains from the tables.

At the other end of the table was a set of electrical equipment. At least it was a series of boxes, cables, and switches emitting small sparks and hisses. Standing in front of the equipment was a tired looking man in glasses, twisting a screwdriver on one box to adjust some dial. A red-haired woman, dressed very neatly in a tan jacket and a black blouse, leaned over his shoulder.

I nearly called out to them, but then I saw their audience.

A group of men stood around the lab watching. There was something in their gaze. The eyeball in its jar looked upon the world with greater sympathy. All the watchers were dressed alike in brown suits with very white shirts and dark ties underneath. Despite being dressed like clerks, they stood like men in uniforms, very straight and grim. I had never had any luck with such men. I drew back a little in the hopes of hiding from them.

"Dr Maleson," the woman said to the man working on the equipment, "I cannot agree with these changes. The research clearly shows this path cannot be opened using such means. Incantations are indicated. Incantations which are sung. Broadcasting a series of sounds, such as you are attempting to do, may well upset the entire balance of this method."

"Incantations," retorted the other. "Superstitions of the last century. This is 1924! We use science to solve these puzzles. I agree sound frequencies are important, but those created by the human throat are subject to infinite variation. This device–" he patted the thing emitting sparks, then jerked his hand back quickly as if it was stung or hit hot metal. "This device," he continued, "will allow us to duplicate the process precisely every time. When tuned correctly, we will be able to journey to whichever period, whichever moment, we want."

"Dr Maleson," said a tall man in a brown suit. "I have half a dozen federal agents here on Christmas Eve. The paperwork to make this possible, as well as the funding my Bureau has already given your experiment, is staggering. Can you or can you not produce results today?"

"Agent Tawney, of course I can," said Maleson. "This is the start of something big, something undreamed of."

"Not by HG Wells," said the woman with a sour look. "I believed he dreamed of it quite effectively years ago."

"Wells? Miss Thompson, he is a writer!" exclaimed Maleson. "A political radical. Not a scientist. What I have proposed here is something completely different. Not a machine of fiction but a creation that can carry us forward and backward as desired."

"It's my research you're using to create the phenomenon," she said. "I'm telling you that you interpreted it all quite wrong."

"And I'm telling you if this doesn't work today," said the man in the brown suit, "I am shutting off your funding come New Year's."

"Agent Tawney, Miss Thompson," said the scientist. "Prepare to be amazed." He flipped the large lever in front of him and a series of musical notes erupted from the brass metal screen on one end of the box.

A scent rose in the air, not of burning but of something more terrifying than fire. I could smell the forest, the terrible damp fog that breathed from the ground, full of decay and death. I dared not turn around and look. If I did, I was sure I would be engulfed in its horrible depths again. Instead I began to think how I could reach the door. Perhaps if I ran fast enough, hard enough, I could escape this room and whatever was growing behind me. None of my attempts had succeeded so far, but anything was better than standing frozen in fear, every muscle straining as I fought not to look behind me.

"Did you use a music box as the guts of this thing?" yelled the woman over the tinny but loud notes coming from the box.

"Of course," Maleson yelled back over the noise. "The cylinder is larger than normal, my own design in fact, but based on the same principle. As it passes by the comb, the same combination of notes played in the same order resound. Based on the accounts written by Agatha Crane–"

"Yes, yes," Thompson yelled back. "I told you about Crane's research and Sharpe's encounter with a time traveler. But you can't use this method to open the path this way. Didn't you read the account of the grimoire cited by Walters?"

"The grimoire is a family myth of some inbred Innsmouth family, supposedly drowned with the Titanic," replied Maleson. "I refuse to be harnessed by superstition. Or the work of Harvey Walters! He's not a scientist."

"Stop arguing," said Tawney. "Something is happening over there." He pointed to a corner of the room. The shadows shifted, taking on some vague shape. I knew it immediately. It was the shadow of a hound. But only a shadow. The creature was still not in the room. But I swear I could hear a rising whine coming from the corner. A hungry sound shivering through the air. I began to sweat even as I shook from cold terror. So far I had only caught glimpses of those terrible creatures. I never confronted them or stayed long enough to truly look at them. Once they began to howl, I always ran.

Tawney reached under his jacket and withdrew a gun.

"You can't fire that in here," cried Maleson. "There's chemicals."

"There's research! Specimens!" said Thompson. "You could destroy the whole lab."

Something was unsettling about the tune. I knew it vaguely but had never heard it done in such a dirge-like rhythm. The world around me was falling away, the shelves becoming translucent, turning into trees. I finally gave a shout of horror as creatures began emerging from the corners of the room turned into forest.

"The time traveler!" screamed Thompson, pointing at me. I blinked at the woman, as confused as she looked. I was a prisoner of the forest, no traveler, but there was no time to explain.

"Look, Agent Tawney, he just appeared," she said. "By the specimens. It's exactly as Beatrice wrote in her journals."

Tawney swung his gun toward me. "Stop! Halt!" he shouted. "You're under arrest."

I walked toward him, my hands held above my head, knowing that a jail cell would be far safer than this room. But as I stepped forward, a howl sounded through the room and a terrible, scaled creature appeared in the corner filled with shadows.

Tawney screamed as the beast leapt into the middle of the brown-suited men. With one swipe of its long reptilian snout, it bit a man's head off, shaking it briefly like a terrier shakes a rat, and then tossed it across the room. The grisly object sailed through the air and through the trees. I saw a tree whip out an extended tongue and latch onto the head trailing bits of spine and muscle. The tree gulped down its catch.

I sprang away from the shelves, banging into the table.

"Run," I shouted. "Run!" Instead, Tawney fired his gun directly at me. Given what was appearing in the room, a bullet would have been a mercy, but I swerved to avoid a hound and the shot missed me. "Run," I screamed at him and then scrambled to save myself.

Even as I ran, the room lengthened, twisted, and turned into a distorted part of the beach beneath the trees. I struggled toward the door.

More shouts and screams erupted as the place became half forest, half laboratory, and complete chaos.

The beasts charged among the men. With horrible wet sounds, they bit bodies in two, even as the men emptied bullet after bullet into the hounds. Tawney kept firing wildly at the creatures, screaming at the others to "Save the box!"

I stumbled back from the carnage, trying to find a way out as the path flickered on and off beneath my feet, as the tune stuttered and stopped and started again from the box now sitting on a flaming laboratory table.

"Get out!" yelled Thompson at the two men next to her. "Get out. It will stop as soon as that stupid box stops. The hounds only appear when time shifts. If we get away from here, they shouldn't be able to follow us."

"My box," cried Maleson, suddenly turning to grab at it. "Mandy, I have to get my box!"

Thompson screamed, "Leave it!"

Tawney shoved Maleson away. "*My* box!" he yelled. "I paid for it. This is mine."

"You traitor," yelled Maleson as the two men wrestled over the wretched music box. One hound lifted its bloody snout from the body of a man that it was efficiently tearing into smaller parts. It fixed its gaze upon the pair fighting over the music box.

"If the music ends, this ends!" yelled Thompson as she picked up a pair of tongs, the type used for handling test tubes, and swiped at the music box. She knocked it to the floor with a resounding crash. The music stopped.

Tawney howled in rage: "That's government property!"

"Look," cried Maleson, "the forest is fading."

Even as I struggled toward it, the door vanished. Maleson, Thompson, and Tawney began to dissolve.

The screaming stopped, leaving a terrifying absence of noise punctuated only by the crackling of the flames. All the beasts, the people, and the music box disappeared.

I was alone under the trees save for a jar containing an eyeball and some parts of men who moments before had been watching an experiment in a laboratory. Beyond that was a hound, still splattered in blood. It raised its head and began to howl.

I walked backward away from it, step by slow step, not daring to breathe, only retreating, forever retreating, under the trees which swiped their tongues along the path and ate the remains of once living men.

CHAPTER SIX

Inevitably, Reggie fiddled with my headset to improve it, which made it both better and worse; he was fascinated by anything that amplified sound. After he worked on it, I could hear some things better. But I also had a much worse time with phantom voices.

However, I'm trying to tell my story in the order that things happened, and I mustn't get ahead of myself.

The voices, or rather one particular voice, became a regular companion on the day after my walk.

As Nova explained over lunch, Tuesday was also a rather slow day as the Diamond Dog didn't offer dances in the evening from Sunday through Tuesday. She once again suggested I take time to see the sights of Kingsport, but I felt I had explored its shops and looping roads enough. Besides, the weather had taken a turn for the gloomy, with overcast skies and a promise of sleeting rain. However, recognizing my aunt might like some time to herself, I went in search of others downstairs.

Reggie and Johnny had finished their noon broadcast

and were in the process of locking up the radio station. I'd talked to them the day before about my surprise at being featured in their Saturday broadcast. They'd expressed their remorse for causing any embarrassment. Johnny tried to persuade me into coming on a future broadcast to give "a woman's view" of dance music, but I declined. As fascinating as it all was, I couldn't see myself as a radio personality. I didn't like drawing attention to myself and felt too many people were already staring at me in Kingsport due to my hearing device.

Billy, Harlean, Ginger, and Cozy rehearsed on Tuesday afternoon to prepare for the Wednesday evening dance. As much as their music drew me to the ballroom, the heartbreak of not performing made me want to leave. I knew I was being unreasonable. Billy would have gladly shared the piano with me, or I could have played when he was gone. But I wouldn't be as good as I once was. I tried several times after the infection left my ears, and I could feel in my heart as well as my head the difference in my playing.

As I looked around the Diamond Dog that afternoon, I saw no place where I was needed nor anyone requesting help on a project. Sitting idle in my aunt's apartment for another day definitely did not appeal to me.

When I mentioned that I didn't know what to do next, Johnny told me that they were planning to go to the movies in Arkham, a city not far from Kingsport. "You should come along," he said. "You could see something of Arkham. It's bigger than Kingsport and we could find a good place for dinner too."

This plan sounded much more attractive than anything I could think of, so I said that I would love to go to the movies with them.

"There's a Buster Keaton short," said Reggie.

"And the latest episode of the Flapper Detective's aerial adventures," added Johnny. "That's one of the reasons to go to the Arkham theater. They have the first showing of this adventure."

"My aunt's quite a fan of Betsy Baxter," I said. Nova had written to me about meeting the actress who played the Flapper Detective and her admiration for the woman.

I must admit I liked Baxter's current serial, all about a mystery surrounding a new type of long-distance airplane. I still hadn't figured out who was the villain and who was the hero although I knew the Flapper Detective would save the day. The stunts were spectacular, particularly her shoot-out while walking on the wing of a plane. I certainly wouldn't have the courage to do such a thing.

Reggie pulled a rolled-up newspaper out of his pocket, scattering a few screws and a bundle of wire, and opened the paper to the movie ads. "There's an early screening this afternoon," he said to Johnny and me. "We can just make it if we take the car."

"Let me fetch a coat and hat," I said. I ran up the stairs to the apartment, meeting Nova coming down to check on the stock. As she'd mentioned at lunch, Tuesday was the day that Nova spent in the basement taking inventory and reconciling the books. The basement, which I'd briefly glimpsed on an earlier tour, stretched the entire length of the building. There was a cozy little office tucked next to the basement's boiler where Nova and Lily worked on the accounts together. The office was crammed full, with two desks, two wooden chairs, a very large safe, and a pair of filing cabinets. When both women were in there at the same time, there wasn't room for anyone else.

"Are you coming in or going out?" Nova asked me as I passed her on the stairs.

"Going out," I said. "Reggie and Johnny want to spend the afternoon at the movies."

"Sounds like fun," said my aunt. "If you need cash, there's some in the top drawer of my desk. Look for the red leather wallet. Take the men to dinner if you want. I'll be working until late and Thelma has the afternoon off. It will be leftover chowder and rye bread here for supper."

As much as I liked the fish chowder, I wasn't as addicted to it as Nova. "Johnny mentioned that there were some good places to eat in Arkham," I said as I reached the top of the stairs. Looking over the rail at Nova, who was continuing to descend at a calm pace, I said, "If there's anything you need from Arkham, I'm happy to fetch it for you."

Nova shook her head. Waving one hand at me, she said, "Nothing at all. Enjoy yourself!" Daylight from the windows sparkled off her diamond rings and her favorite purple cat brooch pinned to the front of her dress.

Upstairs I picked up my hat and coat from my room. By Nova's desk, I hesitated. I had quite enough money to pay for my ticket to the movies and my dinner. But I knew my aunt meant it when she told me to offer the men dinner at her expense. She was casually generous with all her employees, which was probably why the rest of Kingsport's business owners complained about the sudden interest in jobs at the Diamond Dog.

I opened the top drawer of the desk, the one drawer that Nova kept unlocked since it held stamps, envelopes, and the grocery money for Thelma. I spotted the red wallet immediately and took out enough to cover everyone's dinner after the movies. As I put the wallet back in the drawer, I saw another letter from Chilton Brewster. It bore today's postmark, so Nova must have dropped it into the drawer when pulling out other supplies. Perhaps fetching a stamp for her reply. Nova did write in response to Brewster's nearly daily letters of complaint, usually a quickly dashed note acknowledging the receipt of the letter and no more.

"It befuddles him to receive a thank you for his unkind words," said my aunt with a chuckle one evening. "I do enjoy keeping him off balance."

I started to take the letter out of the envelope but then thought better of my action. As curious as I was to learn why Brewster wrote to my aunt daily, I couldn't invade her privacy in such a way. If she wanted me to read it, she would share it. Or so I told myself as I shoved the tempting envelope back under the red wallet and slammed the desk drawer shut.

Our drive to Arkham took us through the pleasant, if chilly, New England countryside. Both Reggie and Johnny were talkative companions, pointing out various places of interest including the obligatory spot in the road where the redcoats clashed with the Colonists. I told my own tales of walking through Boston, searching for where Paul Revere and his fellows had met and plotted against the British.

I found Arkham to be a small but interesting city. Like Boston, Arkham felt more like a place of yesteryear than today. It lacked the energetic hustle of New York or the intriguing newness of Denver.

Reggie drove us past a Georgian manse built of mellow brick and fine marble facing which dated from the last century, built well before the Civil War. "That's the Arkham Historical Society," he said with a nod. "There's some very good exhibits inside if you're interested in the history of the Miskatonic River Valley."

As soon as Reggie had pointed out his favorite place, Johnny insisted that we tour what he called "far more interesting spots" including Velma's Diner, the Curiositie Shoppe, and Hibb's Roadhouse. When we slowed past the latter, Johnny made me promise that I wouldn't tell my aunt that he'd directed me there. I assured him that I had no interest in visiting roadhouses with or without him.

We missed the first reel of the Keaton comedy, but it was such silly fare, we soon found our place in the plot, laughing and clapping with the crowd as Buster boxed his way to a romantic conclusion. I truly enjoyed the organist accompanying the film, who took full advantage of the Wurlitzer's more specialized sound effects to add emphasis to Buster's antics. Although I didn't need the hearing aid at the movies, I still wore it. To save the battery, I switched it off during the show. The Wurlitzer was loud enough, I could practically feel every note in my body.

When I mentioned to Reggie how much I liked the organ, he told me that the theater management had added it last year. "Before, they had an upright piano and sometimes a small quartet to accompany the bigger films," he said. "They made quite a show on the first evening that they unveiled the Wurlitzer. Even brought back several big movies, including Fairbanks' *Son of Zorro* movie, to demonstrate all the effects of the organ."

The afternoon was as entertaining as expected. I always liked films as lighthearted as Keaton's *Battling Butler*. Betsy Baxter also didn't disappoint and her appearance as the Flapper Detective was loudly cheered by the audience.

At dinner after the movies, Reggie and Johnny told me about how they'd seen the actress in an aerial circus earlier that summer. "She was performing with Wini Habbamock," said Reggie. "A bunch of real stunts, including jumping off a motorcycle onto a rope ladder dangling from Habbamock's plane."

"I can't imagine such a thing," I said.

"Have you ever been up in an airplane?" Reggie asked as he mopped up a piece of apple pie. Due to the early hour, the restaurant that the men picked was quiet enough for me to clearly hear everything that was said and there were no distracting crowd noises.

"No, I've never flown, and I can't say that I have any desire to," I responded. What I left unsaid was that the physicians all advised against it. Nova had discussed having me fly to California to try a new surgical procedure. With the damage already done to my ears by the fever, the doctors felt a plane flight was too risky. There was even some discussion about whether it was safe for me to return to the higher altitude of Denver.

After so many conflicting doctor visits, I decided to ignore the gloomier predictions and planned to return home eventually. However, those warnings had helped make my case for staying with Nova for a little while longer. To her, I said that it was a chance to make sure that my ears were fully healed and recovered from the infection. Of course the delay in corresponding with my family was not so easily explained. But my reluctance to write bad news at Christmas was between me and my conscience. So far, my conscience had lost that particular battle.

On the drive back to Kingsport, I sat up front with Reggie, chatting about radio technology while Johnny gently snored in the backseat.

Reggie glanced over his shoulder at his friend and smiled. "I told him the turkey and gravy were a mistake if he wanted to stay awake."

"Let him sleep," I said, wedging myself more comfortably in the corner of the front seat. The hills rolling by us were anonymous mounds of white, turning slightly blue in the twilight. The bare hedges and long black branches of the trees overhead once again reminded me of the sinister Currier and Ives print back at the college. The skies were still overcast so there was no friendly moon or stars visible. Such a cold and lonely landscape made me glad that we were headed back to the cheerful warmth of the Diamond Dog.

"Do you like working for Nova?" I asked Reggie. As soon as I said it, I realized how awkward the question was. What could he say to Nova's niece?

"Very much," said Reggie without hesitation, apparently not even aware of the oddness of the question. "There was nothing like the Diamond Dog or the radio station before she came to Kingsport. No matter what they say about people from Innsmouth, she has fantastic ideas. You know she is talking about hooking into the National Broadcasting Company's network. We could be heard from coast to coast. Imagine sitting in California and hearing the band playing in Kingsport."

"It sounds like magic," I said, remembering Harlean's excitement about the idea. Then, thinking more about what Reggie said, I asked, "What do people say about Innsmouth? I've never been, although I know Nova and my mother grew up there. Whenever I ask Nova about it, she changes the subject. My mother does the same."

Reggie shrugged. "I don't know much about Innsmouth, just that they're supposed to be unfriendly."

"That's not Nova's personality," I laughed.

"No, your aunt seems to attract friends," Reggie agreed. "But folks like Chilton Brewster sometimes mutter about bad blood in Innsmouth. I really don't know why."

"Did you grow up near here?" I asked. From earlier comments, I gathered Reggie had moved to Kingsport as an adult.

"I grew up near Boston and moved to Arkham to go to the university there," he replied. "Then I worked for the phone company after I graduated. I modernized the switchboard in Kingsport and made some other improvements, but I was always more interested in radios than phones. Nova's job offer was a dream job for me."

"So you weren't one of the employees that Nova stole from Chilton Brewster?"

"Oh, him!" said Reggie. "There's a man who loves to tell the rest of the world how to think and act."

"I've heard his editorials on the lack of decorum in the modern generation," I told him. "Did you know he also writes letters to Nova? She gets one almost every day."

"Brewster writes notes to everyone," Reggie said with a laugh. "I've helped Elmo out once or twice with his transmitter. He showed me a stack of letters from Brewster, practically one for every broadcast, detailing everything that Elmo could do better or should do better. You think working with Elmo five days a week he could just talk to him after a broadcast if he wanted to change something. But no, Brewster goes home, writes a letter, and then posts it! The odd thing, says Elmo, is that when Brewster is in the same room, he hardly talks to Elmo at all. Just goes in front of the microphone and reads out his bits."

"I wouldn't want to work for a man like that," I said.

Reggie nodded. "Elmo's been hinting that he'd like to come over to our station. If Nova does expand the broadcast, we could use the help. But I hate to think how many letters that Brewster would write to all of us if he lost another employee to Nova!"

When we reached our destination, Johnny roused himself from the backseat and wished us a pleasant evening. He was, he informed us, off home for a quick wash and brush up before venturing out on his date of the night. He'd return for the car, which he shared with Reggie, in an hour or so, he said.

"Two dinners in one night," said Reggie, pretending to be scandalized. "You won't fit into your suits if you keep this up!"

"We plan on dinner and dancing at the Purple Cat," responded Johnny in his velvety voice. "In my case, a light dinner and much quickstepping."

He disappeared into the twilight gloom with a final cheery "Good night!"

When Johnny left, I wondered if I had a book in the apartment to entertain me. My aunt kept no more than one or two shelves of reading material, and she favored nonfiction accounts of polar exploration and sea voyages. My own books were crated up for shipment home. I regretted that my beloved copy of Lang's *Red Fairy Book* was in the boxes stored upstairs in Nova's attic. I'd packed up my boarding house room and shipped everything to the Diamond Dog before departing to New York with Nova, unsure if I'd be returning to Boston or heading to Denver after seeing the doctors. Since then, I'd regretted packing up my childhood favorite. Lang's stories had traveled all the way from Denver with me. I spent many long days stuck in bed with the fever, and the book had been my greatest comfort. The twelve dancing princesses, Jack and his beanstalk, Rapunzel, and Snowdrop were all old friends of mine due to a long-ago birthday gift from Nova. But I supposed reading about Amundsen had educational benefits.

"Are you heading home also?" I asked Reggie. Nova was sure to be in the basement, still working on accounts, or perhaps she had taken the Rolls to the Purple Cat. I hadn't been to the cafe, but I knew Nova held a small dance on

Tuesday nights there when the Diamond Dog was closed. Thelma was gone as well. Suddenly the thought of returning to the empty apartment didn't appeal. I had spent enough time there.

"I'm going into the studio to make some adjustments to the transmitter. I have a few ideas for improving the microphones too," said Reggie. "Would you like a tour of the space?"

"Very much so," I said, cheerfully abandoning my resolve to finally figure out the differences between Arctic and Antarctic exploration. Amundsen could wait for another day.

In the studio, Reggie made the technical aspects of broadcasting as understandable as possible. He was a lively and well-informed guide for a novice like me, pointing out many similarities between the equipment in the studio and the device which sat so uncomfortably on my head.

"Do you mind taking it off?" he said, pointing to my headset. "I'd love to take a closer look at it."

"I'd be delighted," I said truthfully. The gadget was beginning to drag uncomfortably on my neck and shoulders. I was happy to surrender it to him.

"Do you mind?" he said, gesturing at the device. "I'd love to see what's under the cover."

"Not at all," I said. If in my heart I hoped he'd break it, it was a very small wish. Nova would not be pleased if the thing was in pieces in the morning. I, however, was relieved to have it gone for even a few moments. A number of sounds might not be as distinguishable without it, but what I heard felt more natural.

"I'll be careful," Reggie promised as he took the hearing aid from me. He produced a screwdriver and began taking the earphone apart.

As he worked, I mentioned to Reggie the recent distortions of sound that I had heard as well as how the device failed to live up to all the promises made by the salesman. "I know it's the best that there is," I said, because Nova had made very sure of that before purchasing the hearing aid. "But nothing ever sounds exactly as it did before the fever. I suppose it's studying music that's made me so fussy. I do know when something doesn't sound quite right."

Engrossed in the device, Reggie mumbled something back about pitch and microphones failing to catch all sounds. Thinking of the opera singers that I'd heard on the gramophone, I thought I understood what he was saying. The full tone of their singing was missing from the recording, while perfectly audible in the theater with no amplification at all.

"It's all to do with the range of what we pick up and translate into broadcast sound," Reggie said. "With the older microphones we could only capture a narrow segment of the audible spectrum. But Western Electric's new microphones and signal amplifiers are making a huge difference. You can definitely hear it in some of the newer recordings. Those systems let us reproduce a much broader frequency range."

"But will it sound the same as going to a concert hall?" I asked skeptically.

"It will sound better," he replied, "and everything that

I've seen in the past few years promises broadcasts and recordings will continue to improve. There's even a guy experimenting with broadcasting pictures with sound. Imagine seeing talking movies on your radio!"

I thought of the Wurlitzer resounding through the theater in Arkham. "I prefer the movies the way that they are. With live music in a theater."

"Nobody is going to be broadcasting pictures tomorrow." Reggie tapped the equipment around him. "But even now we can broadcast more of the highs and lows. And softer sounds. I've been telling Harlean with these new microphones she doesn't need to belt out every tune. She could even whisper into the microphone and our radio audience will be able to hear her perfectly, as if she was singing in the room to them."

"A more intimate sound?" I guessed.

"Crooning is what some of the singers are calling it. They're not singing for a theater full of people. They're singing for and to the microphone, and it's a very different technique."

"I'd love to hear it," I said and meant it. I wondered if such microphones and amplifiers could bring back the full range of music to me. Even as radio improved, hearing aids had to improve as well, I told myself. But nothing would ever be the same as it was, I thought a moment later.

Reggie nodded. "Come into the studio during the next dance. I'll put one of our headsets on you. You can listen through it to Harlean and Billy when they're playing for the broadcast. It should be clearer than listening to Nova's radio upstairs. You'll be hearing what I hear when we broadcast."

"Tomorrow night?" I asked, thinking it would be fun to sit with Reggie during the Wednesday broadcast.

"Tomorrow night!" Reggie affirmed. He screwed the plate back on my earpiece and then held it to his own ear, speaking softly into the microphone. "Better," he pronounced, handing the whole contraption back to me. "But not perfect. I'm still hearing something, just at the edge of my range, a slight ringing. Do you hear it?"

"Not quite a ringing," I said, adjusting the headset and hanging the microphone around my neck again. "More like the faintest buzz. Although sometimes it sounds like a dog barking."

"It probably isn't a dog. The animal would have to be in the room for your microphone to pick it up. More likely the microphone is amplifying something that we don't normally hear, like your heartbeat. A piece of jewelry or a button could rub against the microphone while you're walking. It could cause distortions that you wouldn't hear when sitting still."

"No jewelry and I wear the microphone outside my clothes, so the heartbeat is unlikely," I said as I gathered up my hat and coat. "But thank you for looking at it and for the lovely day. I enjoyed the movies, and the dinner, and the lesson about microphones very much!"

"So did I," said Reggie with a smile. "Johnny's right. I'm mad about this stuff." He waved his hand to encompass the whole studio. "Radio is going to be even bigger than movies someday. When we truly understand how to record and broadcast sound so it seems natural, like someone sitting beside you telling a story, we'll change the world."

"I'm sure you will," I said as I left the studio. "Goodnight, Reggie."

"Goodnight," he called back.

I crossed the empty ballroom. The place was nothing but shadows, only a few small lights left on for latecomers like me or Nova working down in the basement. I felt more than heard the clack of my heels as I crossed the wooden dance floor. To amuse myself, I began to hum Billy's rendition of "Jingle Bells" to see how it would echo in the empty room and sound in the microphone slung over my chest. Just as I reached the end of the first verse, I heard a man's voice coming from my earpiece.

He spoke very low and intimately, just as Reggie said people would sound on the new microphones. But he wasn't broadcasting from the stage. There was no one there. He wasn't in the room speaking into the microphone resting over my now wildly beating heart.

With a gasp, I spun around just to be sure that I was completely alone. There was no one there at all.

But still I heard him speak to me. I froze, glancing about me. There was something familiar about this sorrowful voice. I had heard this man before. But I knew the microphone didn't have the strength to pick up anyone outside the room. Reggie had been certain about the range and if anyone knew microphones, it was Reggie.

"Ghosts," I whispered to myself. Clara and I often scared ourselves silly playing with a Ouija board when we were younger (a gift from Aunt Nova, of course). But I never truly believed the dead could speak to us. Because if ghosts existed, it would have been my brother Benny's voice that I heard. This was a man, I decided. Someone my age or older, with a deep soft voice full of sadness and, I was sure of this, an undertone of fear.

"Once upon a time, something happened. If it had not happened, it would not be told," the man said in my left ear as if he was crooning a story just for me. But there truly was nobody there.

I pulled the headset off and slung it around my neck so I could no longer hear any whispers in the earpiece. I switched off the battery as added protection from disembodied voices. Then I ran upstairs as fast as I could, banging into Nova's familiar apartment and hurrying into my bedroom. Luckily, Nova was still out and I didn't have to explain myself to my aunt.

I divested myself of the hearing aid as quickly as I could and retreated to my bed. I sat there for some time just staring at the headset, microphone, and purse containing the battery pack. It was just a collection of wires, I told myself, not a conduit to phantoms.

The longer I looked at it, the more my initial fear faded. I listened to voices coming out of Nova's radio every day. Such sounds couldn't hurt me. To be frightened of a man's voice in my earpiece was ridiculous, I told myself firmly. Just because I didn't understand how I was hearing him, there was no need to be afraid.

My own shillyshallying annoyed me. I used to be a person who made plans and moved forward with those plans. I was never frightened by shadows or odd noises (three brothers cured me of any squeamishness quite young).

"Raquel Malone Gutierrez, don't be a cowardly lion,"

I said, echoing my brothers' favorite call to bravery when their sisters failed to take a dare. I marched to the dresser. Once again I went through all the bother of placing the hearing aid correctly on my head and then switched on the battery pack. Perhaps Reggie's fiddling had changed so it could broadcast as well as receive.

"Hello?" I said to the night. "Are you still there? How can I help you?"

Because I was sure of the sorrow and the fear that I had heard in the man's voice, I was sure that he needed someone to help him.

I called out again.

Nobody answered me.

INTERLUDE

"Once there was a princess who was such a dreadful storyteller that the like of her was not to be found far or near," a boy in Norway began his story to me. By which he meant the princess was a liar. I'm worse than the princess. Once I told a man that I was raised on a chicken farm in Iowa, when I didn't even know where Iowa was, much less anything about chickens.

But I'm trying to tell you a story, a story about a dreadful liar that I met, only this one was a prince and not a princess.

I heard him whistling as he walked around a corner. Where I had been a moment before, I couldn't remember. But now I was standing on a street full of fancy houses with evergreen wreaths upon their doors. The sky was as dull as old iron above.

It was all so normal, so calm, that I could hardly believe I had walked into such a place after the nightmares that I had experienced.

"Hey, can you spare a dime? Even a nickel will do," said the man as he walked up to me. Then he shook his head. "Looks like you're as broke as me. Nice jacket! I had one like that, but I threw it out when I got a nick on the sleeve. Those were the days."

I shifted my hand across the cut on my left sleeve. The handsome American facing me was dressed like a wealthy man, with an overcoat lined in fur and a fine suit under that. But the hems of his trousers were frayed and his shoes were unpolished. Even his mustache seemed a bit ragged at the edges and his chin was shadowed by stubble, as if he couldn't afford a good razor or a barber.

"Lovely house, isn't it?" he said to me, but he looked over my shoulder as if seeking a bigger audience. "I once owned the biggest house of all. Of course, the crash took care of all that. Put your money in stocks, Preston, you can't go wrong. You'll always be rich, Preston, just do what your daddy did and you'll never want for anything."

His laughter rang out, a bitter sound. "What does the song say? Traipsing through hell? Walking through it? Slogging, slogging, that's the word," he said to me. "Heard it on the radio and I knew the song was about me. Because that's what I did." He thumped his breast with one hand. "Helped them out, didn't I? Gave them money, didn't I? Slogged through hell, didn't I? And everyone loved me because I was a millionaire."

He waved his bare hands wildly in the air. Each hand was chapped red with cold. The littlest finger on his left hand was crooked, as if he had broken it not long ago. His hands were not the hands of a rich man. His hands were the hands of a poor man, a man who dug ditches or washed plates to eat. His hands looked like mine. So I knew all his talk of wealth was lies.

"Good old Preston," he said, shaking his head. "Good old chump. Thought the money would never run out until it did. Thought I'd spend all my days dancing at the Clover Club and the Diamond Dog. Seems like yesterday, seems like forever ago."

His look turned sly, the glance of a rogue, and he said again to me, "Sure you can't spare a dime? Pay you back twice over. Pay you back with as many silver dimes as your pockets can hold." He tapped the side of his reddened nose. "I have friends, you know, my father's friends. All I have to do is talk to them. Then I'll be me again. I'll be rich again. Just need a small investment in the outer appearance." He gestured at his frayed trousers and shabby shoes. "Get the suit brushed, the shoes shined, and the hair trimmed. If I look like I'm worth something, they'll want me, same as before."

Digging my hands deep into the pockets of my leather coat, I backed away from him, because all his wild talk, all his tall tales, frightened me. Then I felt it, small, and round, and cold as ice in one corner of my pocket. I pulled out the silver coin and tossed it to the desperate man.

He snatched it out of the air and whooped. "A dime! It's my lucky day and yours, too, my friend. 1933 is turning into a good year after all. I wonder what sort of supper they serve for Christmas Eve at the Order. Why don't you come along and find out? I'll tell them you're a friend of the family. What's one more little lie going to hurt?"

I answered his question. I don't know why I did, but it seemed that this man needed to hear what I had to say.

"I have spent all my life lying about who I am," I said. "I

did it to eat. I made up stories to stop men from beating me. I lied so I could join an army. I lied again so I could desert my post. I lied every time I crossed a border and became someone new. I have told so many lies about myself that I don't know who I am. I can no longer remember. It would have been best to tell the truth."

He stood completely still, one hand still clutching the dime that I had thrown to him. This poor man in a rich man's tattered suit looked at me with eyes filled with agony, a look I could feel on my own face.

The door of the fancy house opened, and a woman stepped out on the porch. "Preston? Preston Fairmont, is that you?" she said.

He whipped around to face her. "Oh Daisy, darling Daisy, how are you? How is my favorite librarian? Merriest greetings of the season and so on."

"Merry Christmas," she said, coming down the steps with her arms outstretched. "You dear, dear man. It's been too long. When did I see you last? Cairo?"

He sidestepped from her embrace. "Mustn't hug me," he said with a little sadness in his voice. "Not fit for man or beast tonight. I slept rough the last couple of days. Arkham's flophouses lack a certain cleanliness. Not like the Ritz, not like the Ritz at all."

"Oh, Preston," she said with a tender smile. "Come in and get cleaned up. We can find you a bed tonight."

"I don't like to impose, dear lady, I had plans for quite another destination, but–" and he glanced at me, "–perhaps it wouldn't hurt to talk it over. You always were so much wiser than me, darling Daisy." Then he turned and tossed the dime back. "Here, buddy, you need this more than me tonight."

A little boy appeared in the doorway. One hand was wrapped around a candy cane and the sticky evidence of the treat ringed his mouth. The other fat fist clutched a string of bells. "I figured it out," he yelled. "I know when to ring my bells, Auntie Daisy, when the others sing. Come listen to us." He shook the bells at us.

Then they were gone, like a dream, and I was in this place with no stars. For once, despair did not engulf me. My hand was wrapped around the dime that the poor prince tossed to me, and it was warm in my fist. I hoped he would tell the truth to his Daisy.

Unlike the tales that I have told before, the ones I told to deceive and survive, the stories I am writing here are true. But how do I make you believe? When I can barely believe what I see when I raise my eyes from this page.

But I believe you are real. For I heard your name and you spoke to me.

CHAPTER SEVEN

Over the next few days, I heard the unknown man several times more in my earpiece. Sometimes when I was in the apartment, but more often when I was downstairs listening to the band and dancing. Mostly his words sounded like someone broadcasting fairytales.

I'd always enjoyed stories which began "once upon a time." Starting when I was five, Nova had sent me Andrew Lang's fairy books, a few volumes every birthday, until I had all twelve colors, which I loved to read to my baby sister and brother. Nova also shipped us the new Oz book every Christmas.

So when I heard the man's voice saying "Far, far away, across the great waters," I wasn't sure if I was hearing someone outside my head or simply repeating to myself the start of a half-remembered story.

Then, like the miller's daughter in *Rumpelstiltskin*, I discovered the stranger's name. It happened when I was dancing with Johnny at the end of Saturday evening, while Harlean sang "What Can I Say After I Say That I'm Sorry?"

As Harlean gave the final line a nice upbeat twist, Johnny spun me around and the dance ended.

Up on the stage, Billy was joking with Harlean while his fingers rattled out the opening bars of "Jingle Bells." The crowd gave a shout and Billy waved at them. "Next one!" he promised as the band took a break.

In my left ear I heard the stranger say, "My name is Paul."

Without thinking, I responded, "My name is Raquel" just as the music stopped.

Johnny looked at me with a puzzled twinkle in his eyes. "Hello, Raquel," he said to me.

I stepped away from Johnny, scanning the late-night crowd of couples slowly leaving the dance floor. Most were intent on returning to their seats and gathering up their belongings. There would be a call for the last dance in a minute or two, but many would leave now. None seemed interested in me, nor could I spot anyone who might have just declared his name.

I knew it was a man who spoke. That much I was certain of. Every time I heard the stranger, his voice was clear enough for me to judge him a man, not a boy, and – although I was less certain of this – probably not an American. There was something about his accent that reminded me of the Jewish immigrants I had met before, the Yiddish speakers in particular. But, remembering a few visiting musicians who came to play with the college orchestra in Boston, he could have been German or Ukrainian or Polish. I simply wasn't hearing enough to tell, and I was certainly no Sherlock Holmes to instantly know a person's ancestry from their accent.

"Raquel, are you all right?" Johnny said, laying a hand gently on my shoulder to guide me off the dance floor.

"Yes, of course," I replied, sitting down at the small table in the corner that we had taken for our own. "I'm sorry. Just a little distracted. I thought I heard someone I knew."

"See them now?" Johnny asked.

I shook my head, feeling a bit foolish. Could I be suffering from auditory hallucinations? Was such a thing even possible? Joan of Arc, of course, heard voices. Many saints did. But I didn't think this was any angel giving me instructions. This man, this stranger, speaking into my left ear always sounded too ordinary. Just the sort of conversation anyone would overhear by accident. Except it didn't feel accidental or a trick of the microphone dangling from my chest. It felt like someone was trying to talk directly to me.

Sometimes he sounded very far away, but sometimes it was as if he was in the same room with me. As if I could speak to him, if only I knew how.

Still, every time I tried to speak to the stranger – to Paul if the name I just heard was his – I received the same response as I had on Tuesday night. Silence.

"Want me to fetch you a drink before I go do my bit?" asked Johnny.

Johnny announced various songs and spoke a little about the Diamond Dog from the stage during the live broadcast.

"No, I'm still working on this ginger ale," I said, tapping my glass. "I'll wait for the others."

At the end of the evening, Ginger, Harlean, Cozy, and

Billy joined me at the table I held for all of us, joking about the evening or speculating about the various couples who circled the floor. They knew most everyone from Kingsport, but the radio broadcast brought many from Arkham and other towns nearby.

Reggie would join us after the broadcast ended. Sitting in the booth and listening through Reggie's headset had been a thrilling experience. On his headsets, I didn't hear the barking of the dog which still disturbed me now and then when wearing my own earpiece. Nor did I ever hear the stranger, I realized, when I was wearing the radio station's headset.

"I'm off then," said Johnny, but he gave a worried glance over his shoulder at me. I resolved to be more discreet in responding to the stranger, to Paul, when next I heard him.

Johnny moved toward the stage to announce the last dance of the evening. Harlean stood at the microphone in a beautiful silk dress with a velvet scarf draped across her shoulders. Her hair was held fast under a sequined bandeau which caught the light and made her sparkle even more.

"She's really good," said a Black man settling into a chair next to mine. He wasn't much older than myself, perhaps he was even a little younger. A good-looking man but one whose face had lines on it that I guessed came from hard times rather than age. He slid an instrument case under his chair. "And Billy Oliver is a genius at the keyboard."

I smiled to hear such praise of my friends. "I couldn't agree more," I told him. "Are you enjoying the dance?"

"Very much," he replied. "Miss Nova holds a swell party.

I visited the Purple Cat once or twice. I always thought she had a good ear for performers. These are the best yet."

"I'm her niece, Raquel Gutierrez," I said, holding out my hand to shake his. As soon as I gripped it, I recognized the calluses of a musician. "You're a trumpet player?" I guessed, glancing down at the case now hidden under his chair.

He grinned and admitted it. "Jim Culver," he said. "I do play the horn when I have a chance. Haven't had much work lately, at least not for folks like these."

I raised my eyebrows in inquiry.

Jim shrugged. "I prefer my daddy's horn over any other instrument, but I promised Miss Nova that I wouldn't play it here or any place of hers. Guess she's got a right to say whether it's the living or the dead dancing the night away."

That's what I thought I heard Jim say, although I almost instantly doubted the words meant what they seemed to mean. I told myself that he was speaking as a musician about the quality of the audience. We'd all had performances where the audience seemed dead to the music, unable to respond no matter how hard we tried.

"But I sure do like the way that Billy plays this song. I mean to try that when I get to the graveyard. It will make the old bones hop," Jim said to me.

I wondered if the Graveyard was a club in Kingsport or Arkham, but before I could ask, Billy had swung into his rendition of "Jingle Bells" on the piano. Harlean was shaking a string of bells in her hand while Ginger made her saxophone trip through the notes as Cozy gave the drums the beat of the horses' hooves. As Billy predicted, the couples were dancing with delight, the men swinging their partners about and the ladies kicking up their heels.

Jim mimed the pressing of keys on a horn as he listened, obviously hearing his own horn in his head as he worked his way through this jazz version of the sleighing song. "Yes," he said, "it's downright rambunctious. Should shake a few awake tonight."

He slid a hand under his chair and pulled out his battered old trumpet case. Then, tipping his hat to me, Jim stood up and wandered away through the dancers.

Over the past few days at the Diamond Dog, I'd grown used to folks quite different from those I met in my small Boston college. But there was something about the horn player which bothered me for quite a while after he left. As I sat puzzling through the end of the band's last song, I realized what it was.

The whole time that we were talking, I'd heard very faintly in my earpiece the sound of a horn playing. But Ginger was blowing the sax and Billy was pounding on the keys of a piano. So why had I heard a trumpet playing along with them in that final song? A horn whose notes became more ghostly as Jim Culver danced away from me clutching his closed trumpet case.

Then Paul's voice crackled in my ear again, starting again with "Once upon a time." I forgot all about Jim as I listened to him. The song ended and so did Paul's story. I heard nothing more unusual than the clattering of plates and glasses as the waiters swept around the room, cleaning up the Saturday night dance.

I sat at the table, rapping my fingers against the top,

thinking about the stranger who named himself Paul. For the more his voice haunted me, the more I needed to solve this one puzzle. I needed to believe that I could do something for him, even though I hadn't been able to solve anything else in my life.

INTERLUDE

I saw a strange phrase in a book once. The book was old and tattered and sitting on the very bottom shelf in a public library. When I first came to America, I found cities full of libraries built at the wish of a rich man so even a poor man could sit and read without fear.

One day, in a library with tall, curved windows which let in the foggy sunlight, I opened up a book about knights and ladies. I thought at first it was a child's book so I read it to practice my English.

But it was written in a very strange way and many words made no sense to me. Finally, I went to the librarian and pointed at the chapter heading. "Please," I said, "what does this mean?"

"Divers grisly ghosts," she read out loud, but very softly, as it was a library and people only whispered in its rooms.

"Divers are men who swim underwater?" I asked her, which made no sense in a book about knights and the way she pronounced the word sounded different than what I had heard before.

"It's old English," she said with a shake of her head. "It means diverse or many ghosts."

I remember the Kingdom of Ghosts in the book, where smoke and fumes choke the air and spirits chatter with iron teeth.

Between one step and the next, I walked out of the place where I was and found the kingdom and the musician who rules it. Fog swirled around me as I stepped amid trees dripping with water but thankfully no teeth. As always, it was cold, and the mist made the light so dim that I could not tell if it was morning or evening. I pulled my coat tight around me. If it wasn't Christmas Eve like all the other times, it was certainly the dead of winter. And more than winter was dead in these woods.

In a clearing before me, at the edge of an open grave, a Black man played the trumpet, a song I almost knew.

Staring at the trees, he called, "Mr Ghoul, you should have danced to my tune before. Time to dance, time to shake those bones into the ground."

Something shambled under the trees, something which stank in the darkness there, and groaned with a wet gurgling sound.

"Oh, they ripped out his heart and they ripped out his lungs," said the musician, "but they left the soul for me." He played a more somber tune upon his horn and the moaning creature crawled from beneath the dripping wet bushes. On hands and knees, it crept forward, a gray and ghastly corpse heading for the open grave.

I had never heard such a song before. In Hollywood, I worked for a director who made stories about men being hypnotized and lured to their doom. If he had met this musician, he would have cast the horn player in one of his films. But no movie audience could have heard what I heard or felt what I felt, the terrifying urge to follow the music.

The horn player kept up his tune. I stumbled forward step by involuntary step, seeking only to lay myself down in that muddy grave with the thing that slithered on its belly like a worm into the gaping hole.

But the musician blew one last note and grabbed me by the arm. "You're too late," he said to me with a mournful smile. "Ten years too late and this place isn't for you. Leave the grave for Mr Ghoul."

I stumbled back, too overcome by the silencing of the music to find words.

Shaking my shoulder with his free hand, the musician said, "Go back, go back and try again. Listen for old Jim Culver but listen for a younger Jim. When you hear me playing this, dance to my tune." Lifting his horn to his mouth, he played a jangling tune.

"I know this," I started to say but his music drowned me out.

As the musician played the trumpet, he circled away from the grave. I followed Jim because I had no will to do anything else. He said to me, "You come dancing again on Christmas Eve. But 1926, not 1936. Remember. It's important. You come dancing when Billy Oliver starts playing and Ginger wails on her fine sax. Listen and dance when Cozy beats the drums, or it will be the last dance they'll ever dance. You remember and stay out of Dunwich. This is no place for you!"

Arkham Horror

Then his music danced me out of his haunted wood with the song I had heard before and names I didn't know. But now I hear your voice. I think you hear mine. I write this warning in hope that you will understand and never see the Kingdom of Ghosts.

CHAPTER EIGHT

We were halfway through the month, and every night brought bigger crowds to dance at the Diamond Dog. All the town was buzzing about how Nova would decorate the place for her Christmas Eve event. Expectations ran high that the decorations would rival the Parker House in Boston. I spotted boxes of crepe paper and festoons being carried into the basement at all hours by Otis and Tim.

Strings of electric lights were draped around the room by Reggie, who constructed the most bizarre switchboard in a corner of the room to control the whole lot. One afternoon he ran me through the switches, showing me how to light up various corners of the room or plunge everything into darkness except the stage. Apparently one of Reggie's past hobbies was amateur theater and he had, in college, run the lights for an amateur theatrical troupe until the theater burned down. The latter piece of information alarmed me until he explained that the fire had broken out on stage during a bizarre play being directed by Sydney Fitzmaurice.

"The film director?" I asked. My older brothers had been

huge fans of Fitzmaurice's nightmare movies, although I never liked them much myself.

"This was before he went to Hollywood," said Reggie. "When we both attended the university in Arkham. It was a long time ago, before the war. He was fascinated by the occult and staged this strange show all about a hooded stranger. A fire broke out on opening night. I didn't like Sydney much, so I decided not to work on the production. In fact, I joined the amateur radio society and built my first transformer around that time."

"Didn't a fire destroy Fitzmaurice's final film?" I said, with some vague memories of the headlines around the time that I started teaching in Boston. My students gossiped about the fire for months afterward, as several were fans of Fitzmaurice's leading lady Renee Love.

Reggie nodded. "About three years ago. He came back to Arkham to film in his family home. The fire destroyed the place and his last film."

"Hey, Reggie," said Johnny, walking over to us. "Mrs Orne is here with her recipe for pepper nuts. Do I have the name right?"

"Pfeffernüsse," said Reggie. "It's a great cookie."

"What kind of cookie would use pepper?" I asked.

"Find out along with our listeners. You'd like Mrs Orne," said Johnny. "Come on the air with her?"

"No. I need a walk and to do some shopping." I wanted to buy a gift for Nova, but I couldn't think what she would like. Obviously diamonds, but such jewelry was well outside my budget. Then I remembered the hardware store with the bicycle in the window. I wondered if they carried some small electrical appliances. Nova loved gadgets. I suspected even a clever toy might amuse her.

Outside, it was a simply splendid December day. Not too cold and enough sun to make the snow on the roofs sparkle. Even that slush trodden underfoot didn't look too bad.

I found myself humming Billy's version of "Jingle Bells" as I walked along the streets, smiling and nodding at several friendly faces. In the short time that I had been in Kingsport, the townspeople, especially those who loved to dance, had become familiar to me. And I to them. Nobody stared at my headset anymore or seemed much perturbed if I asked them to repeat their words into the microphone. I began to think that perhaps I could live with the contraption. At least in a place like this, a small town where people could see me as more than a woman with a hearing device. How I would manage in a city like Denver, or how I would tell my family, I still had not decided.

Then, as I stepped from the sunlight into a pool of shadow on a side street, I heard the stranger's voice in my ear. "My words may frighten you. Do not be afraid. Please do not be afraid. One of us must be without fear," he said.

He sounded so sad and so lonely that I spoke without thinking, "I am not afraid. I swear I am not. I wish I could help you."

A sigh, or more accurately, a suddenly indrawn breath sounded in my ear. He said, "How can you hear me?"

"I don't know," I said. "But are you Paul?"

Another ragged breath and with almost a sob, he answered, "I am Paul."

"My name is Raquel," I said.

"I heard you say your name," he said. "Oh, a long time ago, I think. But it gave me such hope."

"It was at the dance a few nights ago," I said. I must have looked so strange. A woman standing on a street corner talking to the shadows at her feet. Luckily this quiet street was deserted so nobody saw me. But I didn't care. I'd finally managed to speak to the stranger, who didn't feel like a stranger at all. I knew Paul, I felt, almost as well as I knew the doubts in my head. During the conversation, I absolutely believed that he was real, a living man, and no ghost of my imagination.

"Time has no meaning where I am," he said. "Tell me what you see."

"I'm on a street," I said, struck by the inadequacy of my words. I tried again. "It's a street in Kingsport, a very pretty town, and it snowed last night. The trees and the bushes are all covered. Oh, and the sun is shining. The sky is perfectly blue."

I stopped, appalled at my lack of ability to accurately describe something right before my eyes, because there were so many details I hadn't mentioned. The small birds hopping in and out of the bushes in search of seeds or bugs. A lopsided snowman decorating the lawn of a house across the street.

"Perfectly blue," Paul repeated. "I look into a sky of nothing. No stars, no moon. Just nothing. Thank you, Raquel, for reminding me of sunlight."

"I wish I could do more," I said. What he said was so strange, so unreal, yet still I believed him.

"You are a voice of hope," he replied. "I have nothing here but despair."

I thought of my own sorrow and anger at losing my hearing through no fault of my own.

"Don't despair," I said as much to myself as to the voice in my ear. "There is a way out of this."

A man rounded the corner of the street, walking toward me. I stepped back to let him pass and Paul was gone. I don't know how I knew that, but I felt his absence keenly.

"Miss Gutierrez," said the tall gentleman as he passed me, tipping his gray fedora.

It took me a moment, but I recognized him as the man who had been meeting with Chilton Brewster the other day.

"Do I know you?" I said.

"We haven't been introduced," he said. "But I was hoping to speak to you. Agent Ralph Tawney, the Bureau of Investigation." He flipped his coat open to show me a badge. Beneath his brown suit jacket, I could clearly see the outline of a gun in a holster.

"I'm sorry," I said, stepping back in surprise. "Why would you want to talk to me?"

His next words shook me even more. "It's about Chilton Brewster. He's made the most peculiar claims about your aunt Nova Malone."

INTERLUDE

"Snip, snap." I think that is an ending and not a beginning. But the cook made me think of it.

You spoke to me and something stirred in my heart. Not quite hope, it is hard to know hope in this place. But I did not feel its absence so completely. I did not despair as I walked among the trees, not even when I saw the bones of a man lying tumbled at the base of one trunk.

I smelled baking and between one step and the next, I stood at the back door of a restaurant. I had washed dishes in enough places to know this was a good restaurant since the smells coming out of a propped open door were heavy with spice and comfort.

I stepped inside and saw a cook going from tray to tray, icing small ginger cookies in the shapes of stars and crescent moons. From a small box on a shelf, a song crackled through the room. I had to look twice to realize that it was a radio. I had never seen one so small.

"If you're here to help serve today's lunch, you're early" said the cook as she bent over her task, humming a bit to herself; around her neck hung a large silver cross, "And if you're the fool who was supposed to help me with the baking, you're late. It's two hours past dawn already. I need all this done by ten this morning, so I can get started on the entrees. It's not every day we host the Mayor of Kingsport for Christmas Eve."

"A very pretty town," I said to the cook, remembering how you described Kingsport to me.

"What?" said the woman, putting aside her icing to reach for a spatula to transfer the cookies to a rack. "Are you here to work or just hoboing through?"

"I can wash dishes," I said because I knew all good cooks need somebody who is willing to clean.

This cook stopped her work to look at me properly. "Been on the road long?" she said, glancing at my worn leather jacket and stained pants. Even my shoes bore marks of the path's often sudden descent into blood and mud.

"Forever," I replied as honestly as I could.

"Well, the Lord helps those who help themselves," she said. "But there's a lot to be said for charity, especially in this season." She pointed to an alcove behind the kitchen proper where I could see a sink and a large counter with dish racks and draining boards set upon it. "There's a pile of dishes already waiting for a pair of honest hands to clean them. Expect more as the day goes along. Get it all done and I'll pay you."

I set to work. Behind me voices rose and fell as more people streamed into the kitchen.

"Hurry up," said one waitress to the other. "They want the desserts to come out before Mayor Brewster's speech."

The washing continued past lunch as dishes came back to

the sink. I had never stayed in one place so long, I thought, since I became lost under the trees. I began to hope that this time I would remain in the pretty town of Kingsport. I was afraid to step away from the sink at all, afraid I would find myself back in the forest.

Eventually the noises behind me died away as people wished each other a "Merry Christmas" and departed. Still I scrubbed, rinsed, and dried, convinced each action would anchor me in one time and place, even though I didn't know what year it was. Whenever it was, there were dishes to be dried and stacked. A job for me. No matter where I wandered, work always made me feel anchored to a place. For a time at least.

Finally, the cook came to tell me that I was finished. "There's not a single dirty dish anywhere," she said. "Just a plate with some leftovers for you. Sit down and eat something before you go."

As I ate, the cook fiddled with the radio dial until eerie music filled the room and a deep voice intoned, "What evil lurks in the hearts of men, the Shadow knows…."

With a sigh, the cook collapsed into a chair and rested her feet on the rungs of the chair opposite me. "I love this show," she said to me. "The first time I heard it I knew Lamont Cranston understood about the monsters lurking out there. Sometimes I'm so tired of fighting, but then I think someone must keep battling. Just like all the people who help the Shadow on this show."

She sighed and shook her head. "I reckon people all over the world are learning the hard way that we must fight evil. Ten years after the crash, I guess we thought life would be getting better by now. But I read the newspapers, all the stuff happening in Europe because of Hitler, and I just don't know."

I ate as slowly as I could as the story of a detective – a detective with the power to cloud men's minds – unfolded on the radio. Children were reunited with their father. At the end, a rich man gave his girlfriend Margo a puppy and the actors wished the audience a "Merry Christmas." I had never heard anything like it before, but it was marvelous. I told the cook how much I enjoyed it.

The cook smiled at me. "It's sentimental," she said. "I know it is. But we need shows like this. Things just keep getting worse, but this gives me hope. Makes me feel like someone will take up the fight."

"But does it have to be us?" I said as I finished the last of the sandwich. It was a question that I had wrestled with all my life. Driven from place to place, I had heard many men and women standing on soapboxes at street corners shouting for change. I'd seen them cut down and I'd seen them rise to power. It seemed to make very little difference. Men slept cold and hungry in doorways. Women still wept at the death of children. If the newspapers of 1939 piled on the table beside me were true, war was once again engulfing the world.

But here I was warm and safe, and for the moment I was content. That much I had learned in a wandering life. The events of the world can change our lives, but we can do little to change the world. All I wanted was a safe and pretty town and to live my life in peace. But the woman across the table from me wanted something very different.

Arkham Horror

"I don't know about you, son," the cook said as she tapped the cross around her neck, "but I know I have a duty, a calling, to put down monsters. There are days when I am tired, and there are days when I wish the Lord could find another to bear my burdens, but I always know that what I do is good. And I know something more important than the evil in men's hearts."

"What is that?" I asked, touched by her kindness toward me.

She reached out and touched my chest. "I know the good in the most ordinary of people. How much a cook, or a waitress, or a mechanic can do to keep the world a safer place. I have met some extraordinary folks on my travels. I hope you become one of them."

She reached for a handbag and pulled some dollars from it, counting them on the table in front of me. "Use this wisely," the woman said to me. "You're a good worker. I'd have you back, but I'm leaving tonight. There's something in Dunwich that I need to take care of."

As she said the last name, I remembered the grave and the ghoul. "Don't go to Dunwich," I said, thinking about the warning from the trumpet player.

She shook her head. "I don't have a choice. There's a job to be done. Good luck to you."

Even as I gathered up the money, I knew my dream of staying in this Kingsport was impossible. This was not the time, this was not the place, as Jim Culver had predicted. I could feel the world fading as I walked toward the door. The music on the radio became a familiar tune. The kitchen disappeared.

I wish the cook well on her journeys and am sorry that I never learned her name.

CHAPTER NINE

Agent Tawney escorted me to a small diner and insisted on buying me a cup of coffee.

"I'd rather have an Ovaltine," I told the waitress in a small bid for independence. In truth I wished I'd walked away from him when he first invited me to talk to him. Except I was a little overwhelmed. I'd never been stopped by so much as a policeman, let alone a federal agent, and I wasn't sure if I could just walk away. I wished Nova was with me and, at the same time, I was glad that she was safely back at the Diamond Dog, working in her apartment.

"Miss Gutierrez," said Tawney. "Raquel, can I call you Raquel? Please call me Ralph."

"I'd rather not," I muttered, but very quietly and he may not have heard me.

"Mr Brewster has been writing to the Bureau for some time," he said.

"He writes to my aunt daily," I said and then wondered if I should have kept quiet. Perhaps saying that would make Nova look as strange as Brewster.

"I am not surprised," Tawney replied. "He seems to be the very best customer of the US Postal Service. Nevertheless, we must investigate even the most outlandish claims. For the safety of the nation, as I am sure you understand."

"Not at all. What could my aunt possibly do to threaten the safety of the nation? She runs a small cafe called the Purple Cat near Innsmouth and the Diamond Dog in Kingsport. Right now she's home planning a Christmas Eve dance for her ballroom with a live broadcast on her radio station. How could that be of any concern to your Bureau?"

"It's true that investigations of your aunt's activities have fallen to the Prohibition boys until now," he said.

"Oh dear," I said without meaning to speak out loud. Mother would not be pleased if she learned that her suspicions of her sister were shared by the Federal government.

"However," said Tawney, speaking over my interruption, "this is much more serious and well outside the US Treasury's mandate."

"What do you mean?" I asked, while thinking "What could Nova have done?"

"According to Mr Brewster, your aunt – and possibly others employed by her – can travel through time," said Tawney.

I blinked. "I'm sorry, I don't think I heard you correctly," I said. Tawney had one of those rough and slightly low voices that I found hard to understand, even with the help of the hearing aid. But I was looking directly at him and was almost certain he had said "time" as he raised his coffee cup to his mouth and took a sip. Around us the normal clatter of dishes and other people talking also made it harder for me to clearly distinguish his words from others. I shifted the scarf draped across my chest so there was no chance of it muffling or obstructing my microphone. I must have looked like a maiden aunt fussing with her jewelry, except my aunt never fussed and would have demanded answers immediately from Tawney.

"Can you repeat what you said, just a little louder?" I asked, my embarrassment overridden by my curiosity.

"I'd rather not be overheard," he said, leaning across the table toward me. "Read this."

He slid a letter into my hand. Unfolding the heavy cream paper, I immediately recognized the blocky, neat script that covered the entire page. I'd seen Chilton Brewster's distinct handwriting on nearly a dozen envelopes since I had come to stay with Nova.

"To whom it may concern," the letter began. "I have proof that Nova Malone can disrupt the proper progression of time or knows someone who can. She has taken advantage of her knowledge to provide safe passage of illicit goods from one country to the next. Further, her actions have caused an unsettling of previous events to the point of endangering the future of our good town of Kingsport."

I read it twice and then looked at Agent Tawney. "I still don't understand," I said in genuine puzzlement. I could understand an accusation of bootlegging as I had my own suspicions. But time travel? "What does he mean?"

"I asked Mr Brewster that very question. He claims your aunt has traveled through time to accomplish her purchase of the Diamond Dog, an act which may very well impact the history of our nation or at least this corner of it. Since then, he claims she employs time travelers to smuggle liquor into the country for distribution throughout the Eastern seaboard."

"That's ridiculous," I said, pushing the letter back to Tawney. I must have spoken louder than I intended because he made shushing motions with his hands. But I was in no mood to be silenced. "My aunt purchased the Diamond Dog in October after many months of negotiations with the owners. She told me about it herself. She had no need to time travel." I did not bother to comment on the rest of his accusations, which were just as ridiculous. Even if my aunt smuggled liquor, I doubted she had magical employees capable of manipulating time. Plenty of bootleggers existed throughout the state, and they all seemed to manage just fine with cars, boats, and planes. However, I couldn't say that to Tawney.

At the same time, I wasn't completely naive. There'd been a great bustle of activity around the Diamond Dog these past few weeks. Even if I'd never seen liquor served in the ballroom, I resolved to take a closer look at the boxes and boxes of decorations being carried down to the basement of the Diamond Dog. It was past time that I confronted my suspicions about Nova's other businesses head on. Of course, what I would say to her after I found proof, I had no idea.

Tawney continued, "The records of your aunt's purchase of the Diamond Dog seem clear. But Brewster's letters do suggest something strange happened here. He says he lived through the same day twice. This may be due to somebody's manipulation of time."

"Brewster must be lying," I said, unsure why Tawney would be taking this all so seriously. "Time travel isn't possible!"

Tawney shook his head. "I cannot reveal all our sources but some of Brewster's claims seem to be true. We have evidence something did happen to him on December 24, 1925."

"He says he lived through Christmas Eve twice?" I said. "You can't truly believe him." It seemed a very imaginative claim for a cranky banker who spent most of his time writing editorials about how the "dry" laws enhanced public morality and penning letters of complaint to his neighbors.

"He says he was knocked out of the correct day by a time traveler," said Tawney, as if this was a rational explanation.

All around us the diners continued their conversations. Through the window I could see people hurrying down the street with all the packages associated with Christmas errands. Oddly enough, I found my brief talk with Paul just moments ago felt far more real and urgent than this conversation. My doubt and bemusement at what Tawney apparently felt was a major revelation showed clearly in my face, for the agent reacted very strongly to my disbelief.

"I do have evidence," Tawney said with some ire. He reached into his upper vest pocket and pulled out several small snapshots. "These photos support Brewster's story," he said, thrusting the first picture at me.

Peering at the photograph, I recognized the entrance of the Diamond Dog. Brewster was standing on the doorstep with a portly man that I did not know. When I said as much,

Tawney answered with such emphasis that I shushed him, much as he had asked me to drop my voice earlier. "That's one of the former owners, Samuel Morrissen. Who is also a suspected bootlegger," Tawney said with a glare that contradicted all the friendly chatter of "just call him Ralph" only a few minutes earlier.

"Why are you showing this to me?" I asked with some justification and equal brusqueness. "I haven't been in Kingsport before this month. I don't know this person." Which was true, but not completely so. I did remember the name from conversations with Nova about her purchase of the Diamond Dog. The suspected bootlegger part she had not mentioned.

"This was taken during a stakeout of the property by a Prohibition agent. Which is confidential information. I would appreciate your assurances that you won't discuss this conversation with others," Tawney said, completely ignoring my question and increasing my uneasiness.

I murmured something noncommittal. I wasn't about to argue with a man with a badge, but I also wasn't going to gag myself unless I absolutely had to.

"The photo was logged as having been taken on December 24, 1925. As was this one," said the agent.

Tawney slapped down a second photo. Like the first, it showed Morrissen standing on the steps of the Diamond Dog. In this one Morrissen was talking to a man in a leather coat whose face was turned away from the camera. Something about the set of the second man's shoulders and the way he was stretching one hand toward Morrissen seemed desperate. Rather like a man making a plea for help.

"Who is the other man?" I asked.

"Chilton didn't know," Tawney said in such a way that I immediately wondered if the agent recognized the man in the picture. He was certainly scowling at the picture as if the blurred figure was a known criminal. "Brewster claimed that he was an employee of your aunt's, sent to disrupt his business deal by knocking him down. I want to talk to this man and find out what he knows."

"But how is this evidence of time travel?" I said. "Two photos, taken of the same place, showing people on the steps of the Diamond Dog."

"One photo shows Morrissen talking to Brewster on the steps. The other shows Morrissen talking to the stranger in the leather coat, our time traveler," Tawney said as if laying claim to the unnamed man in the leather coat. "Both pictures were taken at exactly the same time." He tapped the ends of the two photos. On each, handwriting noted the date as December 24, 1925, and each did indeed state in the same handwriting that the time was 3:27 PM.

"One of these was labeled wrong," I said with some conviction. The whole thing was too absurd, no matter how convinced Tawney sounded. I wondered again how a federal agent could take such claims seriously.

"The photos were taken with a Vest Pocket Autographic," said Tawney. "The photographer always noted the time and date on the film at the time he snapped the picture."

"He read his watch wrong," I insisted.

"Then this photo appears on the roll and is dated exactly three minutes after the other two," said Tawney, laying down a third picture.

In the third picture, Morrissen was walking away from the entrance of the Diamond Dog, heading toward the photographer. A little further away a figure came down the street. Tawney claimed this was Chilton Brewster, delayed from reaching his destination. Then, in a fourth photo, the man in the leather coat reappeared. Or rather almost appeared. Something must have gone wrong in the exposure, for the man in the leather coat was nearly transparent, a corner of the Diamond Dog improbably visible through his body.

The waitress made another pass by our table, asking if we needed anything. Tawney shook his head at her. I noticed he was careful to shift his hands and cover the photographs, hiding them from her view. But as soon as she walked away, he lifted his hands away and pushed all three closer to me.

"Then there's this photo," said Tawney, setting out a fifth picture like a fortune teller laying out the cards. He shoved it face up across the table to me.

In the picture, again dated December 24 and just a few minutes after the third one, my aunt Nova stood on the street outside the Diamond Dog. She was very oddly dressed for winter, wearing a light summer dress that was torn across the shoulders. Something else about the photo bothered me. I peered closer to be sure. Nova's hair and clothing appeared to be dripping wet. Standing next to her was Chilton Brewster. Once again, a blurry almost translucent figure could be seen further down the street, the man in the leather coat.

"Brewster claims your aunt materialized in front of him

and demanded his coat," said Tawney. "She told him that she'd fallen off a pier."

"In the middle of Kingsport?"

"Seems unlikely," Tawney agreed. "Also, at the very time this photograph was taken, the Purple Cat was holding its Christmas Eve dance. According to photos of the event which were published in the *Arkham Advertiser*, your aunt was there. I also have the sworn testimony of two Prohibition agents who attended the dance that your aunt was visible to them for the entire evening."

"She can't have been in two places at the same time," I protested, trying to think of a logical explanation and failing.

"If Nova Malone's accomplice can time travel," Tawney shot back, tapping the figure in the background, "then he could transport her to any number of places at any time that they wish. Imagine, Miss Gutierrez, what damage even one man could do with such knowledge. What malicious attacks could be made by a hostile government agent. As a patriot, Miss Gutierrez, it is your duty to help me apprehend this time traveler." His hand slapped down on the picture of the man in the leather coat.

"But I don't know who he is!" I said.

"Nova Malone does. She was seen with him. Ask your aunt," snapped Tawney.

I nearly retorted, "Ask her yourself." But I held my tongue. I truly couldn't believe a time traveler worked for Nova. Despite Tawney's persistent questioning about the man, I wondered if the agent concocted the photos as an elaborate sham. Did he think to scare me into giving him information? Why would I help him when it was so ridiculous a claim as time travel? No, I decided, he must be looking for evidence of bootlegging.

What I wanted, I thought, truly was time. Time to find my courage. I needed to question my aunt about why she left Innsmouth for Kingsport and where her money came from.

INTERLUDE

"One, two, buckle my shoe," I sing to begin this story.

The hounds are here. I see them emerge from places beside the trees with teeth. Teeth bloodied by their attack in the laboratory. Their howls sound as hideous as their bodies appear. Their faces are so foul that I cannot look them in the eye. They make the ghoul in the Dunwich woods seem clean.

But I found a lady who taught me a way to trick them. This is how it happened.

I don't remember why I left the beach. But I was running under the trees until I burst into an open square. The sun was setting behind large, impressive stone buildings. I stood in a snowy patch of lawn. Around me the walkways had been shoveled to reveal mellow brick. The surrounding buildings were connected by these pathways which all ran in neat lines forming squares and triangles separated by the snowy grass. A group of carolers stood on the steps of one building singing loudly while others gathered around them.

A man pushed past them shouting, "I'll rest you if you don't get out of my way. Classes are over for the year, why can't you students leave us in peace?"

The carolers shouted back, "Merry Christmas, professor!"

In this quadrangle, young people hurried past me, dressed the way that the wealthy Berliners did in my youth. When I was a boy of fifteen or sixteen, years before I was a man lost in the trenches, I'd loiter on the street corners and watch people like these descend from carriages and motorcars, hurrying across the newly shoveled pavement and disappearing into the light and warmth of a theater or restaurant. The women then wore coats of velvet hanging to their ankles and fur collars framing their faces. I once worked for furriers in Berlin, the workshops specializing in trims for the best tailors and dressmakers. I still remember the sable, seal, mink, lynx, and fox furs lying in piles on the back tables to be fashioned into collars and cuffs.

A pair of young women passed me, angling toward a brilliantly lit building at the edge of what would be a great green lawn if it was not covered in snow. These women also were dressed in the slim coats and large fur collars of my youth, but they were not Berliners. They laughed and joked in English, and the coats were cut from more practical cloth, made of tweed or blue wool.

"Hurry, Beatrice," called one woman. "You don't want to miss this party. They promised sherry and cake."

"Without even tasting the sherry or the cake," answered a pretty lady with brown curls springing out from under her hat, "I can predict that with seven members of the Math Club being male, and only two of us being female, the odds of this party being a success are virtually nil."

"That's why Lillian and Gloria are coming," answered the other. "And possibly another girl from the English department, if she hasn't left for home yet."

"That's still seven to four, not quite outnumbered two to one, but far too close for my liking. If Gloria's additional friend does appear, we will be seven to five, Judy," said the one called Beatrice.

"Beatrice Sharpe! You just want to go back to the library," Judy replied. "You've had your nose stuck in that old almanac all semester."

"It's interesting," said Miss Sharpe to her friend. "There's something about it. Every time I read it… well, I can't explain it, not yet, but I will. There's a pattern there. I only need to determine the correct formula."

"Enough studying," cried Judy, linking her arm with Beatrice and pulling her a little faster down the neatly shoveled walkway. "Let's go to this party. Even if it's dismal, it's still better than sitting alone in our rooms tonight."

"Tonight is simply the 24th day of the twelfth month," said Beatrice with a smile as she walked quickly by the other's side. "There's nothing magical about this date. They changed the calendar in 1752 to correct the errors in calculating leap years. But if we want to be mathematically and historically accurate, we should be celebrating in January 1914 and not December 1913."

"Oh look, there's Gloria, and she did bring some friends," said Judy, interrupting her friend's lecture. Three more women joined the group. "Enough talk about numbers and history, Beatrice."

"There will always be math, it is the formula which underpins the universe," said Beatrice, unhooking her arm from her friend so she could gesture with both hands. "And may I point out that we are going to a party of the Miskatonic University Math Club being held in a classroom still reeking of chalk dust due to the equations written on the walls and chaperoned by two members of the faculty. Which makes it unnecessary to even calculate the odds of math being discussed."

I drifted after them, unwilling to approach them but drawn to the comfort of their bright chatter, more warming to my soul than a fire. As a boy, if I had talked to such ladies I would have been chased away with shouts and blows by their gentlemen companions or the police. I would not have dared. But there were no uniformed police here and glancing down at myself, I was no longer the skinny boy who slept in the doorways of furriers, hoping not to freeze overnight or die of starvation. Something about the one called Beatrice made me wonder if I could ask her for help.

As they made their way up the steps of a large and impressive stone building, Beatrice paused at the top of the stairs. She fumbled with the bag hanging off her wrist. "Oh drat," she said. "I left my notebook in the library. I really must fetch it. They'll be locking up soon and the building will be closed for the rest of the week."

"Beatrice!" exclaimed her friend. "You promised to come with me."

"You now have three other women with you who care

nothing about mathematics!" said Beatrice. "The odds are in your favor, ladies, especially without me, of having at least a few minutes of casual conversation over the sherry before the talk once again turns to esoteric data. Good luck!" She hurried down the stairs toward me.

"Beatrice, you traitor!" cried Judy, but she swept into the building with the others, still laughing as the door clanged shut behind them.

As Beatrice reached the spot where I stood hesitating about approaching her, she looked directly at me and said, "Do you know that you appeared in this square approximately seven minutes ago in that patch of snow?" She pointed to a white area between the brick walkways. "I observed your footprints begin there and proceed to here. But there's no indication of where you came from."

In the twilight gloom the dark track of my steps was clear, as was the fact that all around them the snow lay white and undisturbed. "Would you mind explaining to me exactly how you did that?" said Beatrice.

I was touched by how she looked at me so directly. Others had spoken to me, but Beatrice saw me. "I don't know what is happening to me," I said. "Do you?"

The carolers behind us launched into a song about a good king.

"I've been calculating and calculating, but I can't find a reasonable explanation for your apparent appearance out of thin air," said Beatrice as if my strange waking nightmare was the most natural thing in the world. "Not unless you want to apply some of the more outlandish but quite interesting theories of that Zurich mathematician Einstein.

His papers on Brownian motion, classical mechanics, and electromagnetic fields do suggest time, motion, and energy may be more complicated than Newton imagined." She paused for breath. "Also, the creature following you seems to be untethered to normal patterns of movement. Look how it keeps popping in and out of the corners of the square."

I whirled around and saw one of the nightmares from the forest slinking toward us. Its tongue lolled out of its mouth and it crawled forward on scabrous paws which left no marks upon the icy ground.

"Let's move away," said Beatrice, reaching out to pull my sleeve and tow me after her along the path. "I do want to talk to you, and we can't concentrate with such a thing bothering us."

"Go, go," I said, suddenly afraid I would see her torn apart like the men in the laboratory. But this strange young woman seemed to have no sense of fear. I pushed her away from me, hoping the beast would concentrate on me instead. "Don't let it touch you." The hound behind us had disappeared. Then it popped in front of us, rising out of the corner where one walkway met the other. The stink of the other place, the smell of decay and destruction, drifted through the cold air.

"Very interesting indeed," said Beatrice, cocking her head with curiosity and still no signs of fear. However, she backed up a few steps. "It does like angles, doesn't it? Can't seem to stay away from them." She stepped off the pathway and began to circle the beast. Behind us I could still hear the carolers singing about Wenceslas, but there was nobody else in the square to observe us. The others had gone into the warm and lighted buildings surrounding us on all sides. The hound flickered from spot to spot, increasingly hard to see in the gloom. I could hear its harsh panting and the liquid plop of its tongue swiping in and out of its mouth.

"You must run," I said to her. Running was the only solution. Fighting it would fail. I'd seen these creatures ignore bullets as they tore men apart.

"I was studying the most interesting almanac this morning, and it was all about circles and lines," Beatrice said, not moving at all to my horror. "And nursery rhymes. Most annoying, because I didn't want to be reading children's songs, even one called 'Arithmetick.' But now I wonder."

Because the young lady would not run, I tried to put my body between the hound and her. I had failed those men in the laboratory, thinking only of my escape. This impossibly brave young woman did not deserve their fate.

"Come along, do, you're worse than Judy for lollygagging," she commanded me even as I tried to protect her. "Follow in my footsteps, follow the circle."

She sounded as imperious as the Berlin ladies who once commanded me to sweep the street to keep their hems clean. But kinder too. For still she spoke to me as if I was someone who mattered. As if she wanted to help me as much as I wanted to save her.

So I stepped where she stepped, my larger feet overlaying the prints of hers as we tracked a giant circle around the hound. The beast began to sway back and forth, hunting blindly, always sticking to the straight paths and sharp corners.

"One, two, buckle my shoe; three, four, lay down lower," Beatrice sang as she danced along the curved path we had made in the snow, coming back to where we started. "That rather confused me because I learned it originally as 'knock at the door' but it makes sense here. We don't have a door, do we? I'd duck if I was you."

The hound sprang but Beatrice pulled me aside and down into the snow. The creature sailed over our heads with an odd twisting turn in midair, as if it struck some invisible wall cast up by the outer edge of our circle. It landed back in a sharp corner of the path. It threw up its head and howled, but it seemed as if only we heard it. Behind us the carolers continued to sing loudly, and that may have been the most terrifying moment of all. To know the beast hunted us and only us, and no one could intervene.

Beatrice pulled open her bag and drew out a handful of sharpened pencils, tossing them onto the ground in a pile. The hound whined, a terrifying sound that cut through me, but it was no longer looking at us. Instead it stared at the pile of pencils in front of it.

"Five, six, pick up sticks," said Beatrice, grabbing the pencils on the ground. "Seven, eight, lay them straight." She set the pencils down again in a pattern of triangles. In the sing-song tone that people adopt with pets, she said, "There you go, ugly doggie, look at the nice sticks. Isosceles, equilateral, scalene, obtuse, acute, and right angles. All for you. Good dog, good dog."

She backed away, still walking in a curve, slowly circling

us toward the outer edge of the square, closer and closer to where the group of jolly students sang upon the steps of a brick building. The hound dropped its head down, nosing the pattern before it, and, this I swear is true, flickering in and out of existence. With each appearance, it became smaller and smaller until it faded away, no larger than a mouse.

"Fascinating," said Beatrice. "Congruence seems to have confused its ability to hold to this time and place. I wasn't sure so I made a few patterns. Descending patterns would be best if you meet it again, by which I mean a continuation pattern of ever smaller triangles. And, of course, if you go in circles it will have a hard time tracking you."

I tried to stammer out some thanks. All my stunned mind could produce was the broken phrases of my youth, begging on the streets of Berlin. But my gratitude was far truer than when I begged for coins. "Thank you, lady, fine lady, thank you, without your help today we would have died." As soon as I made this speech, I felt foolish. What American would understand me?

Beatrice answered me in far crisper and aristocratic German, "Don't be silly. The book told me exactly what to do. And I was not about to let the creature eat us. I have so many questions to ask you."

As I blinked in surprise to hear the language of my youth, the group of singers on the steps finished up their carol and all pulled strings of bells from their pockets. With much laughter they shook the bells and began to sing again, marching down the stairs toward us.

"Oh, drat that glee club, can't they shut up for a minute?"

said Beatrice, switching back to English. "Let's get out of their way. Wait, wait, don't go!"

But I was under the trees again and the hounds were howling in frustration as they tried to find my scent. I began to run back to the beach, and I ran in a wide curve, circling, always circling, to confuse my pursuers.

CHAPTER TEN

Although I would regret my decision later, I did not immediately return to the Diamond Dog and tell my aunt about my encounter with Agent Tawney (I never could bring myself to call him Ralph). Instead I left Tawney and his impossible photographs at the coffee shop while I hastened to the camera store down the street.

When I questioned the clerk about an autographic camera, he immediately knew what I was talking about. He pulled one out of his case and proceeded to tell me about how this particular model was known as "the soldier's camera" as so many had been sold during the war. He demonstrated how to use the autographic feature that allowed the photographer to inscribe the date and time that the photo was taken. "Or you could write the name of a place or the name of the person being photographed," he enthused.

The camera also folded up quite small, perfect to fit into a pocket or purse. "You can always have it with you and never miss a single shot," he assured me.

"That would be quite handy for a detective," I seethed. He looked confused at my bitter statement. Of course he didn't know how a certain Federal agent had thrown down pictures taken by such a camera as the evidence of time travel. Technically, what Tawney said seemed possible. The photos could be dated exactly when taken. But that didn't mean, I told myself, that the two different photos had been snapped at exactly the same time.

Feeling a little sorry for the man – for I shouldn't be snapping at him but rather at the world which continued to complicate my life – I asked about the price. While twelve dollars was not cheap, it was affordable. I purchased the camera and some of the special 127 film to go with it. He wrapped the camera together with the film, adding a beautifully tied bow as a finishing touch. The clerk told me that he would be happy to give instructions about the camera's use to the gift's recipient. I responded that it was for my Aunt Nova, at which he seemed quite delighted.

"Oh, I've been dancing at the Diamond Dog a few times," he said. "I am looking forward to taking my gal to the Christmas Eve dance. We already have our tickets."

"Do you listen to the radio broadcast too?" I asked.

"Always when I'm at home, and I enjoy the noon broadcast while eating my lunch in the store." He pointed to a radio tucked behind the counter, one of the newer table models. "The owner is thinking about offering a few radios for sale along with the cameras. There's a big demand these days."

"It's quite an expense," I said, thinking about the handsome radio sitting in my aunt's apartment and the rest of her new appliances. Only a fool would discount Agent Tawney's claims of bootlegging given the extent of my aunt's mysterious wealth. But bootlegging through time travel? That was a foolish story, a fairytale.

Then I remembered Paul's voice whispering in my ear: "Once upon a time."

The clerk tried to discuss time payments to afford larger items like radios, but I simply thanked him for his help with the gift for my aunt and left the store.

Thinking about Paul, and the fragments of fairytales that I'd heard him speak over the past few days, I set off for the Diamond Dog with my package tucked firmly under my arm. I wished I knew where he was and how I could help him. At that moment, rescuing a phantom man that I'd never seen and only heard through my earpiece seemed so much easier and, frankly, more appealing than sorting out my complicated relationship with Nova. Or deciding what to do with my own future.

Nothing made any real sense. But nothing had made sense to me since the day I realized a simple fever had changed my hearing forever.

To keep up my spirits, I began to whistle the jazzy bouncing rendition of "Jingle Bells" that we now played every night at the Diamond Dog. Billy's version had proved so popular that the dancers demanded it at least once in the evening.

As I turned the corner I heard a howling wail, both like and unlike a dog. Glancing back over my shoulder, I saw nothing behind me. But the sound repeated in my ear and I began to hasten down the street.

Kingsport had played its usual tricks on me and, suddenly, I was walking down a street that I'd never seen before. I paused to get my bearings and figure out the best way back to the Diamond Dog.

Convinced I needed to retrace my steps, I went back to a street that looked vaguely familiar. The buildings in this part of town lacked the overall prosperity of other places, but something about the area reminded me of the streets running behind the Diamond Dog.

The brightness of the afternoon faded away. Clouds gathered overhead, sullen with the threat of snow, and the town which had so charmed me earlier in the day felt unbearably dreary. I noticed an undertaker's storefront, the name and business written in gilt letters on the dark glass. Unlike the shops I'd passed earlier, no warm and welcoming lights brightened these windows or the dark doorways of the other shabby buildings huddled close by. Even the streetlamps cast a sulfurous yellow glow that did nothing to lessen the gloom of this street.

I found myself wondering if this was one of the parts of town that Chilton Brewster wanted to clean up and clean out.

A pair of shabbily dressed women stepped out of a doorway. Both seemed weary, moving with a shuffling gait away from me. One stopped and bent to adjust her shoe while the other leaned against the window of the mortuary. A large white hand appeared in the center of the window. The rest of his body invisible behind the darkened glass, the man rapped sharply against the window. The woman gave a little gasp and sprang away. Tugging at her friend's arm, they hurried down the street and disappeared around a corner.

A completely unreasonable fear settled upon me. While a few people continued to go by, intent on their own business, I suddenly felt unbearably alone and lost. Yet I knew friends and family waited for me back at the Diamond Dog.

My earpiece buzzed and whined enough to set my teeth on edge. I reached my hand into my purse, intent on switching off the battery, convinced the cold or my walk had caused the device to malfunction. But even as I laid my hand upon the battery, I heard Paul's voice more clearly than ever before.

"Five, six, pick up sticks," he chanted.

I passed a wrought iron fence. Laying against the fence were a couple of long sticks. I remembered my brothers grabbing sticks like this and rattling them along a fence for the sheer pleasure of making a racket.

Something about Paul's voice compelled me to act. I snatched up the sticks and spun about, convinced that something stalked me along the street. The fear, the certainty that there was something to fear, nearly overwhelmed me.

Of course I saw nothing. I knew there was nothing there. Yet I also knew my eyes and ears were deceiving me. I could not see it. I could not hear it. But something followed me. It frightened me as much as a hand rapping against the glass of a window had frightened those two women a few moments earlier. Yet the hand couldn't touch them.

But fear is never reasonable, and it was fear that made me believe that something lurked just at the edge of my perception.

"Seven, eight, lay them straight," Paul sang. I tossed the sticks down again so they fell in right angles to the fence. Then I spun about and took to my heels, running all the way back to that afternoon's shops and eventually the Diamond Dog, running as if pursued.

INTERLUDE

When Ivan met his Baba Yaga, she told him to set about his business and his business was all about escaping her with the help of birds, lions, and bees. Made brave by my meetings with the faithful servant and the clever lady, I began to search, as Ivan searched, for a way back to the world that I knew. When I met my Baba Yaga, I tried to follow her home.

Standing on the beach at the edge of the ocean without waves, I heard a tremendous splash. Afraid of what was coming out of the sea, I was retreating under the trees when a woman said, "So much fuss for a book."

Turning around, I saw a large woman wading out of the water. Her dress was torn along the shoulders and her hair was wild about her face. I knew her immediately for the Baba Yaga who walked through the stories of my childhood. On her breast winked a purple brooch shaped like a cat. I could see that she was a woman of great strength and cunning, as a Baba Yaga must be.

When she reached the shore, the woman wrung out her

skirt. Then she looked at me and said, "I don't suppose you know the road to Innsmouth?"

I gaped like a fish caught on a hook. It seemed impossible that someone could simply fall into this place like me. I often thought it was my own particular nightmare, and strangers do not join you in nightmares. Besides, I knew bargaining with a Baba Yaga could lead to your head upon a pole in her yard. She frightened me and fascinated me at the same time.

"Perhaps Innsmouth would be a bad choice," she said, and I could not tell if she was talking to me or to herself. She gave me a sideways glance. "I'm not even sure if you're real. Things often aren't here. Try not to turn into anything nasty. I lost my gun in the sea."

Behind me I heard something slither and whine.

"Patterns, I need a pattern for someplace other than Innsmouth," the woman said, walking past me down the beach, still chattering to herself. "Songs make very good maps! But why such a silly tune? Well, it's the one stuck in my head right now. It might fit Kingsport. Here goes."

She began to hum, and it was a tune that I knew. There was a rhythm to it like the ringing of bells. I'd heard this song before in the alley where Pete found me. At the end of the dock when I talked to Captain Leo. I could almost name the song, which had been sung in a beer hall as the faithful servant told me to take heart.

"And soon Miss Fanny Bright was seated by my side," sang the woman, stepping in time to her singing. She began to shimmer around the edges.

With a cry, I sprang after her, more afraid of losing her

than losing my head. "Wait, wait!" I wailed like a child chasing after his mother.

Then I was running down a street, an ordinary street lined with shops. People walked slowly along, chattering with each other and clutching parcels in their arms. I dodged around the shoppers. A few glared at me but most simply moved aside as if they barely noticed me. Ahead of me was my glowing Baba Yaga but nobody else seemed to see her. I bumped into a man and he fell into a snowbank. His hat went flying and his round eyeglasses were knocked crooked across his face.

"Watch where you are going!" he yelled at me, but I ran on. I needed to find my Baba Yaga so I could learn her trick of stepping so confidently away from that terrible place. Or I knew it would pull me back under the trees again.

But the street was deserted. Another man, well fed and well dressed, stood on the steps of a long white building. He appeared to be watching for someone.

I ran up to him and held out my hand. "Have you seen her? My Baba Yaga?" I stumbled through the words. I may not have spoken in English. I was so anxious and confused, I may have used the Russian of my childhood.

"What?" he said, turning and looking at me. "What do you want? I don't have anything for you. Get away." He glanced over my shoulder and swore. "G-man. Should have known this was a trick. I'm out of here. Tell Brewster that he can't force me to sell the Diamond Dog by writing letters to the law. They can take all the pictures they want, they have nothing on me."

The man hurried past me to rap on the window of a

parked car. "I see you! Hope you captured my good side! Merry Christmas, nosey parker!" Then he laughed and walked away, whistling the same tune that my Baba Yaga sang.

In the distance I heard her voice, still singing. Spinning around, I saw her almost dancing down the street, her feet flying in time to her song. She bumped into the very man that I had knocked into the snowbank only moments before. The two clutched each other, swaying back and forth, but she broke away first. I hurried toward them, determined not to lose Baba Yaga until I learned her tricks.

"This isn't Innsmouth," she said with some certainty. "So the song worked!"

"Madam," said the businessman, resettling his glasses on his nose and glaring at her. "This is Kingsport, and you appear to be drunk."

She laughed at his sour expression. "Liquor never touched my lips today. But I am indeed one of the wet tonight. Dropped off a pier and into the drink. What's the date, bub?"

"Christmas Eve, of course!" said the man.

"I think I have some time and distance to go tonight before I find myself in the right place," said Baba Yaga. "Be a good sport and lend me your coat. I'm not dressed for this weather."

Apparently wise enough not to argue with such a woman, the man took off his coat and tossed it over her shoulders. "Do not mistake my charity for my approval," he said quite sternly. "Your lack of decorum is appalling. Take yourself home, madam, and be glad that I did not call the police!"

"Bells on bobtail ring," she sang and stepped away from the gentleman with a merry wave of her hands. On every finger sparkled a diamond ring. "Making spirits bright."

Then my Baba Yaga was gone. I was once again on the beach where something slithered underneath the trees near the shore. But I had received a gift from the witch. I knew what I needed: a tune to lead me out of the woods. I know what we must find. Raquel, dare I ask you to go to Baba Yaga and steal her song for us? For if Ivan's friends failed him, their heads would have ended on a pole in Baba Yaga's yard.

CHAPTER ELEVEN

The morning after my encounter with Agent Tawney, Nova asked me to take the previous evening's receipts to the bank. Normally Lily did this, but she'd been feeling poorly. Nova sent her home and told her to stay home for a day or two until she was fully recovered. Knowing my aunt, she probably sent over a pot of fish chowder to aid Lily's recovery. Nova believed in the healing properties of fish chowder the way that other people believed in chicken soup.

Nova kept her money in Chilton Brewster's savings and loan. Whether she did this to annoy him or to placate him, I cannot say, although I suspect it may have been the former. Generally, Nova rarely showed dislike openly, and she often counseled her employees against carrying grudges (despite this, there was a long-standing feud between one waiter and one cook that resulted in a terrible kitchen disaster on a Saturday night).

However, Nova had little patience for those she considered "fools and damn fools too." So it was entirely possible that she wanted Chilton Brewster to be aware of her success at the Diamond Dog by deliberately depositing her increasingly large profits with him.

I had my own reasons for wanting to visit the bank. Following my conversation with Agent Tawney, I decided to question Chilton Brewster about his duplicate Christmas Eve. I still wondered if the whole story was something of a ruse by Agent Tawney – and possibly Brewster – to gain greater knowledge of my aunt's business.

Declining the offer of Nova's car, I set off across Kingsport by foot carrying a remarkably heavy carpetbag. Business at the Diamond Dog apparently had been very good the night before or else Nova had also added the receipts of the Purple Cat to my load. I considered that some of the cash may have come from elsewhere, but I lacked the courage to question my aunt directly. After all, how do you ask over toast and coffee if your host and relative is a bootlegger? It was a question that I had not answered yet in my own head during our breakfast, and one that would continue to plague me on my walk to the bank.

Otis trailed along behind me, which meant my aunt was not completely confident about the safety of Kingsport's streets on a Thursday morning. Although I felt none of the strange chill I experienced the day before, I was glad of Nova's largest employee walking steadily after me.

When I, and the carpetbag full of dollars and coins, reached the bank, Otis watched me climb the steps to the entrance and then left. Presumably he thought the likelihood of me being robbed inside the bank was minimal or simply not his business. I had safely arrived and that was his task completed.

Brewster's bank stood out from neighboring buildings due to its very solidity. Built of stone, it boasted three wide shallow steps leading up to a stout pair of oak doors. Inside, the floor was marble and the counters also oak, with well-polished brass cages to protect the tellers from the patrons. Nevertheless, the customers upon my visit seemed a mild enough lot, waiting in two neat lines for the next available teller. When it was my turn, I heaved the carpetbag onto the counter and said, "Deposit from Miss Nova Malone."

There was a little sighing and fussing, as the bag was too large to pass easily through the teller's window in the brass cage. Instead, I was informed that Miss Malone's deposit was usually handled by the manager and I should take the bag to his desk. Presumably Lily would have done this but why they expected me to know where the bank manager sat, I couldn't guess.

After more fussing, somebody came out from behind a half wall of golden oak to fetch me and the bag to the proper place. My guide turned out to be no less than Chilton Brewster himself.

"Miss Malone?" He bowed me through the open gate that led from the public area to where the officers of the bank sat.

"Miss Gutierrez," I replied. "Raquel Malone Gutierrez," I added in case he thought I was trying to deny my connection to my aunt.

"I don't believe we have seen you here before," he said. I found it hard to reconcile this rather bland man with the one who had shouted accusations of bootlegging at my aunt on my first day in Kingsport or who wrote hundreds of letters to others about their failings.

I wondered if there was a Mrs Brewster and what she thought about his activities. Did the man have any time for her, or did he simply disappear into some office at home to write out all those neatly printed envelopes? Later I would learn there was no Mrs Brewster, which was something of a comfort as things turned out.

"Lily was not feeling well," I explained, "so I offered to bring the deposit for her."

Brewster waved me into his own office and pulled out a chair for me. He circled the large desk (oak again!) in the center of the room and settled into his own chair. An equally impressive bookcase filled the wall behind his desk. It appeared to hold ledgers and a number of smaller leatherbound books, all neatly arranged on the shelf according to the year stamped in gold upon the spine.

Brewster's mouth pursed in an expression of concern at my earlier comment. "I am sorry to hear about Lily. Her work here was always excellent and she was very well liked. I'll instruct my secretary to send some flowers."

That concern, so quickly expressed and apparently genuine for a former employee, encapsulated the problem I had with Brewster the entire time that I was in Kingsport. While I could never like the man, he had his moments of humanity, or at least of good manners, which made it very hard to dislike him as much as I wanted to.

"Oh, Lily is not very ill," I said, heaving the carpetbag onto the desk. I could have sworn the thing had gained a pound or two during my walk and another one while waiting in line at the bank. It landed with a resounding thud.

"Business seems to be doing well," said Brewster, still very pleasant and polite, so much so that I was beginning to regret my resolve to ask about his time travel story. I couldn't think of a way to bring up the topic that wouldn't make me sound unhinged.

"Yes, quite well," I said. "I don't know much about my aunt's business, but she seems to be a success." I paused, hoping Brewster would press me with questions about Nova's business that would allow me to question him in turn.

Instead, he opened the carpetbag and withdrew the bank book and deposit slip resting on top of the cash. He looked it over carefully and just as carefully pulled out the rubber banded stacks of dollar bills and the rolls of coins. He counted the stacks quickly and said, "I'm sure this is all correct. Lily and your aunt are always meticulous and we haven't found an error yet in their deposits." He took the deposit slip from the bank book and placed it with the currency. Then he made a notation in the book, initialed it, and dropped the bank book back into the carpetbag, which he handed to me.

I sat there with the empty carpetbag on my lap, staring foolishly at him over the stacks of bills. In all the mysteries that I read, the detectives came up with clever jokes or sly questions which led their suspects to spill out every possible clue. I couldn't think of a single way to start the conversation. Brewster continued to look at me with the slightly distant but polite expression of a man who must be wondering why I didn't rise and leave his office now that our business was done.

Brewster, probably due to antique notions of propriety, had left his office door slightly ajar. Glancing over my shoulder, I could see other employees walking across the bank's office. A woman typed at a desk just outside the door, the clatter of the keys loud enough for me to hear. A man leaned over her desk, grabbing a stack of paper from a wooden tray while whistling a few bars of Billy's version of "Jingle Bells." It seemed even the employees of Brewster's bank were fans of the Diamond Dog's broadcast.

Then, suddenly in my left ear, the one covered by my earpiece, Paul's voice said, "I believe in you, Raquel."

Feeling momentarily braver, I turned in my seat, looked straight at Brewster, took a deep breath, and said, quite casually, "I met Agent Tawney yesterday."

"Ah," said Brewster, reaching out to rearrange the pens lying on his desk blotter. He set them end to end in a neat line, looking at the desk rather than me.

"He says you wrote him several letters," I went on.

Three almost as straight lines appeared in Brewster's high forehead as he frowned at his desk. "Hmm," he said.

"Did you write to him?" I said, now sounding a little desperate and wishing that somebody, anyone, would tell me exactly what to say. Paul might whisper words of encouragement to me, but how did those smart ladies in Rinehart's mysteries solve the cases? "Did you write to Agent Tawney about my aunt?" I said and hoped that was the right question to ask first.

Brewster raised his eyes from his contemplation of his

neat row of pens and looked at me directly. "I wrote to several agencies about your aunt's activities in Kingsport," he said finally. "In my position as a business leader in Kingsport, I am charged with a civic responsibility toward our city. I did not think it would be prudent to keep my observations to myself. Rather, when I saw that significant changes were occurring, and that those changes could be traced to your aunt's acquisition of the Diamond Dog, I felt it was no more than my duty to bring forward the conundrum which I personally experienced on December 24 of last year."

At this I straightened up a little. Tawney claimed that Brewster's letters spoke of a "time travel" incident on Christmas Eve. As I was just about to ask him what happened, he launched into another speech.

"Kingsport can be so much more than it currently is," Brewster said, warming into a cadence that I recognized from his editorializing on his radio show. "I can bring our city to a new level of excellence, a model for all other cities, through programs which harness our resources, both natural and manmade, to serve the greater good."

He spoke very rapidly. I know I lost a word or more, but I've tried to reproduce in this account the general self-important emphasis that he gave to his statements. Although he held no elected office or official position, he truly believed himself to be the center of Kingsport's civic life as his next unsolicited speech would prove.

"To use such a discovery as your aunt has made for the mere satisfaction of a recreational vice can only be abhorred by right-thinking individuals, as I am sure our governmental agencies would agree with me," Brewster continued. "It is my duty to inform them what was happening here in Kingsport. We cannot become another Arkham or Innsmouth."

My own unease grew as I sat there listening to him.

Still he did not shout as he had the first time that I met him. Later I decided he was one of those men who cared greatly about outward appearances. If he had yelled at me in the bank, he would have been heard by his employees through the open office door.

"The Diamond Dog provides innocent entertainment, as do the radio broadcasts from Nova's station. Neither, I think, can hurt Kingsport's reputation," I argued while I tried to figure out how to say, "I'm sure my aunt doesn't use time traveling as a means for bootlegging" without sounding like an idiot.

Brewster frowned at me. "Are you so certain about the innocence of those broadcasts? Have you listened closely to what is said? I have. I advised Agent Tawney to do the same. The cookie recipes threaten us all with a deluge of liquor and vice in our fair city."

I blinked. "The cookie recipes?" I repeated back to him, certain that I heard his words wrong. Weren't we talking about time travel and bootlegging?

"Pepper nuts," said Brewster, "should never contain white pepper according to Mrs Orne. Yet Johnny Carl told the listeners to add two shakes of white pepper. A direction," Brewster emphasized the last word, "which makes no sense in the baking of cookies but contains a great deal of information for others."

He looked triumphantly at me, but I had no idea why. "I

don't understand what pepper has to do with anything," I said.

"No?" said Brewster. He pushed back his chair and stood up. He stepped to the bookshelf behind his desk and reached for one of the leatherbound books on it. Like its fellows, the dark brown leather cover was stamped with a year on the spine and, when he opened it, I saw the front cover bore his initials in large gold letters: a prominent CB on the lower right corner.

Brewster flipped a couple of pages and then nodded. "Here it is," he said. "I keep quite meticulous notes for posterity. Someday these will be of great interest to my biographers. Three times in the last two weeks, Johnny Carl has added directions following a recipe. The first time it was 'a pinch of saffron,' a ridiculous spice to use for the cookie in question. Next it was 'improve with an extract of peppermint' and today was the questionable addition of white pepper. About the only flavoring that he's mentioned which makes sense is nutmeg, and even then, he told people to add a dash to a maple cookie recipe which already contained a full teaspoon of nutmeg."

"Johnny jokes around with people when they are on the show," I said. "He would suggest spices to create conversation."

"Do you think so?" said Brewster. "I found the entire pattern of comments suspect, as I informed both your aunt, Agent Tawney, and those laggards in Prohibition who are doing nothing to keep the cities around here dry."

"You told Nova? When? How?" But of course, I should have known the answer.

"I wrote her a letter yesterday after hearing the mention of white pepper. Her code was ridiculously easy for me to decipher," said Brewster. "The idea of sending directions over the air is quite ingenious." Brewster's tone indicated he considered himself quite ingenious too for figuring it out.

"What are you talking about?" I said, completely bewildered on how we had progressed from bootlegging and possibly time travel to cookie recipes in one conversation.

Brewster set his journal upon his desk with a self-important thump. "Directions," he said. "Johnny Carl always says, when he makes those suggestions for the recipes, that he has an extra direction to improve the flavor. Which, obviously, translates to certain listeners as a direction of where to go with their illicit cargo. Extract of peppermint for east, nutmeg for north, saffron for south, and white pepper for west. The last is quite clever, there's very few spices with w in their name."

I remembered how intently Nova listened to the noon broadcast while she generally ignored the evening one. Was she checking each day at noon to see if the directions to her bootlegger friends were being broadcast correctly?

"I suspect the two dashes, one shake, and so on refer to either distance or time, or perhaps a combination of both. Johnny Carl makes other comments during the cookie segment which obviously translate to further instructions on where to go and when to leave a cargo behind," said Brewster.

"So you think my aunt is smuggling liquor into Kingsport," I said with the sinking feeling that his story of radio codes would sound very plausible to law enforcement, however lax Brewster found the local Prohibition agents, and far more plausible than time travel. Still, I had to ask: "Why tell her in a letter that you know how she is doing it?"

"As I said, I am not unaware of the scandal that it would create to have liquor raids in Kingsport," said Brewster. He still stood behind his desk. My neck ached as I craned my head back to watch him. Brewster leaned one hand on his journal and tucked the other in his jacket, obviously striking a practiced pose.

"It is not in our best interests to have our town become as notorious as Arkham. Let Arkham have its Clover Club and its wars among the bootleggers. Let Innsmouth keep its foul secrets. I assumed if Nova Malone realized that her tricks were revealed, then she would cooperate with Agent Tawney, allowing him to gain the information that he seeks. In return, he could grant her certain protections and immunities. In fact, I wrote to her that I would be happy to attend a meeting with both of them and facilitate a dignified exit from Kingsport for her."

"How could Agent Tawney help my aunt?" I asked. "Why would he do so?" Yet Tawney had also hinted during our conversation that he could make "deals" with Nova. Could Tawney be so obsessed with finding a time traveler that he would bend the law or even ignore it? It seemed absurd but Brewster seemed terribly certain a deal could be struck. I wondered how good that deal would be for Nova.

Brewster bent a look at me that I often saw on the faces of certain male professors who could not resist lecturing their fellow faculty members, especially the women, on the most basic of facts. "In return for your aunt's full cooperation, Agent Tawney assures me that she will be removed from Kingsport peacefully. Our town will avoid the shame of harboring such a criminal character as well as, sadly, having lauded her as some type of civic hero. The number of people who have praised her broadcasts and the entertainment at the Diamond Dog is simply appalling. I cannot imagine why they venerate a woman so lacking in decorum." He paused here, perhaps realizing how petty he sounded or perhaps only marshaling his thoughts.

A "peaceful removal" sounded a bit ominous to me. I started to ask for more information, but Brewster continued.

"If Nova Malone cooperates with our government, I will have done my duty and would then be in an even better position to aid my party and my country. I hesitated to run in the recent special election but there will be a Senate seat open again in 1928. I could do a great deal of good for this nation if I were in the Senate," he concluded.

In other men, Brewster's ambitions might have been labeled commendable. But there was something about his tone and his preoccupation with himself which made me uncomfortable. His absurd belief that his private journals held secrets desired by future writers was even rather pathetic.

"Mr Brewster," I said as firmly as I could and not letting him interrupt me again, "my aunt is an honest businesswoman. Not a bootlegger."

Brewster bent a skeptical look at me. "You must hope

that is true," he said finally. "But if Nova Malone does not leave Kingsport soon, I will insist the Prohibition agents raid all her places of business. According to the newspapers they've already had considerable success in confiscating liquor bound for Arkham in the last few months. A dry city is a safe city, Miss Gutierrez, and I intend to make Kingsport the safest place in the state."

However odd Brewster was, I realized that he could stir up a great deal of trouble for Nova. My aunt needed to know about his letters to Agent Tawney, I decided. She could no longer wave off this banker's editorials on the radio or write polite notes back to him. Brewster's actions posed a real threat to all my friends at the Diamond Dog.

With all the dignity that the niece of an honest woman should display, I rose from my chair, collected the carpetbag, and left his office. As I hurried out of the bank, my fear was mixed with annoyance. While having a slightly shady aunt was an enchanting tale for children to whisper on Christmas Eve, in reality it was appalling. If the Diamond Dog was raided and I was arrested, the list of things that I could not bear to write to my family about would grow infinitely longer. For people like Harlean, Billy, Ginger, Cozy, Reggie, and Johnny, such an arrest might well end all hopes they had of careers in radio and entertainment. I knew how bitter it was to lose such a dream after giving up my own hopes of being a concert pianist. How could Nova have mixed me up in such a business, I fumed, well aware that my anger was a bit misplaced.

For hadn't I come to Kingsport with Nova willingly and

never questioned where all her expensive gifts came from? And didn't I love her, my big, brash, and loud auntie with her generous heart?

"Oh, pepper nuts," I growled as I stomped back to the Diamond Dog.

INTERLUDE

So the story is told, and here it begins. So the story is told, and here it ends.

Except I can find no endings and the beginnings grow worse. Every time I step out of this place, I lose more of myself. I am no Shadow, adept at fighting evil. I'm not even a cook determined to be brave.

Courage. I tell myself to have courage, but I don't even know what the word truly means anymore. Around me the trees weep blood and all I can remember is the old story of Bluebeard's bride stepping out of the little locked closet. Her shoes are covered in blood. Her heart is cold with terror. The key in her hand cannot come clean but drips blood whenever she picks it up. Courage, her sister tells her, courage for our brothers are coming to save us.

"Down she went, down she went, until she reached the little closet and turned the key," I recite to myself; this story is the only memory that I can keep in my head as the blood pours across the ground and rises around me. "She walked into the little closet and her shoes grew sticky with blood."

No sooner than I thought of the closet full of blood than I stood in the hallway of a house. Light filtered through a dirty window to show a floor gray with dust. I did not know the place, although I had lived in so many houses like this. A remembered smell made me sneeze, a fog of cabbage soups and despairing lives crammed under one roof. I was certain that I stood in the upper hallway of a boarding house. Yet I was equally certain that I was alone, trapped in my nightmare forever.

As I walked down the hallway, I saw my footprints behind me were the only prints on the dusty carpet. All the doors swung into empty rooms, stripped of furniture. A broken window in one room let in the cold wind. An icicle dangled on the windowsill and the walls were blotched with a dark fungus.

Then I heard the bang of a door. I looked back behind me before I realized that the sound came from below me. At the top of the stairs, I found myself overlooking an entryway.

Leaning over the railing, I spotted a woman and a man. All I could see was the top of their heads, and the woman wore the large hat of another era. Their voices sounded neither young nor old. Still, there was an undercurrent of affection and exasperation in their tones that spoke of a couple long used to each other.

"Agatha Crane," said the man. "I don't want to spend our Christmas Eve in a deserted house, not even one with ghosts."

"Wilbur," replied the woman, "there are no ghosts, at least as far as the accounts of this house go. Just a room where the ceiling drips blood, to be precise." She sounded like a woman who always wanted to be precise. When I was very young, I remembered a neighbor who spoke in such a way, a very grand lady in my memory, and one who commanded politeness from small boys. I suspected Agatha was such a woman.

"I don't want blood dripping on my suit either," replied Wilbur. "We're supposed to be at my mother's for dinner tonight."

"We'll be there in plenty of time. Just let me put a new cylinder in the Dictaphone. This will be a very quick experiment. Please rewind the Edison. I have a theory that music causes the vibrations in the ether which trigger the manifestation. You play the song while I dictate what happens for my records."

"We bought the recorder for the office," said the man. "Not as an aid for your research. Why can't you just use your notebook?"

"Wilbur, it's 1908. We must move forward with the century. Why record my thoughts with pen and paper when I can preserve them for posterity on these wax cylinders, which will last for centuries? Imagine, Wilbur, a hundred years from now, two hundred years from now, fellow researchers will hear exactly what I am thinking at the very moment of discovery. These machines are invaluable for research."

"Look, I don't mind you taking the Edison, the thing's nearly ten years old and you can play your old song until the wax melts off. But the Dictaphone is brand new. I don't want blood on it," said the man with a grumble as he cranked on the handle of an old-fashioned phonograph. "It would be the devil to clean, Agatha."

"Don't you 'Agatha' me. If it is blood, it will be spectral blood – ectoplasm, according to all the newspaper articles," Agatha said. "I'm sure any essence produced won't gum up the works or stain your suit."

"I've heard that before," Wilbur said with a sigh. "I love you dearly, Aggie, but you have no respect for machines." He let go of the crank and clicked a switch. The little phonograph began to play a jingling tune.

As the Edison played, the hall where I stood started to melt away. I smelled the scent of blood. Beneath my feet I could see the path through the trees begin to form again. With resignation, I turned away from the landing, knowing nothing I did would prevent me from falling back into the forest. Sometimes I could speak and act with those around me. This time I felt as if I was still half in the other place, dreaming about this couple in the boarding house. Yet beneath my apathy ran a current of fear as I knew that this dream, like so many events before, could turn into a nightmare.

"Hush," Agatha said. "Do you hear dripping? But it's not coming from the closet. Do you suppose it is just a leak in the roof? Blast, I forgot to turn on the Dictaphone. Stop the music. Let's try again."

A click halted the rotations of the wax cylinder player. The hall formed again under my feet, but I still had no power to move or do more than listen to the conversation below. My memories seemed more faded than ever before. If this pair called up to me and asked me my name, I was sure that I could not answer. I stayed silent and watched, like a man in a theater watching a film flickering past him, unable to influence the actors on the screen.

"Aggie," said Wilbur, "we are going to be late for dinner."

"We'll be there on time," she promised. "And I'll play two hands of pinochle with your mother. What I fear is that we will have wasted this time on nothing more than a rumor."

The wind moaned through the broken window in the abandoned house, but Wilbur answered stoutly, "Don't you say there is no wasted research even when it fails? Courage and continue on, that's the motto of my Agatha."

I heard her give a watery sniff. "You old softie," she said with affection coloring her voice. "Now, start the music when I open the closet door. Courage, indeed, Wilbur, and let us continue – the answers are almost within our grasp!"

"Good for you, my dear," he replied.

There was a click of a second machine. Agatha's voice rose from the entryway as she spoke very clearly and slowly into the Dictaphone. "Pursuant to my research, I have determined that in specific circumstances sound waves can manifest certain phenomena which the ignorant might call supernatural. However, I believe these manifestations are natural occurrences created by an intersection of sound and light. The propagation of this wave, passing through the interface between one medium and another, may produce an appearance of matter with varying density."

As the music rose through the empty house, the hallway faded away but the memory of the fond words between Agatha and Wilbur remained with me. Like the others I had seen, they continued with courage. Perhaps it is fear which makes it hard to hear the song, and all I need is the courage to listen for it, the courage to continue the search for a way out of this place.

Then I heard your voice singing. My heart grew a little easier. When I looked down, there was no blood on the ground. I knew my name again and I knew yours.

Courage, Raquel, courage. There is a way through this forest. We will find it together.

CHAPTER TWELVE

I wasted considerable time on my trip back to the Diamond Dog, stopping at the same small cafe where Agent Tawney had bought me a cup of Ovaltine. I may have had a vague idea of questioning Tawney about Brewster. Unfortunately (or fortunately), the man wasn't to be found there so I was spared a very awkward conversation. Instead, I chewed my way through a bacon sandwich and drank the bitter black coffee served from the dregs of the pot. I lacked the will to send back the coffee or request sugar, being so preoccupied with the thoughts buzzing around my head.

The carpetbag sat on the chair next to me at the counter. During my lunch, I avoided the attempts of the waitress to discuss the upcoming Christmas Eve dance. Apparently Johnny chatted up the event on the noon broadcast. I almost asked if he'd given any directions on how to spice Christmas cookies but didn't. I paid for my sandwich, left the coffee to grow cold in the cup, and marched on with the carpetbag now tucked under one arm like a bad puppy.

Finally, I arrived back at the Diamond Dog in the deadest

hour of the afternoon, the time when everyone scattered to prepare for the evening. Normally Nova used this break in the day's activities to take a small nap in her apartment, but a quick check proved she was out. With some relief, I left the now hated carpetbag on the kitchen table.

A look outside showed the Rolls parked in the garage. If Nova had left the building, she'd left on foot. This seemed unlikely as Nova liked using her Rolls whenever possible. It was far more probable she was still within the Diamond Dog.

The radio station side of the building was locked up tight as Reggie was scrupulously careful about this whenever he left the building. I knew neither he nor Johnny would return until evening.

After no small debate with myself, I stood at the top of the basement stairs and stared down into the depths of the one area that I hadn't explored thoroughly. Nobody had told me not to go into the basement, or so I reassured myself. But nobody ever went down into the basement except Nova, Lily, Tim, and Otis. If something was needed from there, Tim or Otis fetched it. Lily worked on the receipts in the basement office because the safe was located there. But I gathered from Lily's comments that she never went beyond the small office right at the base of the stairs. Nova worked in the office with Lily, but she also "took stock" on Tuesdays. The latter had something to do with a clipboard, several sheets of paper, and, oddly enough, a small screwdriver that I'd seen her clutching in one hand when she descended.

This was Thursday and not Tuesday, I reminded myself,

and it was unlikely Nova was taking stock below. On the other hand, she was nowhere else in the building. I considered climbing the stairs to the roof but knew nothing was there except the antenna for the radio station. The basement remained the most logical place to find Nova.

Switching on the light by pulling the long string that dangled over the top of the stairs, I made my way down to the basement office while humming one of Billy's medleys of holiday songs to keep up my spirits. But the office door was closed.

When I tested the knob, I found it locked. I rapped on the door and called Nova's name. No answer came. Which left only the long hall leading past the boiler and into the storage spaces beyond. The lights were on, indicating that someone else might be in the basement although I heard nothing.

I opened my purse and checked the battery for the hearing aid. Everything seemed fine. When I tapped my microphone with one finger, the tap echoed in my left ear. The silence of the basement was a true silence and not my impaired hearing. Which was not a comfort.

"What fun it is to ride and sing," I sang as I walked down the hall, still intent on making my presence as known as possible.

"Courage," said Paul's voice in my left ear.

"Can you hear me?" I said in surprise, but the reply that came was not in response to my question. Rather it sounded as if he was reciting a story out loud.

"Down she went, down she went, until she reached the little closet and turned the key."

I knew the tale as soon as I heard it. The terrible story of Bluebeard and the closet full of blood had been a favorite of my family, with Clara and I alternating between which was the sister treading in blood and which was the one in the tower watching for their fierce brothers.

By this time, I was so used to Paul's stories that I didn't even consider why he was reciting Bluebeard. Which was altogether foolish of me. For the story was not about a man who liked to murder his wives. It was a warning about how you can never hide from a family secret once you have found it.

"There's nothing in this basement," I said to Paul, even though I was sure that he couldn't hear me. Paul responded directly to me only a few times. Usually hearing him was like listening to the fragments of radio broadcasts from very far away. Reggie demonstrated to me one night how the skywave bounce brought moments of other broadcasts briefly into range. Going up and down the dial, we heard music, news announcements, and call letters fading in and out.

There was something magical about it, as Reggie said, this ability to pluck random voices out of the air. Also, in a cold and seemingly empty basement, something slightly terrifying. Thoughts of phantoms and ghosts intruded. How could we know the voices in the air belonged to here and now, that the people speaking to us were warm and living human beings?

"Courage, Raquel Malone Gutierrez," I said to echo Paul. "There's nothing here to scare you." But I don't know if I believed what I was saying.

No doors were locked in the basement except the door that I just tried. Locked because the ledgers and safe were inside, I told myself, not because seven brides hung on the wall dripping blood upon the floor. Perhaps Nova's gifts of fairytale books were to be deplored for their influence on small children, as the images in my mind were far too vivid.

"Courage," Paul said again, and I took his words for encouragement to explore further.

Walking down the hallway, I opened doors to storerooms full of boxes. When I pried open the lid of a box marked "decorations," ornaments twinkled in the light cast by the bare bulb in the ceiling. I found no sign of illicit booze and began to consider if Nova had been telling the truth about the Diamond Dog being a dry establishment.

Further away from the stairs, the items became more the type of thing stored away in the hope that it would be repaired and useful again someday or else someone would finish discarding it. Tables which rocked sideways on their pedestals, chairs with broken legs, and a pile of chipped dishes. I grew more upset with myself and my suspicions. There was literally nothing of interest here.

The hallway took a sharp turn and suddenly the world wobbled. I can't describe the moment everything changed better than that. One moment I was in a chilly, dimly lit basement and then I wasn't. The smell hit me first, a damp boggy smell, like the areas where water collected in the forest and couldn't drain away. I'd hiked through places like that in the time between winter and spring, when the snowmelt caused flooding and brought down dead trees.

It was an old memory, long before my younger brother

and sister were born, when I was the youngest desperately running to keep up with two older brothers who had forgotten the little sister trailing behind them. The trees bordered a graveyard. The boys had dared each other to go through the dark woods and climb over the fence. A fierce winter rain had turned the ground below the trees into stinking mud.

As if I'd tumbled back into my old memory or a dream, I found myself stumbling again over tree roots. Jagged bushes snagged at my clothing. The same queasy fear of my four year-old self returned to me in terrible clarity; I was convinced the forest went on forever and I would never be found. The real woods, the ones I remembered, were a scraggly patch of uncleared land barely wider than a city block.

In this place, I struggled to see in a gloom that still oddly resembled the flickering lights of the basement. There was no beginning or end as I spun around, trying to find the corridor where I had been walking.

I took another hesitant step. Paul's voice sounded in my earpiece. "And her shoes grew sticky with blood."

The mud covering the ground squelched under my feet and splattered over my shoes and stockings. The smell rose with an iron tang, less bog and more like the stink of the sickroom where my youngest brother coughed out his life as I played the piano to distract him.

I fell into a new and worse memory, one which had become a recurring nightmare for many years.

I played, and played, and played, in the hours between midnight and dawn when Benny's coughing always intensified, and my little brother wept with the pain. Overhead, I heard the creaking of the rocking chair as my father held Benny in his arms and sang to him as I played the piano in the parlor below.

The smell increased, the smell of blood and sickness and the shadow of death, all accompanied by the creaking of the tree branches moving overhead, like the rocker I could always hear, no matter how loud I played the piano. The rocker that we could all hear throughout the house as we waited.

I remembered those terrible weeks so clearly, a stronger memory than many things that had happened to me more recently. I played to distract my mother and Clara sitting in the parlor with me, handkerchiefs stuffed in their mouths so my father wouldn't hear their sobs. I played for them and to comfort the pair creaking overhead. I played to console myself.

My father wouldn't allow Clara or me in Benny's room, terrified that we would fall ill even though we'd had lighter bouts of measles as infants. I couldn't hold Benny, my beloved baby brother, but I played all his favorite songs.

After my mother fainted through exhaustion one day, my father also insisted on hiring a day nurse and taking over himself in the evening.

But he couldn't make us sleep through the night while Benny wept from the pain of his fever and rash or coughed up his lungs because of the terrible pneumonia that followed.

I remembered again all too clearly the chilling silence when the rocking chair stopped, when my baby brother no longer cried and moaned. It surrounded me now in this forest place that was not real but felt too real, the silence of my father weeping with his son clasped in his arms. The hideous silence as I closed the lid over the keyboard and sat in the stillness of the dim parlor unable to look at my mother or Clara.

Without thinking, my hands began to move in the pattern of playing those final songs of comfort for Benny, the simple tunes he loved so much, and the music resounded in my head.

Between one step and the next, I was walking through a dimly lit corridor in the basement of the Diamond Dog. Glancing down, I could see my shoes were clean and unstained with mud or blood or any evidence that I had done more than walk through a dream of a best forgotten past.

Shaken, half convinced I had been dreaming but terribly afraid that I had been awake, I continued around the corner. The walls and floor changed again, but for logical reasons. Bare wood rather than painted plaster and a certain roughness of timber indicated a much newer and rather slipshod construction quite different from the basement of the Diamond Dog. Although I wasn't sure of exactly how far I had gone, I wasn't surprised to find a second set of stairs leading out of the basement and into another building altogether.

The narrow wooden stairs ended at a closed door, beyond which I could hear the muffled sound of voices, including the distinctive tones of my aunt. I stood on the top step and eased the door open.

"Seventeen crates of champagne," Nova said quite clearly. "And two more of the port."

A man answered, a voice I didn't recognize. "The boss wants it delivered by Monday. There are big parties planned next week."

"Everyone will have their bubbly by December 20," Nova replied. "Give me your list and we'll take them straight to your customers."

A deep laugh rumbled through the room, but it didn't sound friendly. I crept up one more step and eased the door open. Nova stood in the center of a great bare space, a former garage to judge by the work benches and large barn doors at one end. Near the doors was parked Nova's delivery truck with Otis leaning casually against the hood. As relaxed as his stance was, he never took his eyes off the equally big man confronting Nova.

The stranger was dressed like a businessman in a good suit and heavy overcoat. But his broad shoulders and heavyset features made him look like a boxer. Something about his stance or the way he kept his big meaty hands relaxed at his side also shouted that this was a dangerous man. He ignored Otis, keeping his own gaze fixed on Nova.

"The boss says everything comes to us and we make the deliveries," he said to her.

Nova smiled. "Don't trust me with your list of clients, Chuck Fergus? The Christmas truce holds as far as I'm concerned. We won't overstay our welcome in Arkham."

"Don't forget we helped your people when Innsmouth was raided in September," Chuck replied.

"Poached a few of my men too. How's Albie doing?"

Fergus grimaced.

Nova chuckled. "Can't say I miss Albie. He never was the brightest bulb of a bootlegger."

I held my breath and eased the door open even wider. The stairs were dark at the top so I fervently hoped nobody would notice me. Here was the evidence that I hadn't wanted to find, the family secret confirmed. Like Bluebeard's wife, I had absolutely no idea what to do next with the knowledge. But I knew now that my Aunt Nova was most definitely a bootlegger.

"Still, you did help when I was gone," Nova said to Chuck. "Happy to return the favor and best wishes for the season to Naomi. I'll stay out of Arkham as long as she stays out of Kingsport."

He nodded. "Innsmouth and Kingsport are yours, just as agreed. When and where on Monday?"

"Turn on your radio tomorrow. Johnny will let you know," Nova replied.

Chuck laughed again. This time his amusement sounded genuine. "I didn't believe it when Naomi told me that you were broadcasting to all the rumrunners on the coast, right under the Feds' noses. You've got some gumption, Nova Malone."

"I can't believe you're still relying on telephones and telegrams," said Nova. "Don't you know the Feds are tapping lines all the way to Chicago?"

"We're making some changes at the Arkham telephone company," Chuck said. Then he tipped his hat to Otis and added, "See you on Monday." Turning on his heel, he strode out of the door.

Nova motioned to the truck. "Better go pick up the stash. Make sure Fergus doesn't follow you."

"He wouldn't dare," rumbled Otis as he climbed into the truck.

"It's our luck the Feds found most of their champagne and confiscated it," Nova said to him. "I'll enjoy making money from their misery, but I won't be fool enough to trust the O'Bannions too far. Keep an eye out for trouble."

The rap of her heels crossing the wooden floor toward the door drove me back down the steps. The door opened fully and Nova stared at me. Over her shoulder she said, "Get going." The sound of a truck's engine reverberated through the space. I could smell the exhaust even where I was.

Then Nova said to me, "Are you coming up or shall I come down?"

"Courage," I said to myself and called out, "I'm coming up."

Standing in the garage space, I looked through the wide double doors to the street and realized that we were at the far corner on the opposite side from the Diamond Dog.

Nova wore a fur stole draped across her shoulders with a fox head biting its own tail to keep it closed. I felt rather like the fox under her gaze and waited to find out if she'd shoot me or skin me for discovering her secrets.

Of course, she did neither. Being Nova, she just shrugged and walked to the heavy wooden garage doors. She began to slide one along the tracks to the closed position. "Get the other one," she said, nodding at me.

Shoving the green wooden door along the track with

a clatter of wood against the metal runner, I met my aunt in the middle. Once we had pushed the doors into place, Nova dropped a wooden bar across the pair to lock them.

"Used to be a stable," she said, dusting off her hands, "until gentlemen didn't need a place to keep carriages. Then they converted it for automobiles. Morrissen bought the joint a few years ago and added the tunnel from the Diamond Dog's basement to here for his own operation. But after his heart attack this fall, he wanted to retire. Convenient for me."

I circled around the space, not sure what to say, until a closer look surprised an exclamation out of me. "This is smaller inside than it should be," I said, remembering how long the hallway below had run.

"Good eye," said Nova with a nod at me. "False walls were added during the first remodel of this place to cover up part of the horse stalls. Morrissen opened them up again for storage." She walked across the room and leaned one hand on a corner of the wall, causing a hidden door to swing open and reveal a stack of crates behind it.

"We bring the goods through the Diamond Dog and out through here," said Nova with a falsely casual tone. She was watching me very closely.

"And Johnny tells people how to pick it up from Otis when he takes it out again?" I said, trying to act as casual as my aunt.

"Why would you say that?" asked Nova as if we were still discussing nothing more important than what to have for dinner. But this was more important than a fish chowder!

I blurted out, "I met Agent Tawney yesterday and Chilton

Brewster today. They know about the cookie recipes." Like Bluebeard's bride, I couldn't keep a secret any longer. I didn't want to pretend I hadn't seen and heard what I just witnessed.

Unlike Bluebeard, Nova's reaction wasn't murderous, although I had never actually believed my aunt would harm me. Not the woman who had done so much to help me in the past few weeks.

Still, her laughter surprised me.

"That's all right," she said, slipping an arm around my shoulders and giving me a hug like she always did. "We're changing codes tonight. From now on, Johnny's going to slip the directions into the weather report. Slightly cloudy, mostly cloudy, almost about to rain, snow expected at ten tonight. There are so many ways to say the same thing in a weather report and still give out more information than the Feds realize."

"Does Reggie know?" I said. "And the rest of them?" I couldn't imagine Billy or Harlean as bootleggers. Or Ginger or Cozy.

Nova shook her head. "Just Otis, Tim, and Johnny. They were running a small operation in Kingsport. This fall, the Feds started raiding around Innsmouth. Most of my old crew left the area. Some people felt it was better that I leave Innsmouth too." She huffed a little, shaking her head almost sadly. "I couldn't believe anyone in Innsmouth wanted me gone but tempers were running hot after a bunch of lawmen poked their noses into certain concerns. I needed to recruit a new crew from a new town. The Kingsport gang were interested. Especially after I suggested the radio station."

I noticed she left out how she came to be in charge of the "Kingsport crew" but then considering the personalities of the three mentioned, I could guess. Nova would have overwhelmed Otis and Tim, as both struck me as more muscle than brain, content to take the money and let somebody else make the plans. As for Johnny, he was definitely the type to take the easiest route. Hadn't he said Nova offered him the chance that he always wanted, to become a star outside of Kingsport?

"One-Time Johnny," I said, remembering Harlean's comment that the handsome radio announcer only went out once with most women.

"That's how they used to pass messages to customers and pick up shipments. Lots of people notice Johnny but they never questioned what the women with him were doing, even when they were the ones driving trucks or boats to pick him up," said Nova. "The radio saves Johnny considerable shoe leather. The Kingsport ladies can still sigh and tell their families that they just like listening to his voice. But the rest of the Diamond Dog employees don't know. It's safer that way."

"But what about you?" My fears remained that a raid could impact everyone at the Diamond Dog. Nova believed she kept them safe by keeping them ignorant. I couldn't be so casual about her smuggling, which apparently involved half the women of Kingsport! What would Brewster say about the decorum of the town if he knew? I felt certain such knowledge would unleash a barrage of letters to every government agency in the country.

"Aren't you scared of being caught?" I asked my aunt.

"No, I'm never afraid. After all, the worst would be time in prison, and I doubt that will happen. I'm not violent, not like some. I even told the boys to stop carrying guns after… well, let's just say after things went a little wrong earlier this year. I decided I would rather lose a load than have someone lose a life."

Suddenly it was all too much. The whispers in my ear, the strange waking nightmare in the basement, and Nova's decidedly casual attitude toward breaking the law and risking imprisonment. My life had already been upended. I couldn't be expected to cope with all of this.

"Why are you telling me this now?" I said.

"Did you really want to know where the money came from?" Nova said with some force. Then she sighed. "No, that's not fair. We never asked my father why he could continue to outfit ships, even purchase buildings, when the rest of Innsmouth went without. Sometimes it is best not to know. That's the path your mother took. I never pressed her about it. Guess I thought you were the same. Happier not to know."

My aunt wasn't altogether wrong, but I had to ask. "So my mother went west and you took up bootlegging?"

"Continued the family smuggling business, as it were. It's always been done on this coast, but Volstead made it more profitable," Nova said. "Especially after I added a few ideas of my own to the business. Perhaps your mother made the more sensible decision. But I never could resist new science or old ideas. It's fascinating what happens when you mix the two. Even when your neighbors turn you out of town."

Help with the problem in Innsmouth, Chuck Fergus had said just a few minutes earlier. I remembered how my letters to Nova went unanswered in September but received a quick and warm response at the end of October. Nova, I suddenly realized, would never ignore a request for help from family or friends, unless something drastic prevented her.

"What happened in Innsmouth?" I asked more gently than my earlier questions. Because, above all else and against all reason, I wanted Nova to know how much I appreciated all she had done for me, no matter how she paid for it. Because she came when I called for her help, giving me time and space to heal, to sort out what to do next with my life. She invited me into her warm, funny world at the Diamond Dog and I liked them all so much. If I broke with Nova, if I ran away from her, too, then I truly would be alone. That thought frightened me more than any nightmare.

"I may have been a little too bold," Nova confessed, and it would be her last confession of the day. "Two very brave young women nearly died this summer because of me. Then I went on a long journey and had plenty of time to think about what I had done, so much so I came to regret my actions. I was glad that I could help you. It seemed... well, it seemed like the best way to make amends. I've never had much ambition to change the world, not like Chilton Brewster always talks about, but I've always tried to help where I could." She reached out and gave me another of her quick hugs. "But never doubt I would have helped you anyway. You're my niece. We're family. I love you."

Again, my aunt had left me with nothing to say except "I love you too, Aunt Nova. But there's Tawney and Brewster. Are you sure there's no danger?"

"It's nearly Christmas," said Nova. "The Feds may disapprove but they know important people would be furious if they couldn't hold their holiday parties. You watch. There won't be any raids until January. We'll have our dance in every way." With a reassuring pat on my shoulder, she released me.

Her casual attitude toward the Volstead Act was not uncommon. Who hadn't dug out a bottle of wine from a well-preserved stash to give to a friend or even sell surreptitiously to a neighbor in need for a special event? But larceny on this scale was the stuff of big city newspaper stories and movies starring the Flapper Detective. I knew I should disapprove but, being aware of Nova's kindness and generosity toward our family, it was so hard not to love her audacity a little. The more I came to know my aunt, the more I realized that I cared for her a great deal.

"Come on," Nova said, tugging me toward the basement stairs. "Let's go back to the Diamond Dog. I could use a cup of coffee. It's always cold in here and down in the basement."

So I let her lead me back to her warm apartment and an absolutely ordinary afternoon of coffee and cookies. Once again Nova slid away from any hard questions so I hesitated to tell her any more of my secrets too.

Which was foolish. Like the bride's bloody key dripping away no matter how she tried to conceal the evidence, I couldn't hide what I knew. I should have told Nova about

Paul's whispers in my ear and the strange nightmare in the basement. But instead, I decided to keep my thoughts to myself, thinking perhaps I could find the answers I needed with just a little more time.

INTERLUDE

I heard you again and suddenly I think there is a way out of this place. Perhaps more than one. I only need to find the right path. But every time I leave the beach, the hounds appear. They do not block me directly. Rather they slink and slither in and out of the trees, and I cannot walk more than ten paces without a howling beginning.

I know how a sheep feels when it is herded by wolves.

I forget things, I know that I do, but I remember the laboratory and the men who died under the teeth of the hounds. The sounds of bodies being shredded by those teeth and claws. The very wet sound of a man's head being torn off his body and gulped by a tree.

And I pause. I cannot lead the hounds to you. I cannot.

The cook trusted me to be a good man. The prince gave me back the silver dime. The good servant told me not to despair. I turn these pages back and forth. In this writing, I begin to see a way out, but I must not let it create new monsters in the world. I must find a way that is safe.

CHAPTER THIRTEEN

With only four days to go until the Christmas Eve dance, a group of us went to find the perfect tree for the Diamond Dog. Which suited me just fine. Nova and I spent our time not speaking to each other about anything important after I discovered her bootlegging operation. I danced as many dances as I could on Friday and Saturday night and accepted an invitation from Lily to spend Sunday dinner with her family. I didn't say a word when every lady in the family gushed about how much they liked the radio broadcasts, especially the cookie recipes and Johnny's banter. Whether they honestly liked to bake, admired the handsome broadcaster, or were part of a smuggling ring of Kingsport matrons, I simply didn't want to know. In those days leading up to the dance, I could have taught ostriches how to bury their heads in sand.

My one regret was that I heard almost nothing of Paul's voice since that time in the basement. Once or twice during the dances I thought he spoke to me, but it was so vague and far away sounding that it left me more confused than ever before. I wanted desperately to talk to somebody about all I had learned. But I couldn't endanger anyone at the Diamond Dog who didn't already know about Nova's operations. Nor would Johnny, Otis, or Tim make good confidantes. Johnny, I suspected, would try to charm his way out of any hard questions and I probably would let him. As I didn't know anything about the other two, I wasn't going to start such a conversation with Otis or Tim. Besides, they would just tell me to go talk to Nova.

So, by the time the others invited me to help them hunt for a Christmas tree, I was desperately glad for an excuse to leave the Diamond Dog and pretend this was an ordinary Christmas with friends and family.

Otis drove us out to the farm owned by a man named Samuel Cuffe. When we arrived at the farm the owner came to greet us, insisting that we all call him "Cuf-fee, just like cuff and coffee combined," he said.

Cuffe was round and pink, with wisps of white hair encircling his bald head. Across his upper lip was a great curling mustache with enough streaks of red in it to suggest as a younger man he had a fiery set of curls. He was, as Clement Moore might have said, a right jolly old elf in green checked woolen trousers and a simply enormous red sweater that was still stretched a little tight across his belly.

Within minutes, this jolly farmer had Harlean and Ginger giggling. Billy, Reggie, and Johnny all joined the ring of laughing discussion about the best place to find a tree of the size that Nova wanted. Once we found the tree, Cuffe promised a couple of hired hands would cut it down and cart it into town for decorating the day before the Christmas Eve dance.

"The best trees are in the back acres," Cuffe said. "It's too far to walk, so I'll take you in the sleigh."

"All of us?" questioned Harlean, looking at our small crowd. We'd fit in Nova's Rolls, but it would have to be an enormous sleigh to take us all.

Cuffe's face fell. "Probably not. There's two benches and I can harness a double team, but five or six at the most."

"Including yourself," said a tall Black gentleman emerging from the farmhouse. "You must count the driver as well as all the passengers." The man was bundled up in a blue peacoat and heavy knit hat like lumberjacks or sailors wore. His beard was full and white, covering most of his lower face. He handed a knit hat, bright red like Cuffe's sweater, to the farmer. "You'll want your hat, too, if you're going driving through the woods."

"You're right as always, Leo," returned Cuffe, popping the hat on his head. It had a great tassel that swung jauntily down the side. "I'll take a few with me to look for the tree. Perhaps the others would like to collect greens and holly nearer the house?"

"And have a cup of something hot with me while we wait for you to return," said the other. "I'm Captain Leonard Pease, at your service. Most call me Captain Leo or just Leo will do."

There was something rather grand about the gentleman. I thought Captain Leo suited him. Obviously the others thought so, too, because there was a chorus of voices then discussing who would stay with Captain Leo and who would go on the sleigh. Otis stated firmly that he would do neither, as he had other errands to run for Nova, but would return with the Rolls later in the afternoon to pick us up.

By the time Cuffe had slid the sleigh out of the barn near the house and harnessed the horses with the help of a burly farmhand, we'd sorted ourselves into two groups. I elected to go on the sleigh with Billy and Reggie. Johnny decided to stay with Harlean and Ginger to pick holly and, if I heard it right, sample Captain Leo's hot buttered rum. Which relieved me mightily, because I wouldn't have to watch my words around Johnny or feel guilty about not pressing him to learn more about Nova's operations. Nova said Reggie and Billy knew nothing about the bootlegging. Which, in my current mood, meant I could pretend I knew nothing about bootlegging while tree hunting with the men.

Cuffe's sleigh was a gleaming beauty, lacquered black with a trim of gold and red stripes along the top edges. Two giant farm horses were harnessed in tandem. The bright silver sleigh bells attached to the straps running across the horses' shoulders rang out as soon as Cuffe led the team and sleigh toward us. He grinned at the sound. "Leo says I put these jingles on the straps as soon as the first snowflake falls. But there's nothing better than the sound of the bells when we're trotting along," he declared. He then whistled and the most beautiful Irish Setter came running around the end of the barn.

"Ready for a sleigh ride, Mab?" Cuffe said to the dog, pulling slightly on her ears while her great feathered tail waved back and forth. "Queen Mab adores riding in the sleigh," he said to me. With a snap of his fingers, the dog bounded into the sleigh. She sat very straight in the front, looking quite as royal as her name.

Reggie and Billy climbed onto the back bench, while I sat in the front next to Cuffe and his dog. He clicked with his tongue to the horses. The sleigh slid smoothly out of the farm's front yard and onto a track winding under the trees. From the tracks of runners visible on the snow and the horses' confident trot, I guessed it was a favorite route. Cuffe soon confirmed that, talking about the woods that we were passing through, the age of a covered bridge that we clattered across, and his enjoyment in being "a hobby farmer." The inherited homestead was apparently too small to bring in much income, but Cuffe had retired from what he called "a city job so boring that its name shall not be stated here." In the winter, he tapped syrup and sold Christmas trees. In summer, he "dabbled" in fresh eggs from the chickens and produce from the garden. Every fall he sold apples from the orchard or pressed his own cider, he told us.

"I write too," he said to me as we swiftly headed to the corner of the farm where he grew Christmas trees. "Over the years I've contributed a few small stories to magazines. Leo is always after me to write something longer and more ambitious, a novel if you will, but I prefer to be the O Henry of Kingsport."

I'd left the hearing contraption at home, not wanting to lug it through a long walk in the woods. Also, I craved a return to what I had known, a world that didn't contain phantom voices, bootlegging aunts, and so much doubt in my own head. The hearing aid was too much of a symbol of everything I had experienced. I needed to leave it behind, I decided, without acknowledging I was once again trying to run away from my problems.

Like the letter that I needed to write to my parents, a letter which was still a blank sheet of paper. Like the questions still unasked and the discussion still not had with Nova about what came next. I even wondered if I was letting Paul's whispers become a way to ignore the other buzzing thoughts in my head. Cuffe's chatter proved an equally good distraction.

With Cuffe sitting on my left side, I could make out what he was saying well enough. The cold air on my face and the friendly ringing of the bells reminded me of Christmases at home, a good memory without any regrets, and that was a blessing too. Mab leaned against my legs and kept my toes quite warm by politely sitting on my feet. I bent to caress her silky ears, very content to be on this winter ride.

Behind me, Billy began to sing in time with the horses' hooves striking on the snow. It was, of course, "Jingle Bells." The rest of us joined in. Cuffe sang with more fervor than perfect pitch. Mab simply thumped her tail a time or two and otherwise ignored our shenanigans.

We crested a small hill and then plunged down into an older, more tangled section of trees with tall bare branches stretching across the narrow road. "The pines are just past this," yelled Cuffe over the singing and ringing of the harness bells.

I peered ahead. A ground mist swirled across the road. In the deeper shadows of the woods, this pale fog appeared almost luminescent above the snowy bushes. From the corner of my eye I saw a strange doglike shadow. When I turned in my seat to catch a better glimpse, I was sure that something was moving in and around the trees, keeping pace with our sleigh. Under my hand, Mab stiffened and then whined.

The air smelt not of snow and pine, but something acrid and almost nauseous, as if a swamp lay beyond the tangle of bare branches or even an open sewer, if such a thing existed in the New England countryside. It reminded me horribly of my waking dream a few days ago.

Billy stopped singing and cried out, "Oh that's a horrible smell. Are you sure there isn't a rotten egg in here?"

Cuffe and Reggie also went quiet. Both sniffed a bit. "Can't smell a thing," Reggie yelled over the ringing of the harness bells, "although I had a terrible cold this week." But even as he spoke, the smell disappeared, as did the doglike shadow that I was watching.

Looking a bit concerned, Cuffe shook the reins and the horses picked up their speed. "This is a bad patch," he said to me. "I forget because most days it's very like the rest of the woods."

The smell evoked the memory of the nightmare in the basement. I stirred uneasily on my seat. Such things couldn't happen here, I told myself. Such things only happened, maybe, in Kingsport. Oh, I was being the perfect ostrich that day!

We left the tall old grove of trees behind and emerged into a patch of cultivated pines where nothing stood more than nine or ten feet tall. The wonderful, fresh and sharp scent of the Christmas trees filled my nose. I quickly, deliberately, forgot the uneasiness of the last few minutes. Cuffe pulled on the reins and brought the sleigh to a gentle halt.

"Go on," he said as we clambered down. He reached down under the seat and pulled out an old scrap of a scarf, as brightly red as his hat and sweater. "Tie that round the branch of the one that you want," he told me. "We'll arrange the cutting and delivery to the Diamond Dog."

One of the many cheerful and completely inconsequential discussions that I carried on with my aunt over the last three days was how she wanted the most impressive tree ever seen in Kingsport. In Nova's words, "One to wow the crowd!" So we stomped through the snow searching for a tree with sufficient wow. Both Reggie and Billy pointed out various candidates, but Reggie championed one with a bald patch and Billy's pick had a distinct bend in the trunk. Mab raced around every tree, a graceful streak of dog giving out a few happy barks before rolling in the snow.

Determined to succeed in finding the right tree for the Diamond Dog, I walked briskly along all the rows. It felt so good to be there with no more bothersome thoughts in my head than the height and width of the perfect pine. When I found it, I summoned Billy and Reggie with a shout. They both agreed the tall Christmas tree with its evenly widespread branches was exactly what Nova would want.

With considerable ceremony, we tied Cuffe's red scarf in a large bow around a branch of what I was already calling "my tree" in my head. I walked a few yards ahead of the others to make sure our marker was visible from the road. Asserting that it was clear and distinct from where I stood, I waved my arms at the others, motioning them to return to Cuffe and the sleigh. Then I turned myself and glanced back at the dark woods bordering this more cultivated area.

The mist was gone but at the juncture where the road angled out of the wood, I glimpsed a doglike shape and two glowing red eyes staring back at me. I squinted, trying to make out what I was seeing. Wolves and coyotes were not unknown in Colorado, although as a city girl I'd mainly seen them in zoos. But though this animal resembled something of that silhouette, there was something strangely wrong about it too.

Mab barreled up to me and barked quite sharply, a warning bark that I felt more than heard. If she'd been a collie, I would have thought Mab was trying to herd me away from the forest. Certainly, she shoved against my legs, pushing me away from where I stood.

"Down," I said, a little more sharply than I meant to. I still strained to see what type of animal lurked beneath the trees. I had a fleeting impression of scales or perhaps even bare skin. When I blinked and looked closer, nothing was there. Wolves and coyotes generally didn't attack humans, I told myself even as I backed away. But if this thing was sick, it might be a danger. The wind shifted and the smell of the mist wafting from the woods was foul, which only heightened my anxiety. The joy of finding the Christmas tree was fading all too quickly.

"Come on, Queen Mab," I said to my companion, "let's go back to the sleigh."

We hurried through the pines. Mab stuck close to me, no longer joyously rolling in the snow or racing her shadow around the trees. As soon as we emerged from the pines, the setter gave a short bark and a wag of her extravagant tail as she rushed to her owner. Cuffe patted her head as he waved us all back onto the sleigh.

The ride back to the farmhouse was quieter. Even the horses' lovely bells seemed muted by the shadow of the older woods. The men said almost nothing, certainly nothing I remembered, and I spent my time peering intently at the shadows under the trees.

But I saw not even a shred of blue mist on our return. For some reason its absence made me all the more uneasy.

At the farmhouse, we found buckets of holly collected by our friends as well as swags of greenery. "There's enough to decorate two dance halls," declared Reggie. "Do you think we can fit it all in the Rolls?"

"Never mind," said the jolly Cuffe. "The men can bring it in our truck along with the tree. Come in, come in." He practically ran up the porch stairs and swung open the door. "You have to try Leo's rum punch."

Inside, everyone was gathered in a long but cozy room. Large, overstuffed chairs were circled around the fireplace while stacks of books covered various patches of the floor nearest the walls.

Cuffe shook his head at the books. "Never mind those. Leo's in the process of moving out of Innsmouth but we haven't enough bookshelves for his entire hoard. We've taken to stacking the books where bookshelves might go."

Captain Leo chuckled as he overheard his friend. "I promise to put it all to rights as soon as Christmas is over," he said.

"You're from Innsmouth?" I asked.

Captain Leo shrugged. "Not really. I lived there for a few years, after I retired from the sea, but the place never took to me nor I to it. I thought it would do for an old sailor who liked to read, but they're odd folk in Innsmouth. I tried opening a bookstore, but nobody ever came into it except a few outsiders, as lost as I was there."

"My mother and aunt were from Innsmouth," I said, "but I've never been to the town. Perhaps after Christmas." Although given Nova's recent revelations, I was beginning to think a trip unlikely.

Captain Leo looked at me. "Are you Nova Malone's niece? The others mentioned you."

"I'm Raquel," I said, holding out my hand to shake his.

Captain Leo started to shake, but then paused. "Raquel," he said in a musing tone. "I have a book for you."

Cuffe overheard him and shook his head with a smile. "Oh, Leo, you try to give a book to everyone that you meet. I don't understand how you can still have so many volumes. Sometimes I think your books multiply when we're not looking."

"Perhaps," said Captain Leo. He walked across the room where he pulled a slim book from a pile in the corner. Bound in leather, it looked very old and battered. "This volume certainly has a strange history, but I think it is meant for you," he said as he held out the book.

"For me?" I said in some surprise, taking it and ruffling the pages. The book appeared to be a journal, the pages filled with a scrawling handwriting that was difficult to make out. I turned back to the first page to see if I could decipher any of it.

"Yes," said Captain Leo, looking very troubled. "I'm sure this one is for you."

I read the first page out loud: "A dying man gifted me this blank book so I could write my thoughts, but my thoughts are birds..." I stopped and stared at Captain Leo, uncertain what the writer meant or why the captain thought this book should be given to me.

The captain must have guessed my doubts because he laid his large hand over mine where it rested on the journal.

"Read it tonight," he said to me, "it's important."

A horn sounded from the yard. Harlean said, "Oh, there's Otis with the Rolls," before I could ask any questions. I slid the book into my purse. We all ran outside, calling our goodbyes to Cuffe and Captain Leo. The pair stepped onto the porch of the farmhouse to wave farewell. Cuffe was beaming and holding on to the collar of Queen Mab to keep the dog from running after us. Captain Leo stood slightly behind him. I thought he looked very sober.

As the Rolls headed back to town, I twisted in my seat and stared back at the strange woods surrounding the farmhouse. As we turned a sharp corner in the road, I thought I saw a flash of something running beneath the trees. The mist rippled along the ground again. I looked again but I could not make it out clearly. It was something like a dog but so strangely twisted and elongated that it was nothing like any dog that I'd ever seen before.

CHAPTER FOURTEEN

Back at the Diamond Dog, Nova wanted to discuss the tree and its decorations. But I wanted to talk about the Wednesday broadcast. During the return from Cuffe's farm, I finally made some decisions, one of which was to persuade my aunt to be more cautious about her radio messages. As much as I believed her repeated assurances that nobody innocent of bootlegging would end up in jail, she clearly wasn't innocent. I had no wish to see Nova behind bars.

"You mustn't have Johnny send any more directions," I said as sternly as I could to my aunt. "Not with Brewster and Tawney listening."

My uneasiness about Nova's operations were justified by the usual warning from Brewster in his distinctive blocky handwriting. Nova shared the letter with me when I arrived back from the farm. I dropped my hat, coat, and handbag on the bed in my room before rejoining her in the sitting area of the apartment. The journal from Captain Leo was forgotten in this new concern. I also dismissed the incident of the strange wolf, if it could be called an incident. We'd been out in the countryside. Strange smells and animals did occur in wooded farmlands.

Instead I concentrated on Brewster's latest letter. I dug through such phrases as "it has come to my attention" and "charged with the ongoing responsibility" while seeing in my mind's eye that impossibly bland man sitting in his journal-lined office penning note after note to the citizens of Kingsport and, apparently, the federal government. When did he find the time to do anything else? I wondered.

The letter exasperated me, full of vague allusions and long words which meant nothing but sounded grandiose and oddly threatening. The word "inadequate" appeared twice for no good reason, although what he found inadequate was unclear. Once he paired it with something about what the larger world should know about Kingsport. Then there was a long paragraph about his ongoing distress that most people outside the town's borders were only aware of Kingsport through the broadcast of music that in no way fit his vision of how the town should be perceived.

"Writes like he swallowed a dictionary," observed my aunt, peering over my shoulder.

"And a thesaurus," I said. "But I think he's saying that if the broadcasts continue to have messages in them, then Prohibition agents will shut down the Diamond Dog and the radio station."

"Since Chilton is not in charge of any branch of law enforcement," said Nova, "his threats don't mean much."

"But what about Agent Tawney? He seems willing to listen to Brewster. I don't think you can count on them staying away until January."

"They haven't done anything yet," Nova pointed out. "Not even come into the Diamond Dog for a bowl of chowder, let alone served us with a search warrant."

"Do they need a search warrant?" I said with some vague memory of a court case in the last year stating the opposite.

"They can search a car, boat, or airplane without a warrant, but not my home or place of business. Or the cars parked in the garage down the street." My aunt grinned at my bemused expression. "I might have left school after the eighth grade, but I make it a point to understand the law. Especially as it pertains to my businesses. Also, I can afford good lawyers and accountants. Accountants are the most important of all. My books are clean. I pay my taxes on time."

"But it's still illegal," I said, trying to sound more disapproving and probably failing miserably. I had never been a heavy drinker, but I didn't objected to others drinking. I'd even thought it was nice how Cuffe and Captain Leo offered rum punch to everyone after hunting for Christmas greenery. If someone as respectable as Captain Leo didn't see the harm, how could I tell others to stay dry? I couldn't. Which, I supposed, was why it was a good thing that I wasn't a politician or a Fed. I suspected men like Brewster or Tawney never doubted themselves. Nova also never seemed to question the rightness of her position, despite the Volstead Act.

Was I the only one, I wondered, who kept seeing the good and bad of both sides and lacked the will to make a decision?

A knock on the apartment door interrupted my gloomy thoughts, somewhat to my relief.

When Nova went to answer it, Lily stepped into the apartment. "There's a man downstairs," she said, handing a card to Nova. "Says he wants to talk to you about some letters."

Nova glanced at the card in her hand and passed it to me. Tawney's name was printed across the top. As she crossed the room to check her makeup and hair in the mirror, Nova said to me, "You should stay up here."

"No," I said, coming to a decision at last. "I want to hear what he says." And, also, I desperately needed to hear my aunt's answers. I went back to my bedroom and rigged the hearing device on my head, settling the microphone around my neck and slinging the handbag with the battery over my arm. As I crossed the room, I noticed my other handbag on the bed with the square bulge of the book gifted to me by Captain Leo. I retrieved the little book and set it on the bedside table. I hung the coat and hat in the closet.

"Are you coming?" said my aunt from the living room.

"Yes!" As much as I wanted to understand what was going on, I'd also been stalling, fiddling with the items in my room. I never liked confrontations and always did my best to avoid them. Perhaps staying with my bootlegger aunt rather than going home for Christmas had been a poor decision. But I reminded myself, it had been my decision, and I needed to live with the consequences. Even help Nova if that was possible. I wanted to pay her back for all she had done for me.

We went downstairs together, with Lily walking a little way behind us, and found Agent Tawney in the lobby area, reading the posters lining the walls.

"Quite the schedule," he said, nodding at the list of upcoming dances. The Christmas Eve dance was printed in red with little holly leaves encircling the line on the poster.

"I do my best," said Nova with a quick shake of Tawney's hand. "How can I help you?"

"Ralph Tawney. Call me Ralph. Do you want to go somewhere more private?" he replied, glancing at Lily and me.

"We'll stay here," said my aunt with a pleasant smile. "I think better on my feet." She raised an eyebrow at the agent.

He raised an eyebrow back at her. Obviously, he'd expected to be escorted to an office or be treated with a bit more trepidation. Nova simply standing there while the rest of us stared at him seemed to disrupt a particular plan.

I admired my aunt's calm and tried to keep my face as polite.

Tawney then shrugged and smiled at my aunt while he fished out some letters from his jacket pocket.

"We've had some complaints from a local gentleman," he began.

"You've been receiving letters from Chilton Brewster," said Nova with a nod at the envelopes. "Same as all of Kingsport. The man is full of complaints and very few facts."

"Do you disagree with his allegations?" said Tawney a little too quickly.

"I don't know what he wrote to you, but I certainly disagree with the letters that he has sent to me. I believe the music played here at the Diamond Dog is of the highest quality and greatly enjoyed by the listeners of our broadcast. Anyone who doesn't like it can simply shut off their radio. Nobody is forcing them to listen."

His bushy eyebrows drew together as if something in Nova's words puzzled him. "What's this about music?"

"Brewster's letters to me are full of complaints about my radio broadcast," said Nova. She quite calmly left out a host of other allegations that I'd seen in Brewster's latest missive as well as the information that I'd passed to her about my meeting with Tawney. "I strongly object to his characterization of the music played at the Diamond Dog or the musicians playing it as harming the reputation of Kingsport."

Tawney scowled while I bit my lip to prevent a smile. He obviously hadn't expected this turn in the conversation.

"Brewster wrote to you about the music heard during your radio broadcasts?" he asked again, obviously trying to find his way back into the conversation.

"Yes," said Nova. "What else could he complain about?" she added with a bland look almost exactly mirroring Chilton Brewster's most aggravating expression.

I thought Nova was clearly enjoying herself, but also felt some trepidation about how Tawney would react. When I was teaching, my students would occasionally fall into a quarrel with each other. Some mornings simply saying "hello" could set off a storm of tears caused by a greater frustration unvoiced. While I doubted Tawney would break out in sobs, he certainly had the look of someone bottling up too much emotion. A storm seemed to be brewing, but how it would break out I couldn't say.

The federal agent slowly replaced the envelopes in his pocket. "What else, indeed?" he said, looking again at Lily with visible frustration. Since he'd already discussed Brewster's claims of time travel with me, I could only assume that he didn't want to mention it in front of Lily.

Lily, in turn, became very preoccupied with the notebook in her hand as if she expected Nova to begin dictating the day's food orders to her. She barely glanced at the agent.

The silence stretched on. If they ever put up a statue of Nova Malone in Kingsport, and a very unlikely idea that was, then she was ready to be carved in stone. Her hands hung loose at her sides, the light winking off her diamonds. Only the slight rise and fall of the purple cat brooch indicated that she was still breathing.

Nova's serene expression flustered Tawney's attempts to control the conversation. He restarted with, "Now, see here, madam," and then stopped, apparently realizing his tone and words sounded too much like a lawman and not a friendly visitor who asked you to call him Ralph.

"We're a little concerned about some of Mr Brewster's claims, as odd as they might sound," said Tawney in a softer voice, not defining the "we" in his sentence. "Perhaps we could take a look around."

"The Diamond Dog is open to the public every Wednesday through Saturday," said Nova. "Of course, we'll be closed for Christmas this Saturday, but the Christmas Eve dance on Friday will be spectacular. Anyone is welcome if they have a ticket. I'd be happy to leave a pair at the box office for you and a companion," finished my aunt with a smile. "Is that all?"

Tawney seemed stumped for an answer, but his face flushed very red. I stepped back a pace or two, not certain what, if anything, I should or could do.

"I think that's all then," said Nova, walking past him toward the doors of the ballroom. "Raquel, come tell me where you think the tree should go. Center of the floor? In the far corner near the bandstand? Or here in the lobby?" She opened the doors with a last nod at Tawney. "Lily will see you out, Ralph… it is Ralph, isn't it? Thank you for your visit."

She walked into the ballroom. I hurried after her, closing the doors behind me.

"I think the far corner," said Nova, surveying the room. "Then it won't be in the way of the dancers or obscure the view of the band. If we make the tree too visible from the lobby, then there's no surprises when they enter here. I do like wowing my audience."

I blinked at her complete focus on not discussing what had just happened. She certainly surprised Agent Tawney and wowed me. However I quickly gathered that this, like all the rest, was falling into the vast bucket of things Nova would ignore. Unless I forced the issue.

Nova pointed to the left of the bandstand. "Right there. When people come in, they'll be busy chattering and looking at all the holiday finery being worn by their friends and neighbors. Then they'll look up and see our tree glowing with electric lights. Covered with all the silver and gold trimmings."

She had a slightly faraway look in her eyes as if she could see the tree decorated and in place already. "It will be spectacular," Nova said with pride.

Like Tawney, I was baffled as to how to continue the discussion of Brewster's accusations. But I had to try.

"What if Tawney had insisted on talking about Brewster's claims of codes being broadcast in the shows?" I said, because that was the easiest question to ask. "That Johnny was giving directions for bootleggers?"

Nova turned around and shrugged at me. "I would have said that people see patterns everywhere, but such patterns mean nothing at all. Spices as a code for directions? What a charming idea for a Philo Vance novel. I'm hoping for a sequel to *The Benson Murder Case*. A convoluted code cracking would be exactly what Vance would do."

"But that's what you did!" I said with rather more force and then looked around guiltily. Luckily, we were the only ones in the ballroom.

"Well, it probably wouldn't be wise to admit to Tawney that such an idea crossed my mind as soon as I read about new transmitters. Really, it is amazing how clear and how far the signal goes these days. Such an improvement over just a few years ago. As for the rest of Brewster's claims, his letters would sound like so much gibberish to a government man."

"But Tawney believes Brewster!" I protested. "Tawney thinks time travel is possible. Tawney is looking for a time traveler."

Nova spun around to stare at me. A truly worried look crossed her face. "You didn't tell me this before."

"How could I? All you talk about is this dance, and

the decorations, and what to add to the Christmas fish chowder. And that's when you weren't discussing cookie recipes with Thelma!"

My anger was perhaps a bit misplaced. I'd been avoiding hard questions as much – if not more – than Nova. But once started, I couldn't seem to stop. "You've said absolutely nothing to me about anything important since last Thursday. Not a word about the bootlegging or what happened to you after you left Innsmouth last fall! I've been waiting days for you to talk to me about your past. About what's happening now! So how could I tell you that Tawney believes in time travel?"

Nova actually deflated a bit before my eyes. I never thought I'd see such a thing from my supremely confident aunt, but she actually appeared sheepish.

"Well," she said after a very long pause. "It's all mixed together. Innsmouth, time travel, and, yes, bootlegging. It started before Prohibition, just a little light smuggling and cutting a few corners to make a better profit in the early days, much like my father did."

I probably looked like one of the fish heads in the chowder with my mouth hanging open.

"There's no reliable way to time travel," said Nova with such calm that I almost believed her. Except what she was saying was impossible. "It's more of a side effect if you like scientific terms. I have a theory that time travel happens when you become lost on certain paths. We used to have a book which helped us avoid such accidental trips."

"We?" I said, rather frustrated with the vague "we" used by both Tawney and my aunt.

She smiled in apology. "The family grimoire. I'm sure your mother never mentioned it. She very much disliked that part of our history."

That I could believe. My mother was a very practical woman who even slightly disapproved of her children receiving volumes of fairytales and Oz books from their aunt. She always gave us novels about plucky orphans.

Nova walked across the room with a brisk click of her heels against the wooden floor that I felt as much as heard. She put a large soft arm across my shoulders and hugged me close for a moment. She dropped her voice low, but I could tell by the way she was pitching her words and speaking directly to my microphone, she wanted me to hear the next bit perfectly. "Our ancestors owned a grimoire once. It let the family smuggle goods along routes difficult to sail without fear. Because of that, they concocted a way to become fearless, a potion of seaweed which left its mark on those who drank it. Your mother always refused her share, which was wise since she moved away."

"And you?" I asked, absolutely enthralled because I loved fairytales and Oz better than Anne Shirley.

Nova gave me another squeeze and stepped back. "Father gave me more than enough when I was a sickly baby." She pushed back the sleeve of her dress and shifted her arm to display a patch of purple scales which glittered like her diamonds in the light. I gaped like a bystander at a carny show and then knew a flush of shame for such a reaction. This was my aunt, no matter how strange the scales, someone who cared a great deal for me.

Nova pulled the sleeve back down. "I never minded the

taste. You don't when you've been drinking something since you were a little baby. But the side effects are annoying."

I simply blinked at her, uncertain what to say.

"I become unmoored," Nova said finally. "Oh, how do I explain this? I know a woman who can do this with a tangle of knitting but I'm not a knitter. Sometimes, not by choice, I step out of the world."

I remembered that moment in the basement when the world wobbled as the ground became blood beneath my feet. "But how do you get home?" I said, because it seemed the most important of all the questions racing through my head. Paul, I thought, was lost in the woods, and searching for a way out, according to the stories he whispered in my ear. How does Paul go home?

And, a more treacherous voice whispered in my heart, how do I avoid going home as such a failure? What if Nova's path could lead me to a new future by changing my past?

"If I'm very careful and use the right tune, I avoid being lost on the path and can step back out again," said Nova. "Of course if I'm pushed off course or distracted, or use the wrong song, I can sail right into another time. It's the devil to correct when it happens. That's why it took me nearly a month to begin answering your letters this fall."

I still didn't understand so I picked out the words that I'd heard best and repeated them. "The right tune? The wrong song?"

Nova smiled a little sadly. "It sounds like one of Harlean's blues numbers, doesn't it? But a person can step out of the horrid place if a set pattern is followed. The hardest part is to not be distracted by what's happening there. Some do it by concentrating on a knitted item of clothing and counting the stitches. I find songs with strong repeated melodies work well."

"So you can time travel?" I said, still trying to pick out the sense of what my now chatty aunt was trying to tell me. I might have paid lip service before to accepting only rational explanations, but I wanted the irrational now with all my heart.

"Not intentionally," said Nova. "Because when I do, it causes problems. Like taking Chilton Brewster's coat on December 24, 1925, and not returning it until nearly a year later. I probably should have thrown the coat away. But I try to be honest. Most of the time."

CHAPTER FIFTEEN

According to my aunt, she fell off a pier in Innsmouth at the end of summer and splashed ashore "somewhere else, which means nowhere at all." In leaving somewhere else, she went backward and forward in time, including a stop in Kingsport on Christmas Eve a year ago.

"But why did you fall off the pier?" I asked, because the incident seemed the simplest part of the story and the only part I could visualize.

"A silly battle with a man. I should have known better," said Nova with a shrug and wouldn't say more.

"But why did you take Chilton Brewster's coat?"

"Because I was cold, wet, and angry as a hornet. He looked too warm and too sure of himself as well," replied Nova. She was pacing around the ballroom, checking where she wanted to put decorations and jotting down notes in a small notebook not unlike the one that Lily had held. Although Nova carried hers in her skirt pocket and it had a metal cover set with rhinestones. Like during her conversation with Tawney, she seemed immensely calm, but there was something about the line of her always straight back and the set of her shoulders which made me believe she was gauging my reactions very carefully.

"When did you give the coat back to Brewster?" I asked. Nova's moving about was frustrating me to no end as I had to keep shifting my own position to hear her as perfectly as possible. As usual, her big voice was remarkably clear through the microphone, but I didn't want to miss a single word.

"In October, when I finally arrived back in 1926, close enough to when I fell off the pier to stay here. I popped back into the basement of the Diamond Dog and found the tunnel to the garage across the street. I'd had my eye on the place for some time but that's when I knew it would be perfect for me."

"Perfect for smuggling," I said. "Bootlegging."

"Well, it's been our family business for more than a hundred years. Whatever is wanted at a bit lower price than what is legal. Or whatever is wanted that is completely illegal. Opium was once our trade, and I do think liquor is far less harmful. Your mother never approved of the smuggling or several other things about Innsmouth. She made her choice and a good life too. I stayed and tried to make a difference in the town. I thought the money that fine French wine and good Scotch whiskey brought could make a difference. But Innsmouth hates change even worse than Chilton Brewster."

"And about his coat?" I said, unwilling to be sidetracked in this discussion.

"When I took myself topside, I found it was a warm day for October. I didn't need a coat anymore. I saw Chilton walking by and handed it to him. Unfortunately, he remembered the dress that I was wearing."

"A summer dress with a tear across the shoulder," I said, thinking about the photos that Agent Tawney had laid across the table in the coffee shop.

Nova nodded. "Yes, and more. Brewster remembered not encountering me as well."

"That makes no sense at all," I said. None of the conversation made much sense to me but I kept thinking back to the wobble in the basement and the smell of a decaying forest suddenly surrounding me. Had I been standing in the spot where Nova "popped in" to in October? Was that the place where Paul was? With trees creaking overhead to remind him of old griefs and deep sorrows? A place which felt like stepping into a nightmare for the few moments that I was there.

"Shifting about in time never makes sense," replied Nova with complete conviction. "Some people end up with double memories. What happened when the time traveler interacted with them and what happened when the time traveler didn't. The after and before effect, one theorist called it."

"That's the wrong way round. Shouldn't it be before and after?"

"Only when time is linear. There's a very clever woman named Beatrice who wrote an interesting little paper on an encounter with a time traveler when she was in college. She talks about something similar, that only *after* the encounter can you remember what it was like *before*. Those stuck-up professors at the university simply dropped her work in a cardboard box with some other theories of time travel and forgot all about it."

"How did you read it?" I asked.

"The Miskatonic University professors don't mop their own floors. I pay the cleaning women to bring me information now and then. Earlier this year I was searching for more information about the book I mentioned, the family grimoire. I thought traveling between places by plane would make using those routes outside of our world safer." Nova shrugged. "But it turns out the whole idea is impractical for many reasons. If you're in the space betwixt and between – for I can't call it anything else – you begin losing memories and ending up in the wrong places or the wrong time. Sending codes for normal routes over the radio is much easier."

Nova's revelations left me reeling. But her story also made me wonder if what I had experienced in the basement was possibly real.

Nova closed her notebook with a snap. "Well," she said, looking around the room. "We're almost ready for the dance. Let's go back upstairs."

Which meant, as I'd come to learn, Nova had told me all she wanted to tell me. And I, still trying to understand the information so casually given out, never did mention Paul or what had happened to me in the basement.

Like all relatives who have had an incredibly awkward conversation, or at least as was common in my family, we spoke only of the most mundane things possible over dinner.

With no dance on that night and no evening broadcast

on the radio, we then sat in an even more uncomfortable silence in Nova's small living room. At one point, out of sheer desperation, I suggested a game of cards, an activity I usually avoided as my siblings were all much better players than I was. Clara routinely won pennies and nickels from me in various games of chance.

Nova adored cribbage. I knew the minute I saw her lovely board made from a sperm whale's tooth that I was destined to lose badly. But it was worth it for the smile on my aunt's face as she pointed out the features of the board to me. The scrimshaw around the edges depicted a beautifully rigged sailing ship and, rather sadly, the death of the whale.

"It belonged to your great-grandfather," Nova said to me, pulling out the pegs from a cunningly carved little drawer at one end of the tooth.

"David would love this," I said, thinking of my oldest brother. Like Nova, he had his own cribbage board and always insisted on playing at least one game with the rest of us when he came home for Christmas. He preferred three-player cribbage, but gallantly dealt everyone in, even me. My inability to remember the rules correctly often earned me considerable teasing from my siblings.

As I told this story to Nova, she chuckled and admitted that she was another card shark of the family, so much so that my mother rarely played against her as a girl. "I could always persuade our father into a hand or two," she said. "More if he'd had a good run. But by the time I turned thirteen, he could never beat me. Unless the cards were very unlucky. Your mother, on the other hand, is the best at checkers."

"Oh, we know!" I said, remembering many laughing games when my mother trounced even her youngest child with no mercy. As my father once consoled Benny in happier days, no one could come between my mother and an opportunity to king her pieces.

"But what was your best game?" Nova asked me as we picked up our cards.

"I never liked games as much as the others. We had a piano, an old upright, in the parlor so I'd play that when they dragged out the game boards." I still remembered with great clarity those winter evenings, with people shouting out their favorite tunes while I laughed and joked, and played exactly what they didn't ask for. Unless it was Benny. I always played whatever Benny requested because he was my baby brother, and his smile lit up my heart.

After Benny's death, I hadn't played for weeks. I couldn't. Until one evening my father with great solemnity pulled out the checkers board and challenged my mother to a match. With the same gravity, he sat me at the piano bench with Clara beside me to turn the music and sing as she often did.

It had been a strange evening, with Clara and I at the piano, and my parents at the game table. There was a small shadow in the room, the boy who had always sat at the end of the couch, swinging his legs as he gave my father instructions on how to challenge my mother at her favorite game. I know we all felt it, but we knew a great comfort too. And I had played the piano every day since then until my illness stopped me.

Through the cutting of the cards, the creation of the crib, and the little pegs moving relentlessly around the board,

I told this story in stops and starts to my quietly listening aunt.

"I am sure they will miss your playing at Christmas," she finally said to me.

"Clara plays well enough," I responded. "She never loved piano lessons like me, but she took them all the same. She's a much better singer too."

"But it won't be you at the piano. Play for them when you go home," she added.

I shook my head. "It won't be as good," I said, remembering my frustration with my playing earlier in the fall.

"For them, it will be," replied my wise aunt.

But I changed the subject and kept our discussion to lighter matters, including what I owed Nova by the end of the evening. She waved away all debts but did suggest I bake cookies with Thelma and her the next day. "We always need so many boxes," she said. "I give them away to everyone who works for me on Christmas Eve. It's something of a tradition for me, to bake on the winter solstice. It's the shortest day of the year, so it feels right to warm up the oven. Besides, Thelma hasn't baked anything since Saturday and the cookie jar is almost empty."

"Are you going to make Pfeffernüsse with white pepper?" I said with a little sarcasm.

"It has a certain bite," said Nova, unrepentant at having me repeat one of her bootlegging directions. Which made me laugh. Then Nova decided that a final glass of cold milk from her electric refrigerator and the last cookies out of the jar would make an excellent nighttime snack.

Far after midnight, I went to bed feeling better about

the world and my aunt's shady business. Nova treated the whole affair of Agent Tawney so lightly that I was finally sure that she could indeed escape any serious punishment. As for her claims of a family ability to time travel and former ownership of a mysterious grimoire, I stored that in a corner of my brain reserved for tall tales from relatives. I didn't completely doubt her claims anymore, but I wasn't exactly sure what to do with the knowledge.

As I was turning down the light, I spotted the odd little book that Captain Leo had given me earlier in the day. I adjusted the light next to my bed and began to read the first page.

One sentence leapt out at me. "My name is Paul." I knew immediately I had found the voice who whispered to me and me alone. Next, I read "Do not be afraid. Please do not be afraid. One of us must be without fear."

But I could not follow that advice.

A creeping horror came over me as I read on; the strange mix of fairytales and unworldly descriptions making it impossible to put the book down. One incident seemed to describe both Captain Leo and the jolly Cuffe. Others referred to places that I had at least heard of. All were towns surrounding Kingsport if not Kingsport itself. But the saddest part of all was the man who was telling these tales, a man lost in a terrible place who had never known the family or the friendship that I had taken for granted all my life.

I never believed in love at first sight. I still don't. But I do believe you can read a stranger's words and realize there is a kinship there, a soul that you would like to know better. If nothing else, I wanted to give Paul the courage to find his way out of the terror which held him trapped.

As I turned back the pages and read certain descriptions again, I realized something. As a music teacher, as the girl who always played the piano at family gatherings, I knew the tune that Paul heard, the one sung by his Baba Yaga with the purple cat brooch, the pattern set by Nova Malone. The song which brought Paul back to our world and sent him out of it again.

The tune was Benny's favorite. We played it every night at the Diamond Dog and broadcast it throughout Kingsport. We sang it earlier traveling in Cuffe's sleigh with the horses' harness bells ringing out.

A song I could play from memory, a Christmas song which had nothing to do with Christmas and everything to do with traveling.

I left my bed, wrapping my old blanket robe around me. Then I headed downstairs into the Diamond Dog to experiment on the piano. For I finally knew exactly what I should do next.

I would summon Paul back into the world with "Jingle Bells."

CHAPTER SIXTEEN

Downstairs only a ghost light illuminated the ballroom. The single bulb was left lit in the center of the dance floor all night long in case somebody needed to cross the ballroom or, given Nova's other business activities, wanted to see their way to the basement staircase for a delivery.

I sat on the stool and rested my hands on the keyboard. The cool ivory beneath my fingertips welcomed me home. As much as I hated not hearing the nuance of every note, I loved the music carried from my mind through my fingertips to the piano. While I would never play with the jazz, the fire, of Billy Oliver, I could play, pattering up and down the keyboard mimicking the pounding hooves on the hard-packed snow, the laughter within the sleigh of friends and flirtations, and the ringing, the jingling, of the harness bells. Oh, what fun to know again the life that I had had, to send this tune reverberating through the instrument and the music spilling out into the empty room.

Then I knew it, with the precision that meant I'd always known how my playing should sound, how others should sound, what was perfect for the concert stage, and what was simply acceptable for a family parlor on a winter night: whatever glory, whatever spark, that I had possessed before the fever was still there. I could play – albeit not as perfectly as before, not as beautifully as I had.

So I played the song as ugly as I could.

I hit the keys harder and harder so I could feel it in my hands, my wrists, and all the way up into my shoulders. Harder and harder so I could hear the music shaking through my body, all the anger accumulated and all the sorrow collected. All the love that I had for the music until my body betrayed me. I wasn't even thirty yet. I wasn't supposed to be hampered by illness, weakened by disease. I was supposed to be starting my future, not haunted by the past. I wanted to howl and so I did, screaming through the lyrics until my throat was shredded raw.

I had left the headset behind, forgotten on top of my dresser. In the hours past midnight, I played for my damaged self, hearing only what I could hear without electronic amplification.

As I played, my fury hardened, my intent solidified. I would drag Paul back into the world where he belonged and I would go.

If Nova could fall out of the world, surely I could do it too. I was no longer afraid of the bloody ground, the starless skies, the trees with snapping teeth, and the hounds slithering out of shadowed corners.

I was afraid of the future.

But I did not fear the forest.

I wanted to dive into the ocean with no waves. I wanted

to run in circles to conquer the hounds until the music shook me out into the past.

I needed to change my life. I wished for Benny to be alive. I desired (shamefully, oh so shamefully) to have my hearing back just as much as I wanted my little brother.

If my aunt was a Baba Yaga striding into the past, I set my heart on following the same path.

Sweat poured down my face, making my hair cling to my neck. Beneath the blanket robe, my nightgown stuck to my skin. Still I pounded on the piano and sang, the words running together now in one hideous jangling shriek of rage.

Then the world shifted.

Like before, the room wobbled. As Paul had described it, the falling step and drop of a dream overtook me. But the piano keys shook beneath my fingers and the music still reverberated through the wires. My feet banged down on the pedals.

I saw him. In the pause between one note and the next, he was there. Such an ordinary looking man, such an extraordinary person, he was standing under the ghost light in the middle of the room. He was standing on the shore with unmoving water behind him. Both places in the same moment of time were visible to me. In Paul's hands – and I knew he was Paul – was clutched the very journal that lay upstairs upon my bed. After and before, all muddled the wrong way around as time unraveled in the room.

Paul looked straight at me as I stared back at him. His mouth formed a word. I knew it was my name.

But I could not hear Paul.

The hearing aid, the contraption, the hated thing which marked me as different in the world, was lying upstairs. Without it, I couldn't hear him.

I leaped off the piano stool and started toward Paul. I don't truly remember what I meant to do at that moment. Grab him and pull him back into our world? Throw myself into the still waters behind him and hope to surface in a better past?

It didn't matter.

As soon as the music stopped, he disappeared. I fell with a bone-jarring thud off the stage, bruising my already bruised hands as I tried to stop from crashing down. Curling around myself, I lay on the cold dance floor and wept.

I cried like a child, bawling with temper at being denied my heart's desire.

A door banged open. The steady tread of a heavyset woman in sensible house slippers crossed the floor.

"Raquel Malone Gutierrez," said Nova, "what have you done to yourself?"

INTERLUDE

I saw you. I know it was you. When you looked toward me, I know you saw me too.

You are real. You are Raquel. And I am still here and still trapped and afraid, so afraid now, to hope for more. It was only a moment, but why didn't I act? Why didn't I step forward, grab your hand, and pull myself out of this place?

Even as I write this, the memory of your face is fading. So fierce, so brave, and the moment when I saw you runs out of my mind like sand through my fingers. I must find my way back to you.

If I sit here and tell you a story, then I can keep you in my mind. That's how this works. I think somebody told me that is how this works when they gave me this journal, only now I don't remember. But I wrote it down at the very beginning, that a dying man gave me this pen, this little book, so I could find you.

I turn back the pages to read again the stories that I have told and remember the people who appeared. When I spoke of Bluebeard, it brought me to the house dripping blood and hearts full of courage. When I spoke of faithful servants, I met one.

I know the stories must be told to find you. Somebody told me what to do but I cannot remember who. Was it you?

Can you find me again?

CHAPTER SEVENTEEN

I couldn't confess to Nova what I had done. Not all of it. Not the full extent of my anger or my shameful wish to escape into the past to avoid a future that I didn't want.

Instead I talked about being unable to sleep, playing to distract myself, and then, most improbably, falling off the stage. I let her think the bruises on my hands were from the fall rather than my attack on the piano.

For it had been an attack, an attempt to wrench the world into the pattern that I wanted, and, as I was painfully aware, it was a failed attack.

Nova remained calm and, in the routine that we had established over the last month, didn't ask too many questions. At least not awkward questions like, "Why did you sound like you were murdering the piano?" Hopefully she hadn't actually heard much of my playing.

My big, loud, and often brash aunt demonstrated her own talent for stillness. She sat listening quietly while I clutched a cup of tea and stammered through my story.

Finally, I offered an apology for waking her.

"I never heard the piano," said Nova. "I jolted awake and thought I better investigate. When I was coming downstairs, I heard you fall."

I remembered the whole world wobbling when Paul appeared and wondered if that was what roused Nova. Another thing that I did not confess was that I had been trying for my own "unmooring" from time. Even in my shaken state, I knew Nova would not approve.

After a few more reassurances that I only suffered minor bruising, I retreated to my bedroom. I leafed through the journal again, noting how the writing grew wilder, more sprawling across the page, further into the book, as if Paul was scrambling to put down all the words as quickly as possible. Then an idea struck me. Closing the journal with the final entries still unread, I crossed the room and picked up my headset.

After a moment of thought, I headed back into the dining area to raid Nova's desk for pencils. The lights were out in the kitchen and Nova's bedroom door was shut. I sincerely hoped my aunt had gone back to sleep. I swiped a handful of nice straight pencils out of the top desk drawer and went back to my room.

In every corner of the room, I laid those pencils down in patterns of decreasing triangles as Beatrice had suggested to Paul.

Then I settled myself back in bed and placed the hearing aid on my head. The microphone on my chest, the earpiece in place over my left ear, and the battery placed on the bed next to me. I switched it on, hearing the now familiar electric hum, the faint static just at the edge of my comprehension.

Humming the first few bars of "Jingle Bells," I waited.

"Raquel," said Paul's voice in my ear. As usual, he sounded distracted and worried, even terrified. The howling noise which bothered me before was also audible. I looked at the corners of the room with some trepidation. But nothing appeared.

"Paul," I said as clearly as I could while trying to keep the tune running in my head. Not as simple as it sounds, but I was always good at talking to my pupils while playing examples on the keyboard. Now my fingers drummed silently on the quilt, the same motions as if I played "Jingle Bells" on a keyboard. "Can you hear me? I know how to help you."

"Raquel," he said again, but firmer and more confident. "I saw you."

"You did," I said. My fingers went up and down, playing the melody silently so I could continue the conversation. "I think there's a way to bring you to the Diamond Dog."

"The Diamond Dog?" he said with almost a laugh. "It sounds like something from a fairytale. A little dog who jumps out of a walnut to help poor Ivan."

"I don't know that story." The sounds in my ear were fading, even the howls growing fainter, so I hummed a few bars of "Jingle Bells."

"When I see you again," I heard Paul say, "I will tell you all the stories in my head. That's how I learned to speak other languages, asking for fairytales. I remember them still, all the stories. I heard them everywhere I went. Everyone has a story which begins 'once upon a time.'"

"I always liked the endings better than the beginnings,"

I said very softly. Because I did not need to shout for this man to hear me. Because I could hear him even as his voice dropped to a whisper. Because we were bound together in this strange bubble of time, memory, and music. "I like the endings where they lived happily."

"Ever after," replied Paul.

A bang and thump distracted me, and the tune dropped completely out of my head.

"Paul? Paul?" I called but nobody answered. I called again and then sorrowfully gave up. It seemed the music could only hold him in our world for a short time. I needed to find a way to make it last. To give him a chance to escape. To give me a chance to escape.

Looking up at the windows, I realized it was dawn already. The thump was probably Thelma coming in the kitchen door with the day's delivery of eggs and milk, I decided. I remembered Nova's grand plans of baking and wondered how quickly I could extract myself from rolling out dough.

For I needed to find Ralph Tawney and I needed help doing that. Help that I couldn't discuss with Nova.

Because I knew the secret of time travel now – and I believed this new secret could buy all of us what we wanted.

I would pay my aunt back by protecting her.

But first I needed to speak with Tawney. He'd given a card to Nova, but I couldn't ask her for it, not without revealing my plans. But I knew somebody else who had Tawney's address. I could go to Chilton Brewster, who would be broadcasting his usual editorials this morning and then proceeding to his office at the bank.

After dressing for baking, I met Thelma and Nova in the kitchen. Nova asked how I was feeling and accepted my assurances that all was well. Which was exactly how I felt. All was well. I knew what to do next.

After that… the future could be changed, I told myself, if I could journey into the past. If I showed our government how to do it, surely they wouldn't interfere with my plans. They would owe me a favor, many favors, favors that I intended to use to help everyone, including myself.

Brewster had hinted at immunity for Nova. Tawney had almost as clearly promised it. To save Paul, I needed the sort of help that our government could give me. I realized that I could tell Tawney what he wanted to know. I could bargain for everyone at the Diamond Dog. I would insist on Tawney helping me in return.

I had forgotten, of course, the first rule of all fairytales. You must never keep anything for yourself. You must sacrifice everything for others. Or disaster will strike, and your happy ending will be overturned.

INTERLUDE

In the ruins of my memories, I found a story which will link me to you, my Raquel, my Marya Morevna.

Did I tell you about the old lady, the one who was fiercer than Baba Yaga? She lived in my village in a little red house at the very edge of a field of wheat. She grew poppies in her garden. I remember the wheat, taller than my head, golden in the sun. I remember the red poppies lining the path leading to her blue door and the sunflowers planted all around her house. This was years and years ago, when I was very young. I recall her house so perfectly.

Why can I remember this and not remember how I came to this place without sun or poppies or the wind whispering through the wheat?

But my fierce old lady lives in my mind, the hard rap of her silver thimble on the top of my head if I'd done something wrong. But if I did something right, she would tell me about Marya Morevna.

She was brave and led her army into battle, did Marya Morevna, and she was kind, helping her foolish prince even after he let Koschei out of the dungeon.

If I had married Marya Morevna, I told the old lady, I would never have listened to Koschei.

"Koschei the deathless, an interesting character from Russian folklore. The hiding of the heart inside an egg, inside a box, and so on," said the man with a long white beard to a younger man. The two sat together with cups of coffee in a booth. I sat on a stool at the counter, this book between my hands. The waitress hummed a song, a song I have heard before, as she cleaned the counter.

"Be right with you, hon," she said to me. "Just let me get this next order out."

"I used Koschei with my freshman class to illustrate the possibilities of galaxies hidden within other galaxies, stars which can only be detected by their influence on other stars as it were, the heart within the egg within the box," said the older man.

"Afraid that's a bit more complicated than I can understand, professor," said the younger man. "I'm more interested in your thoughts about time travel."

The professor poured a spoonful of sugar into his cup and stirred it three times, clinking the spoon each time against the edge of the cup. "All astronomy is time travel. The stars we see in the sky each night do not exist in the present. At least not as we are seeing them. What we are seeing is what they were, and yet they are brilliant in the sky and very much a part of what we are now. A conundrum for philosophers, this notion of time travel, Ralph. Didn't you ask me to call you Ralph?"

"Please do call me Ralph," said the other. "Are you saying a mechanism for time travel exists, Professor Withers?"

"Not a machine, like HG Wells' story," said the professor. "But as a theory, it already does. We've known as much since Einstein published his work seven years ago. Even as my colleagues debate what relativity means and how his work applies to their own, it's clear we could experience time travel to the future. Going to the past would be the challenge. Yet, as I said, I see the past every night through my telescope. If I could remove myself from where I was standing in the present to the speck of light I am observing, then I would be in the past. I already am in the past in my mind, as it were. It's the matter of moving the body as well." He took another sip of coffee.

"Fascinating to think about. One of my more unusual colleagues at Miskatonic came across some literature which suggested one could dislocate oneself from one's time through use of pharmaceutical concoctions, traveling both forward and back simultaneously while leaving oneself in the present. I think it would be very exciting if it wasn't all theoretical and possibly poisonous."

I turned around and almost yelled at them both that it was not exciting – it was horrible. But then I recognized the face of the man in the brown suit. I knew him. It was the man who had tried to shoot me in the laboratory. He looked almost the same. But when he glanced up, he did not seem to know me.

"But do you have people at Miskatonic University who are experimenting in time travel?" Ralph said, turning back to the professor.

The professor stared at him as the old lady used to look at me before she thumped me on my head with her thimble.

"As I explained, such theories can have no practical application. Experiments such as you suggest would be incredibly unwise. If one was to travel to the past or the future, I don't doubt that it would have disastrous results, if only for the time traveler. Such a journey would destroy a man's mind. What government agency did you say you were from?"

A bell jangled as somebody pushed the door open and called out "Merry Christmas, Velma!"

Then I am back in this place without stars, but I know where I am now. I am inside Koschei's egg. I remember the story so clearly as the old woman told it to me: "No matter what Koschei does, he cannot fool Marya. He can kidnap Marya and take her out of our world, or he can cut Ivan up into little pieces and set him afloat in a barrel. It doesn't matter. Marya Morevna always finds the egg where Koschei hides his heart."

Even as I tell this tale, I hear you singing again. I know you will find my heart inside the egg which is this place imprisoning me.

CHAPTER EIGHTEEN

Chilton Brewster was writing a letter when I arrived at his office later that afternoon. He put down his pen without comment. Rising from his chair, he offered me the seat opposite him and then sat again.

"How can I help you, Miss Malone?" he said, as if he was expecting me to open a savings account or ask for a loan.

I didn't bother to correct him about my last name. In this town I would always be better known as Nova Malone's niece. Now I needed to concentrate on how best to help my aunt and the rest of the employees of the Diamond Dog.

"I want to speak with Agent Tawney," I said. Then, because my request came out a little blunt, I added, "Please. You offered to arrange a meeting. You said you wanted to help."

Brewster looked a little puzzled. "Is your aunt willing to talk to Tawney now?"

"This isn't about Nova or bootlegging," I said. The rest came out in a nervous rush of words. "Tawney told me that he wasn't interested in enforcing Prohibition. He wanted to know about time travel. I know how it happens. Well, I know what causes it. Actually, I don't understand why it happens, but I know someone who has traveled through several different times in this area. I can introduce Agent Tawney to Paul."

Then I stopped talking, because I realized I didn't know Paul's last name or anything about him other than what the journal said. My rambling explanation was vague, and probably wouldn't have swayed a skeptic, but Brewster wanted to believe me.

"I knew that woman changed things," Brewster said, and it was obvious "that woman" was my aunt. "I found the two journals from 1925." He pulled down two books from the shelf. The volumes looked identical down to the year printed on the spine and his initials stamped in gold on the cover. "Both books start out exactly the same but change on December 24." He flipped the pages. "In this one, I even copied down the editorial I gave that day." He twisted the book to show me how nearly two pages were filled. "And I noted my disappointment in missing the owner of the Diamond Dog and not being able to finish our transaction."

He had written down everything about his day, including a pithy paragraph about giving away his best winter coat to a woman clearly inebriated and in need of help. I was amused to see he also wrote about how he regretted his action and ran after the woman to retrieve his coat. Apparently, Brewster could even be critical of himself in writing.

"But this journal has a completely different entry on December 24," he said, handing the second one to me.

The entry was much shorter, just a few lines to say he was leaving for an appointment at the Diamond Dog and hoped to take possession of the property shortly. In this book, the pages after December 24 were blank while the pages of the other journal, the one that included the entry about chasing after Nova and his coat, were filled through December 31.

"I always knew there was something wrong," he said, taking back the two journals and setting them side by side. "Every time I walk past the Diamond Dog, I remember things differently than I know how they occurred. It's like remembering a dream, but it feels like a memory."

"Moving through time plays havoc with the memory," I said, thinking of Paul's stories.

"I remember her taking my coat and snatching my journal out of the pocket at the last minute," said Brewster more to himself than me. In fact, the entire time that I was in his office, I felt we both were speaking too much to our own memories and not listening nearly enough to each other.

"After I gave my coat to your aunt, I came back to the office and wrote in it. But later I also remembered writing in the journal and leaving it in the office. When I put away my journal for 1925, I found the other one already on the shelf."

"Writing something down may have caused you to retain the memory of the time before you met my aunt," I guessed. "Although I don't know why there are two journals and only one coat."

"I actually forgot about meeting your aunt until she returned the coat to me," said Brewster. "Then I remembered everything and nothing made sense! I had two journals and the handwriting in both is mine. I remember writing both passages, even though that shouldn't be possible." Strains of anger and even confusion roughened his voice, but again it felt more directed at himself than at me. "She stole my coat. She gave it back. Why do I remember a different day?"

"Something you did after was changed by what happened before but it wasn't the same before, so the after was changed, too," I said, remembering Nova's discussion of time travelers causing before and after to become reversed for some people.

"How do you know this?"

I tried to explain, but it was muddled. I was as confused as Brewster about how time travel worked. Still, I persisted on the one point that I wanted to make. "Paul has been traveling to many places and times. He's the man who knocked you into the snowbank. If the government rescues him, he could explain it all," I said to the banker and hoped the government liked fairytales.

The whole time that I was talking to Brewster, I was thinking Paul needed to be rescued. I didn't know how to rescue him. But Tawney would know who to call, I was certain. When your house was on fire, you called the fire department, you didn't try to pour a bucket of water on it yourself and hope for the best, according to my civics teacher in high school.

There was a reason for agencies like the one that Agent

Tawney worked for, and I meant to use every possible resource to help Paul. And protect my aunt. The latter, I was well aware, might be harder. However, I pleaded for her too.

"Nova never meant to be in Kingsport last Christmas Eve," I told Brewster. "It was an accident. She says it is very unsafe, the time traveling, I mean. She never uses it for bootlegging." I cringed a little as I said the last, realizing I probably shouldn't go into details about Nova's philosophies concerning smuggling liquor and what sounded like magic. I did manage not to talk about the grimoire, probably because I was so flustered that I'd forgotten it again.

Twice already in this conversation I called my aunt a bootlegger. But Brewster barely reacted to that.

"I'd forgotten the man who knocked me down," said Brewster. "I was so preoccupied with the coat. I liked my coat and I gave it away! But she was such a demanding woman. I couldn't seem to say no to her. But I regretted it the minute I gave it to her." He shifted uneasily. "I even tried to follow her, but I lost her almost immediately."

"Paul says she's a Baba Yaga," I told him. "And it's probably best if you didn't catch her that day."

"Then, Miss Malone," said Brewster suddenly, focusing again on me and not on the indignation he suffered a year ago, "why are you here? Without your aunt's consent, I think?"

"It's a very good question," a response I'd learned in years of teaching when students asked me a question for which I had no answer. "But to save time," I added without irony, "let me answer it when we meet with Agent Tawney."

I hoped to think out a better explanation for time travel and also a better way to ask for amnesty for everyone at the Diamond Dog by the time we reached our destination. Tawney had promised something like a quiet exit from Kingsport for Nova. How I would convince Nova to accept it, I hadn't decided. But I thought once Paul landed in 1926 and I went to wherever, whenever I could go, it might work out. After all, the future would change. I had great faith that my aunt Nova would survive and flourish in any future.

Brewster finally agreed to help me. He picked up the phone and gave some quiet instructions to someone on the other end of the line. While I was nearly jiggling with impatience in my chair, he put on his hat and overcoat (if it was the one my aunt Nova borrowed, it was a very fine heavy coat with a fur collar).

"I know where Agent Tawney is staying in Kingsport," said Brewster. "I will take you there. You can explain what's happening to both of us."

Tawney was renting a room in a small, neat house on the edge of town. Brewster drove me there in his car, an imposing Chrysler Imperial but not nearly as comfortable as Nova's Rolls. Brewster drove at a slow, steady pace, and stayed silent for the entire drive, which surprised me. I thought he would fire off a dozen questions, but perhaps he wanted to wait to hear what Tawney said to me and what I said to the federal agent.

As usual, after the third turn and twist down Kingsport's picturesque streets, I had no idea of exactly where we were.

One or two landmarks looked vaguely familiar, but I hoped Brewster would drive me back to the Diamond Dog after our talk with Tawney.

The neighborhood where we eventually stopped looked prosperous enough: white painted houses with red roofs and large garages behind several places, horse barns converted into shelters for the automobiles now more practical for so many families. We pulled up in front of a house looking as respectable as the rest. Brewster explained the owner was a widow who took in a few long staying guests for the income. "I always recommend her to any business associates who need a place to stay," he said. Which explained how Agent Tawney had found the place.

The weather was incredibly dreary, with heavy clouds and a wind which bit through the best of heavy coats. We hurried from the sidewalk to the front door. I was glad of a small fire going in the front parlor of the house where Tawney's landlady conducted us. The room smelled cheerfully of pine and cinnamon. Rather than a tree, a small swag decorated the mantel. The widow, like my aunt, apparently favored baking cookies three days before Christmas. There was even a smudge of flour on the edge of the neat collar of her conservative brown dress.

Upon hearing who I was, the widow, whose name was something like Mrs Simon or Mrs Smith, asked me about the dances at the Diamond Dog. She admitted that she didn't own a radio but enjoyed listening to the broadcasts at her neighbor's house. "I was thinking of buying a radio after Christmas," she said to me. "One of the smaller ones to set in the kitchen."

"The camera shop is thinking of selling radios on time payments," I told her.

Tawney came briskly into the parlor, fetched by a timid maid or daughter. I never learned which the younger woman was, as the mistress of the house continued to chat with us. Tawney made some efforts to shoo his landlady out of the room.

Undeterred, the widow asked if we would like coffee or tea. Brewster declined both politely. Tawney practically growled something negative. I started to say no as well, but then called her back and asked for the tea. A warm cup to hold in my chilled hands was comforting, a small bit of courage, as I explained all over again to Tawney what I had told Brewster in his office. I was stalling again, but I almost had my explanation and my plea for Nova figured out.

The second time I managed my story better than my confused explanations in Brewster's office. Again I left out the part about the journal given to me by Captain Leo, from some vague idea of keeping Captain Leo and the amiable Cuffe out of my troubles and an even stronger inclination to hold the journal private. Several passages written by Paul felt as if he had been speaking directly to me and I didn't want to share his confidences.

Outside of that, I told the two men as much as I could about Paul. I suggested my knowledge came from our brief conversations, always audible only through my headset and triggered by the tune of "Jingle Bells." I described Paul's visits to Kingsport and Arkham, forgetting entirely the one incident in Dunwich and deliberately skipping the one in Innsmouth to avoid mentioning Captain Leo.

I did tell them that wobbles, as I called them, were created by music played at certain times.

I even told Tawney that it was Billy's version of "Jingle Bells" which seemed to be the most effective in creating those "wobbles" in time.

Several times I reassured them that nobody else knew about time travel, which was almost the truth, and I sounded much more confident of my facts. I thought from my conversations with Nova that she kept the Malones' tendency for "unmooring" fairly quiet, just family as it were.

Again, the men said nothing as I spoke about the most outlandish ideas. Tawney kept making some notes in a small book he carried in his pocket. For some reason that made me even more nervous. Throughout it all – and it felt like hours but was probably only fifteen minutes or so – I made it abundantly clear that I would only help them meet Paul if my aunt received some type of immunity or protection from Tawney's office.

The whole conversation felt like I was walking along a cliff edge, where an unwise comment would plunge me quickly into worse trouble. But I truly didn't know how else to help Paul or Nova. As much as I wanted to escape into the past and change it, I didn't want to leave more problems behind me.

Most of the names that I recited elicited no response from Brewster, except for Preston Fairmont. He mentioned to Tawney that he'd heard of Fairmont, something of a dilettante and a very wealthy man, not the poor prince that Paul described. "I can't think of any reason why a man like Fairmont would lose his fortune in the future," said Brewster, clearly most intrigued by this story. "Unless he made some very unwise investments or withdrew his money completely from the stock market." It was the only time he spoke during my recital.

Tawncy seemed more taken by the names of Beatrice Sharpe and Agatha Crane. Both women, he said to Brewster, had done research of considerable interest to his office.

In fact, all of the discussion after I stopped talking occurred between the two men. Listening to them, it seemed Tawney had met with Brewster a number of times, which surprised me. In the cafe it had sounded like he'd only come out to Kingsport to investigate a few odd letters. I shifted anxiously in my seat, wondering what a close alliance between the two would mean for Nova and for me. As Brewster and Tawney discussed possible implications of Paul's appearances in the area, they ignored me completely. You might have thought they had discovered all this information on their own and I wasn't even in the room. In fact, the pair reminded me of college meetings where two of the more pedantic professors would always conclude with a long-winded discussion of music education theory while the rest of us longed to escape the room. I have sat through more arguments about the ideas of Calvin Brainerd Cady than any woman should be forced to suffer.

Just as I was considering following my nose to the source of the delicious scents wafting from the kitchen at the back of the house, Tawney turned to me and demanded to listen to my headset. I must have looked startled and indeed I was, as I had drifted off into my own thoughts of cookies and future possibilities. Trying to figure out the "after and before" as Nova described the effects of time travel made my head hurt and the discussions of the two men made the headache worse. Tawney modified his bark of a command to a "Please could I" upon Brewster's look of disapproval. Manners mattered to Brewster, even though he did his own version of yapping through his letters – and the occasional bark, I remembered, like the first time I saw him come into the Diamond Dog and accuse Nova of bootlegging.

But today, Brewster played the gentleman, reassuring me that it would be best for Tawney to try to hear what I had been hearing. He asked me to help the agent talk to Paul.

With some reluctance, I disentangled myself from the hearing aid and passed the equipment to Tawney. To my relief, he didn't pull the band across his head. Like most men, Tawney used a strong-smelling pomade to flatten his hair. The idea of cleaning it off the headband or smelling it on my own hair made me wince.

Instead, Tawney held the earpiece up to his own ear. After a moment he shook his head. "Just a hum and you clinking your teacup," he said to me. The microphone was resting on the table next to the tea set.

"Sing a little," I said.

Tawney looked as offended as a seven year-old boy sat down for his first piano lesson. Teaching children helped pay my way through college, but it wasn't easy.

I hummed a few bars of "Jingle Bells" and Tawney dropped the earpiece. When he saw my surprise, he thrust his trembling hands in his pockets and leaned back.

"I heard something howling," he said. "Horrible noise."

I glanced with some trepidation at the corners of the room. The hounds appear at the intersections, at the corners, Beatrice had told Paul. But there was nothing there and the room still smelled of cinnamon, pine, and woodsmoke. There was no reason to be afraid, I told myself.

"But did you hear Paul?" I said to Tawney.

He shook his head, pulled his hands out of his pockets, and picked up the earpiece again. When he nodded at me, I started to sing very softly.

After only a few words, Tawney nodded. "I hear something," he said. "A man talking." He huffed a bit. "It's nonsense words. Maybe another language."

"Paul has an accent," I said.

"Foreign agent?" said Tawney with a hard look at me and Brewster. "Perhaps this is the result of another government's experiments."

My stomach clenched. I didn't want to rescue Paul only to have him imprisoned. "He's an immigrant, a refugee," I said, because I thought that was probably true.

"Perhaps a Russian," Tawney said with a frown. "Well, at least he's not German."

"The war is over," Brewster said.

"For now. But we are keeping our eye on Germany," said Tawney. "He's talking again. He's reciting something. A name. Marya Morevna. Definitely sounds Russian to me."

"It's a fairytale," I said, stopping my singing to explain. "Paul tells himself fairytales to remember things." Paul wrote those stories for me so I would understand. After and before all mixed up. Paul wrote those stories so I could be brave now with Tawney. Paul wrote once upon a time so I could find a happily ever after.

"How do I see him?" asked Tawney, laying the earpiece on the table with a click. "How do I lay my hands on him?"

I didn't like how he phrased it, but I told him, "Come to the Diamond Dog on Christmas Eve. We always play and broadcast 'Jingle Bells' and he should appear then. I think it must be on December 24. I don't know why, but it's easier for him on Christmas Eve." Luckily, they didn't question me about how I would know that, as I still hadn't explained about the journal. Perhaps they thought I picked the knowledge up from Nova.

Thinking about the hounds, I added, "It may be dangerous too. You should be prepared."

"Oh, we will be prepared," said Tawney and his tone did nothing to reassure me.

"You have to keep your promises," I said to Brewster and Tawney as firmly as Nova would. I missed my aunt and almost wished her with me, but I was still convinced that this was the best way to save everyone including myself. "No prosecutions of anyone at the Diamond Dog. Or I won't help you. And Paul won't appear if I'm not there." The last was a complete guess, as I really had no idea if I could repeat my experiment and force Paul to appear in the ballroom through my own fierce wishing. But I had felt something for a moment, as he shimmered into view, as if we were connected. Like Marya Morcvna, I had to try to find him, even if he was hidden in a bubble, an egg, of time.

"You can trust me," said Ralph Tawney in a voice that I didn't trust at all.

INTERLUDE

Once upon a time, I despaired, thinking I would be trapped here forever. Now I know hope. All I need to do is find your Diamond Dog. I write this down many times, so I will remember. Every time I write your name as well, so I do not forget you. I remember your name, Raquel. As you remember me.

Now I walk with purpose under the trees and across the beach, to burn away my impatience, as I wait for you. As I walk, I write down another story.

Just moments ago, I found myself striding down a street that I think I know.

As I looked around, I recognized it as the street where Baba Yaga led me on her dance. A movie theater with posters occupied the center of the block. A sleigh being drawn by two bay horses went ringing by me down the street. The signs hung from its sides said, "Buy Your Trees at Cuffe's Farm." Cars tooted their horns in response as a jolly round man waved from the driver's seat.

A couple crossed in front of me to examine the movie

posters. "Let's go in," she said to him. "I like Jimmy Stewart."

He turned slightly to her, leaning heavily on a cane. "Looks sentimental to me," he said. "Isn't there an angel in it? And haven't you seen it already?"

"Maybe, and maybe," she said, hugging his arm. "But I haven't seen it with you, and I think it's the best movie of 1946. Let's go in."

I heard the date and looked closer at the street. The cars were wrong, the clothes were wrong. This wasn't my time, not the year I was lost. Not the year that I found you.

"I'd rather go dancing," he said as she pulled him toward the ticket window.

"Baby, they closed down the USO when the war ended. Besides, you just left the hospital," she said.

"Doing a slow waltz with my gal won't put me back in bed. We could go home and turn on the radio, do a few turns around the room," he retorted while still pulling the money out of his pocket to pay for their tickets. "Doctors gave me a clean bill of health at Walter Reed. I'm taking my benefits and heading to college now. How would you like being married to a college graduate, Mrs Parkington?"

"Sounds wonderful to me," she said, hugging his arm a little tighter. "Everything sounds wonderful now you're home again."

As they turned away from the ticket window, the man bumped into me, nearly dropping his cane. "Sorry," he grunted. "I didn't see you there."

"Can you tell me where to find the Diamond Dog?" I asked, being slow and careful with my words, speaking only in English.

"The Diamond Dog?" said the woman. "That's the place where my parents used to go dancing. It's been gone for a long time, twenty years or more." She pointed to the movie theater. "It used to be there." Then, being a kind lady, she paused and asked me, "Did you know it? You look too young to have been there."

"I was there," I said, but so softly that she probably didn't hear me. "I will be there again. I know I will."

The couple brushed past me into the movie theater. Still I did not move, looking at the closed doors and wishing I knew when I would see you next, Raquel. Where are you? How much time separates us now?

A group of boys spilled out of the theater. One of them swung a little silver bell in his hands, small and round like it came off a horse's harness, which he rang and rang. "See! I'm getting my wings," he shouted at the others. One of them swiped up a handful of snow and tossed it in the boy's face. He retaliated by throwing the bell. I reached out and snatched it from the air.

As I shook it for myself, the street disappeared. When I shook it again in the rhythm of the song you sang, the street shimmered into view, but the boys were not there. I almost stepped out again, but I did not know when it was or where you were. If I am to leave this place, I think… I know… I must see you at the Diamond Dog. The more I consider this, the more certain I am.

Jim Culver told me to dance at the Diamond Dog. I will dance with you.

Now I am here again, beneath the trees which no longer frighten me. I have a silver bell in one pocket and a silver dime in the other. With such lucky treasures even the most foolish Simon can find his way out of the woods. I listen for your singing. When I hear you I will start running, ringing my silver bell. This time I will escape.

CHAPTER NINETEEN

On Christmas Eve we could all feel it, the crackle in the air, the anticipation of the Diamond Dog's biggest dance. The tree arrived on Thursday from Cuffe's farm. Nova left it in the yard behind the building to be admired by everyone passing by. A great number of Kingsport residents seemed to find a reason to pass by and speculate on how the tree would look fully decorated in the ballroom.

I was full of nerves, too, but not for the same reasons. I'd made my deal with Tawney and hoped that it would turn out all right for everyone. If I got what I wanted for Christmas, I would disappear into the past and never have to face the future that so frightened me. Paul would be saved. And Nova? Well, I had great faith that Nova would manage no matter what.

On Friday morning, Tim and Otis wrestled the tree through the double doors of the ballroom with the help of two waiters who arrived early to help with the decorations. At one point, as the four men leveraged the tree toward the ceiling, I feared I had misjudged the height and it was too tall for the room. But when the tree stood straight in its cast-iron stand, the very top was still an inch or two short of the ceiling.

"Just enough room for the star," said Nova with considerable satisfaction. Otis and Tim were dispatched to the basement to bring up the multiple boxes of ornaments. As soon as the noon broadcast was done, Reggie and Johnny joined the fun. Reggie doing most of the work and Johnny most of the commentary on what to do next, until the point came when Reggie asked him if he was a consulting engineer or an insulting engineer.

"Bit of both," said Johnny without any shame at all and a merry grin at the rest of us.

Reggie unrolled string after string of electric lights upon the floor to make sure there were no tangles. With pliers, cutters, and extra wire, he cobbled them together to make one very long continuous string to loop around the tree.

"Are you sure that's safe?" said Johnny, overlooking the operation.

"Absolutely," mumbled Reggie, talking around the pliers held in his mouth as his hands busily knotted together the strings. "This way it all goes into one socket."

Then came the debate about which should come first: the wrapping of the tree in lights or the placement of the ornaments. Traditionally, it seemed, most people placed the ornaments first, but Reggie claimed that was because they were used to clipping the candles on the tree as the last act of decorating.

"We should wrap these around the tree first," he said,

lifting the string off the floor, "and then hang the tinsel."

"Give me one end and I'll start wrapping," I said. At home we always did ornaments first, but Reggie's suggestions seemed sensible to me. Time to try something new, I decided.

Once we looped the electric lights round the tall tree, Reggie placed a silver star enhanced with a small electric bulb on the very top.

I helped Johnny rip open the boxes and hand the ornaments to everyone. Ginger and Harlean took charge of the tinsel. If anyone else tried to add a clump of tinsel to a branch, they quickly removed it, flattened it out, and rehung it so it shimmered straight down like the fringe on a flapper's dress. Only Cozy could hang tinsel to their strict standards. His careful application of each strand earned him a quick kiss on the cheek from Ginger that made him blush and retreat behind his drums.

Billy danced all around the tree, adding glittering glass stars wherever he saw a bare spot. All the while, he sang or hummed his way through "Oh Tannenbaum, oh Tannenbaum" in a manner that suggested it would become a dance hit that night. Cozy caught the rhythm from Billy. Harlean burst into a full throated, "Oh Christmas tree, oh Christmas tree" to accompany them. Soon everyone was singing with her, even me. Billy left the decorating to others as he leaped to the piano stool and turned the traditional song into a syncopated dance that could have come from Tin Pan Alley yesterday.

When it was done, we turned off all the other lights. Cozy did a drum roll of anticipation. Reggie threw a switch and the tree lit up. It glowed in its corner, a pillar of gold and silver reflecting the light in sparkles over the room.

"Oooh," said Harlean, standing by my side. "It's so pretty, I hate to think of it ever coming down."

I just smiled and nodded, because it was too beautiful for words.

"We'll leave it up through New Year's Eve," said Nova. The glow in her eyes demonstrated to the rest of us that the tree matched her inner vision. Tonight's dance would indeed be something to be talked about.

With some regret, I slipped away from the crowd. I was afraid that Kingsport would never forget the bootlegger's dance, but not for the reasons that Nova wanted. I looked once more at the beautiful tree and wished as hard as I had as a child that everything would still be wonderful at Christmas. That this Christmas Eve dance would not lead to disaster.

Outside I went to the street corner to meet Agent Tawney as previously arranged. Out of view of anyone standing at the Diamond Dog's windows, he asked me, "When will your time traveler arrive?"

"Billy is playing 'Jingle Bells' at ten," I said. "I suggested to Harlean that she invite the whole crowd to sing along. We're passing out bells, too, for everyone to shake and ring."

I'd suggested the bells earlier to Nova, who had loved the idea and immediately sent me out to buy up every harness bell or small silver bell that I could find in Kingsport's stores. We'd even driven over to Arkham and raided their stores as well. There were enough bells of all sizes to give one to every dancer. Nova had decided to decorate the handle or loop at the top of each one with a red ribbon and a card that said "Gift of the Diamond Dog" as a souvenir of the ballroom's most memorable night. The whole project made her chortle as Thelma, Lily, and I tied ribbon after ribbon on the bells. For if there was anything Nova loved more than gadgets, I realized, it was giving gifts at Christmas.

Perhaps this shouldn't have surprised me so, considering all the wondrous gifts that she'd shipped to my family over the years or her continuing generosity toward me. Before breakfast was done and we went downstairs to decorate the tree, Nova insisted that I unwrap a long box to reveal a beautiful red sweater with white stars knit into the cabled pattern.

"Nobody should wait until Christmas for all their presents," said Nova, looking me over with some satisfaction when I pulled the sweater on over my pajamas. "Minerva Knowles rarely knits sweaters for folks outside her family, but she was kind enough to do this for me. I knew it would suit you."

"It's gorgeous," I said truthfully, for it was as warm and enveloping as one of Nova's hugs.

As I stood on the corner of the street, dressed in Nova's gift, I felt a terrible traitor as I discussed with Agent Tawney how he and his agents would use the pretense of raiding the Diamond Dog to snatch and hold Paul.

However, I had Tawney's assurances that his men could prevent Paul from being dragged back into his nightmare world. Also, Tawney promised nobody would be arrested during the raid.

"We'll take you and the time traveler with us," said Tawney, "so you can answer some questions in Washington. Then you'll be free to go wherever you want. We may need to hold your aunt for a day or two, just to make it seem like a Prohibition raid, but she'll be free to go before New Year's."

I nodded and made my own promises, although I knew I was lying to Tawney. I simply had to believe he was speaking the truth to me. I had no intention of leaving Kingsport with him. As soon as the world shimmered and wobbled into that other place, I meant to jump into it even as they pulled Paul out. If my aunt could sing her way back to the time she wanted, I was sure I could do the same. I would change my future by retreating into the past.

After I returned to the Diamond Dog, I found it impossible to join in the general teasing and merriment as Nova passed out small gifts to everyone. "For I shan't see you tomorrow," my aunt boomed from the center of the ballroom. "You'll all be home with your families celebrating the best Christmas ever. Just as I know I'll be celebrating with my niece."

I felt horrible as I smiled in response to Nova's speech, because I knew I was about to betray her and ruin her dance.

By nine o'clock, I understood what my mother meant when she said, "My nerves are shattered." My stomach felt as if it had turned into a bowl of acid. Every time somebody wished me a merry Christmas, I wanted to scream or burst into tears. I have never been a hysterical woman, but if one more person asked me how I was feeling, I thought I would indeed shatter.

As the clock ticked too slowly toward ten, Johnny led me out for our usual dance. Even he noticed how tense and stiff I was as we circled the floor to one of Harlean's slower, sadder love songs, all about loss and heartache. The song was far too somber for the night, but the couples loved it as it gave them a chance to lean into each other in a way that the faster dances didn't. More than one couple circled under the giant balls of mistletoe hung in the shadowy corners opposite the tree.

"Relax," Johnny said to me. "You'll be great on the broadcast."

I glanced at the door, looking for Agent Tawney, and so missed his words the first time.

"What are you talking about?" I said as we traversed the floor, keeping to the center and well away from the crowd dancing in place under the mistletoe.

"We're calling you up on the stage during the 'Jingle Bells' introduction," said Johnny, executing a quick two step around a kissing couple who didn't seem to mind the lack of mistletoe above them. "Billy suggested that you play together on the piano, but Harlean wants you at the microphone singing with her. Or you can stand by Cozy and ring the bells."

"That's a terrible idea!" I said, startled out of my worried contemplation of when Tawney would arrive. "I don't play in public anymore. Whose idea was that?" But I should have guessed.

"Nova mentioned how you always played for your family

on Christmas Eve. She didn't want you to miss out, so we're being your family tonight," Johnny said. He patted my shoulder as we twirled slowly around the ballroom. "Reggie's got the booth all set up for recording as well so you'll have a record to send to your parents. It's a gift from all of us at the Diamond Dog to you."

"You cannot be nice to me tonight," I said with some emphasis. I probably sounded furious, but it was sorrow rather than anger that roughened my voice.

"Raquel?" Johnny's gaze went from mildly puzzled to completely confused. "What do you mean?"

"Oh, Johnny. I must do something tonight that Nova won't like. It makes it worse because everyone at the Diamond Dog means so much to me."

Johnny danced me to the edge of the floor, back to our regular table, and pulled out a chair for me. "Now, tell me what's wrong," he said, settling into the chair opposite me. "This is more than performance nerves."

But even as he leaned forward, I spotted Agent Tawney entering the room. Right behind him came three more men dressed in plain brown suits. After them came Chilton Brewster. "Oh no," I breathed.

Johnny twisted in his chair and spotted Brewster. "Raquel, don't worry about him," he said, turning back to me. "Your aunt won't let Brewster spoil the fun."

"It isn't Brewster," I confessed. "It's me. I'm going to ruin this dance."

Completely misunderstanding, Johnny patted my hand and said, "Raquel, it's only one song. The whole crowd will be singing along. Everyone will love it."

"They will not," I said, thinking about how the world wobbled and shifted under my feet when I forced an opening with my playing. But I hoped the shift would be as temporary as possible, a few minutes to pull Paul free and for me to escape, and then everything would be normal.

As normal as being raided by federal agents could be, I amended to myself.

The song ended. The excited, chattering crowd drifted back to the tables. With one last pat on my shoulder for reassurance, Johnny made his way back to the stage for announcements. Throughout the evening, a basket with small blank cards had been circulated through the ballroom. The customers were encouraged to write down holiday greetings for people listening on the radio which Johnny then read out loud at every break. As the evening wore on, the messages became sillier and sillier, much to the delight of the clapping crowd who clustered around the stage and bellowed out their own "Merry Christmas!" every time that Johnny paused.

"I see somebody in the audience is a poet," Johnny said, fishing out one card and looking at it. "Or you stole this from somebody else."

"All my own invention," yelled a man in the back.

"Anyway, here we go," Johnny continued. "It takes dough for Christmas presents, all I have is crust, but wish you a Merry Christmas, oh, honey, don't I just!"

"Ain't that like a man," said a woman standing near me. "Any excuse not to go shopping for a Christmas gift."

"I don't know," said her friend, "I think it's sweet."

The group of men in brown suits spread out across the floor, but the crowd was too caught up in Johnny's jokes and their own excitement to take any notice. Brewster remained so close to the door that I could barely spot him, almost hidden behind the rest of the dancers.

Ralph Tawney drew up the chair next to mine and sat down. "Are you ready?" he said, glancing at his watch. "It's almost time."

I wasn't ready at all, but I nodded my head. Near the stage, I could see Nova talking to Harlean and Ginger. In a minute she would turn around. I didn't want her to see me anywhere near Tawney. I stood up and hurried across the room toward them.

Nova turned and caught me in a quick, one-armed hug as I drew near. She seemed so relaxed that I decided she hadn't spotted Tawney, or she truly believed nobody would dare start a raid on Christmas Eve.

"Merry almost Christmas," Nova said to me. "We should have Johnny do messages at every dance. People love knowing their words are being broadcast through the air."

I nodded, unable to say anything. It was almost time for the next song to begin. Johnny kept glancing at me. I waved to him. I had to keep the evening going or Paul would be trapped forever. I would be caught in a future that I didn't want.

"Hey, folks," Johnny said, leaning into the microphone. "We have a special Christmas treat for you. Our own Raquel Malone Gutierrez is joining us tonight for your favorite holiday tune. Give her a big hand and help her send this song out to her family and friends. We may not be with everyone we love tonight, but we can send this greeting out to everyone listening to us!"

The crowd whooped and cheered. Nova gave me a little push toward the stage. Harlean and Ginger hopped up on the bandstand, drawing me after them. Billy slid off his piano stool and offered it to me.

I shook my head. "I can't play in your place," I said as quietly as I could so Harlean's microphone wouldn't pick up my nervous words. Out of the corner of my eye, I saw Tawney and his men spread out through the room. Brewster still remained near the big double doors leading out to the lobby.

"We can play it four-handed," said Billy. "You sit and I'll stand! We'll be fantastic."

"It's your song, Bill. I'll never play as well as you," I said, picking up a string of jingle bells from a pile on the floor near Cozy. Harlean grabbed a string and gave them a shake.

"Come sing with me," she said, looping an arm around my waist and pulling me toward her microphone. Billy hit the keys of the piano with a run of notes that were "Jingle Bells" but also completely his own. Ginger made her saxophone wail in response as Cozy crashed his sticks upon his cymbals.

The dancers yelled as everyone piled back into the center of the floor, men and women stomping and clapping to the music.

Harlean began to sing, "Dashing through the snow."

And the world changed.

In my left ear, I heard Paul's voice through my headset

as clear as if he stood next to me. "Raquel," he yelled. "I see you."

Then there he was, an ordinary man in a scratched leather jacket, tumbling through a crowd of dancers. Something was clutched in his left hand, which he held high above his head as he cried out my name.

"Paul!" I cried out, so relieved to see him safe among the dancers. That much I had done right.

Then the edges of the ballroom disappeared. Walls, ceiling, and floor dissolved into a forest and a beach unlike anything existing in our world. It was completely wrong in a way that can't be described, like a nightmare lingering in your head after you wake up.

The dancers were screaming and crying as I leaped off the stage, running as hard as I could toward the nightmare. Beyond Paul's shoulder, I saw the beach and the ocean with frozen waves. My destination was clearly visible if I wanted to change my past and future.

A horrible smell burst through the room and a howl unlike anything I've ever heard, even in my worst dreams. Creatures emerged from the corners of the ballroom, shaped like dogs and scaled like snakes. The monsters snapped their teeth like crocodiles. The crowd shrieked again and rushed toward the doors.

I saw Brewster swept away by the mass stampede, pushed back into the lobby and out of sight. Behind me, Nova was yelling, "Get out, get everyone out, go!"

Whipping around, I saw Nova grabbing at the stunned Harlean and thrusting her toward the doors to the kitchen. Billy, Ginger, and Cozy jumped off the bandstand. Another horrible creature emerged from the wall, launching itself toward them.

Nova picked up Cozy's cymbals, clanging them down on the beast's head. It howled and twisted away.

I put on a burst of speed. Trying to reach Paul, trying to exchange places with him. In the muddle of my thoughts, I persisted in believing that if I could only go there, then the forest would disappear again, taking all the terror away from the Diamond Dog.

Gunshots rang out. Tawney's men pulled out pistols from hidden holsters and fired away at the creatures. One recoiled and crashed back into the Christmas tree. Accompanied by shrieks from the crowd, the great tree swayed back and forth, toppling over with a shattering of ornaments and a shower of sparks from the broken electric lights. Flames sprang up.

"Out, out, out!" yelled Nova at the remaining crowd, those too stunned to run. She dove toward the wall behind the bandstand, tearing at the curtain there. Johnny and Billy ran beside her, helping her wrestle the giant fire hose off its base. Johnny swirled the wheel, releasing the water. Nova turned the hose upon the room.

As the jet of water hit one of the howling monsters, it leapt straight up, clawing at the ball of mistletoe and garlands hanging from the ceiling. The paper streamers broke away, dumping the creature back down into the flames and smoke.

Nova sprayed the water again, blasting the crowd liberally. I was hit by the water, sliding across the floor. But the water cut a straight line between one of the howlers and the crowd rushing toward the door. Snarling, the beast turned aside, charging for a corner of the room, where it popped out of existence only to reappear on the other side of the bandstand, nearer to the radio station door.

As I passed him, Paul clutched at my arm and shouted my name.

"I'm sorry, I'm sorry," I yelled back as I twisted away from him, still intent on trying to reach the path that would take me out of the current time.

"It's you! The time traveler!" Tawney lunged out of the crowd to grapple Paul to the ground.

I screamed at the federal agent, "Don't hurt him! You promised."

With a cry, I shoved Tawney off Paul. Then I heard Johnny yell. Turning around, I saw a frustrated monster galloping toward Nova. She also yelled and swept the hose around to lay a line of water between her and it.

I dragged Paul off the floor, shoving Tawney away. The federal agent skidded in a puddle of water and went down hard.

Before me I saw a path which led under trees with horrible mouths. The beach beyond that of gritty gravel colored purple and blue, like a lingering bruise, and an ocean like glass, murky and frozen forever in one moment between the rising and the falling of a wave.

All around me was chaos. With Nova using the hose to battle the hounds, the fire was springing up unchecked in other places. Johnny and Billy pulled at the velvet drapes, now also alight, trying to wrestle the curtains to the ground and stomp out the flames. Fire licked against Billy's hands.

He screamed with pain. Harlean shoved Ginger and Cozy toward the back door as she went back for Billy. Without a moment's hesitation, the other two ran after her, intent on saving their friends.

And I had caused all this, I realized. I had started it. I had to end it. I had to help them. I couldn't do that by relying on Nova to save the day. I couldn't do that by running away.

I turned my back on the path. Grabbing Paul's hand, I pulled him toward my aunt. "We have to help them!" I shouted at him. Tawney was coming up off the floor, starting to wave his gun at the two of us and yelling something that I didn't even try to understand. I elbowed him sharply in the stomach, knocking him down again, as I dragged Paul past him.

Paul never paused. He saw the creatures ahead and ran as hard as I did to help my aunt and friends. But we weren't fast enough.

Smoke rolled through the room, mingled with the horrible stench of that other place. The paper decorations exploded into flames as the fire swept through the room. The world still wobbled, one minute a dreadful forest, the next the ballroom engulfed in fire and smoke. I tripped over a root which became a body upon the floor which then turned into a tar pit of bloody mud.

"Raquel!" Paul yelled as I dropped his arm.

I hit the floor which wasn't a floor, dropping as you drop in a dream with a jolt. I could still see Nova through the smoke, turning the hose upon a snarling beast leaping toward her. The flames swept past me, reaching Reggie's switchboard that he'd set up to control the lights. A dreadful explosion rocked the room.

And then there was nothing as I dropped into a void. The string of bells I still clutched in one hand rang out, one last peal of jingle bells.

INTERLUDE

"This is my best idea ever." I met a man in Hollywood who began all his tales this way. He wove stories out of light and shadows to frighten audiences. We called him the Showman, but we should have named him a wizard for he enchanted us all.

He fascinated me, this Showman, so confident, so certain that the world would want his stories. We were much the same age, but so different. Wherever he went, people saw him. Wherever I went, nobody saw me. I drifted from one place to another, never finding a home. I spoke so many languages, collected so many fairytales, but I talked to no one. Around the Showman there was always a crowd, a laughing crowd, so bright and young. I envied the laughter and the friendship. I never knew what to say.

The Showman knew all the right words, how to draw men and women to him, how to make them carry out his plans. I followed like all the rest, certain it would lead me somewhere. But I still didn't know where I wanted to go.

Now I do.

The Showman was unforgettable, but I forgot him until I saw you again, until I touched your hand.

My life has turned into a story, into a series of stories, that run out of my head as soon as I write them down in this journal. I thought I was done with this, but I'm not. Somehow it is worse now, the trees, the beach, the hounds who crawl amid the shadows. Everywhere I turn, it's different, it's wrong. The trees shift. The beach changes color. Out of the corner of my eye, I thought the ocean moved. Or perhaps something moved under the water, disturbing the shape of the motionless waves.

Whatever swims below I do not want to see it.

I touched you. I felt your hand in mine. I knew hope.

Hope is gone. But is hope gone?

I could not stay with you. I am back here but there is a path and I hold a bell. I ring it and I sing as you sang. I will force the path to take me back to you.

But when I rang the bell, I was somewhere else again, standing at a gate, looking over it at an old house with many windows, a rich man's house. Crows flocked around its chimneys. I knew this house.

I gripped the gate and felt it creak beneath my hands. On the other side, on a lawn covered with snow, was a very young boy and a very old man.

"Grandfather," said the boy, "there's someone in the woods."

"Nonsense," said the man. "Nobody is allowed to go there except the families of French Hill, and we are the only ones left with a proper gate and access to the path. Those woods are your legacy, Sydney."

"No," said the boy, pointing at me, "there's a man at the gate."

"Help me!" I said. More loudly, more forcibly than I had spoken in any encounter before, because I was more afraid than ever before. I saw the smoke and the flames surrounding you. I feared the worst.

"What are you doing there?" yelled the old man, waving a cane at me. "Get out of our woods. You have no right to be there!"

I pushed at the locked gate, determined to enter.

The old man strode up to the fence, leaving a trail of footprints across the snow, and stared at me. "Who are you?" he said. "How did you get here?"

I countered his questions with my own: "Where am I? What year is this?"

"You're on French Hill," he said. "As for the year, it's 1890 as any fool knows." Staring at my scratched leather jacket, he added, "You are not dressed like anyone from Arkham. What path did you take, sir, to come here?"

"The wrong one," I said, turning away from the gate. For I remembered the man who played the horn and told me clearly to dance in 1926. So I rang my bell and sang our song as I followed the path into the woods and out of the world.

CHAPTER TWENTY

A faint knocking on my bedroom door woke me up. Or rather, I was awake, drifting in that limbo between dreaming and being fully conscious, when the muffled rapping made me aware of my surroundings.

I sat up in bed, gasping and sweating. I swore the stink of smoke and that other place filled my nose, but I was in the neat little guest bedroom that I'd occupied all December.

From the other side of the door, Nova called, "Are you ready for breakfast? Thelma has made pancakes." Her words were less clear than usual, as if she was standing very far away from the door or calling me from someplace. She sounded much the way people spoke in my dreams, frustratingly obscure and difficult to hear.

Another thump and Nova called, "Wake up, Raquel."

Scrambling out of bed, I looked wildly around. Nothing appeared damaged or changed. My hearing aid was laid out neatly on the top of the bureau. I was no longer wearing the dress that I danced in the night before. Instead, I wore the silk pajamas gifted to me by Nova when we first went to New York, the very pajamas that I remembered wearing on the morning of Christmas Eve while we ate pancakes and Nova insisted that I open one gift early.

With some trepidation, I opened the door of my bedroom. Nova stood in the hall. A magnificent midnight blue velvet robe decorated with embroidered poppies was swathed around her. In one hand, she held her usual cup of coffee, the smell dispersing the last lingering remnants of my nightmare.

For it had to be a nightmare, I told myself, as we walked into the dining room together. Breakfast was laid out on the table, including a pile of pancakes on each plate. A chafing dish of scrambled eggs was kept warm over a spirit lamp at the center of the table, within reach of both places. The silver-and-crystal syrup pitcher was set close to Nova's plate. Next to my place was a long box wrapped in green paper with a gold ribbon. A box which I knew contained a red sweater with a pattern of white stars down the center.

"An early Christmas present?" I said as I slid into my seat, fighting a sense of dizziness and regret. My actions had literally destroyed the Diamond Dog. But nothing had happened apparently. I couldn't shake the sense that something had happened, that the nightmare continued.

"It's Christmas Eve!" said Nova as she turned to the radio as always to hear the first broadcast of the day. However, just as I remembered it happening before, she took her hand off the dial and exclaimed, "Let's not have Chilton Brewster spoil the morning. I'm sure whatever homily or editorial that he's giving today can be missed. Open your present! I never liked waiting for things as a girl. Still don't. I always think there should be a few presents before the presents. I've got a whole basket of gifts for the employees. I'll give them out later today when we finish decorating the tree." She nodded to the packages sitting by the door, the basket full of gifts that I remembered her distributing.

With trembling fingers, I ripped off the paper of the box by my plate and revealed the sweater.

The last time that I had seen this red cardigan, I had called it beautiful and thanked my aunt. Then I wore it to meet with Agent Tawney and plot the raid on her dance.

The memories of smoke and flame rolled over me again. The horror of seeing Johnny and Billy dragging down the burning curtain. The feeling of Paul's hand slipping away from mine. The awful drop into nothingness. It all washed over me.

I sat in stunned and terrified silence, unable to think what to do or what to say.

Nova set down her coffee. Her eyes narrowed as she looked at me.

"Raquel Malone Gutierrez," she said in much the same manner as my mother. "What's happened to you?"

"What do you mean?" I asked, my hands unconsciously stroking the soft wool sweater and tracing the pattern of stars for comfort.

"Between one breath and the next," said Nova, still staring hard at me, "you faded. Then I saw two of you."

Certain that I had heard her wrong, although I usually understood every word that Nova said in her clear deep voice, I asked her to repeat herself.

"You faded," she said again. "Almost disappeared. I could

see the chair right through you when you opened the box. But when you touched the sweater, it was like a double exposure of a photograph. Two women doing the same action in the same place."

She picked up her cup and swallowed almost all the coffee in one gulp. "Time travel can be very dangerous," she said. "And if ever a woman looked unmoored from time, it is you."

"I don't understand," I said. I understood nothing about this day, this conversation, or how I could be holding a gift in my hands that I'd already received.

"Have you seen the forest and the beach?" said Nova.

I thought about those moments in the chaotic ballroom when I almost stumbled on the path, when I'd dropped off it into nothingness. "I ran toward the beach," I admitted, "but then I turned back." Because the Diamond Dog was engulfed in flames, and I wanted to save Nova. But I couldn't find the words to tell my aunt everything that had occurred.

Very calmly, almost too calmly, Nova said, "When did it happen?"

"Today," I reluctantly said. "I think it will be tonight, if this is Christmas Eve."

"It's certainly Christmas Eve for me," said Nova, taking a deep breath as if to calm herself. "I'm not sure where you are, when you are, but I suspect more than one place in time."

I stared down at my hands. If I squinted, I could see two sets of hands, both layered over the white stars, both horrifyingly my hands. In my heart and head, I knew Nova was right. I felt pulled, and pulled apart, as if I was in two places at the same time. Apparently, I was.

I gathered the sweater up, hugging it against my breast. I saw myself do that. I also saw another pair of hands close the lid as I had the first time and place the box politely on the table. The effect was nauseating, making me dizzy. Nova must have had the same reaction, as she set her cup down on the saucer with her usual decisive movement.

But no click. I stared at her and the coffee cup. All month long, I'd sat across the table from my aunt and watched her take a last swallow, replacing the cup in its saucer with a sharp little click. It had always been as clear to me as the ringing of a bell, this click which heralded the start to Nova's day at the Diamond Dog.

But this morning I heard nothing.

Nova said something about correcting what had gone wrong. I looked directly at her and got the sense of the words, both from what I heard and what I saw, but I didn't hear each word as clearly and easily as before. My hearing, my natural hearing, had grown worse since I had stepped on the path and then off it in the burning ballroom.

"You need to do what you didn't do the last time," Nova was saying very slowly to me, like a child who needed instructions, like a woman who needed reassurance. "Turn left instead of right, leave the apartment if you stayed in it, stay here if you went elsewhere."

Even as I stood up from the table, I thought I saw a ghost of myself still sitting there, pouring coffee and discussing decorations. And that version of me had heard every word spoken, every click of the coffee cup, every chink of a fork against her plate as she ate her eggs in stupid, willful ignorance of all the harm she would do in a few short hours.

I was furious with myself, but how could I chastise a ghost from another time who was already fading? As I moved away from the table, the ghostly figure disappeared.

Nova heaved a sigh of relief. "A good start," she said. "We'll keep you moving in opposite directions of where you were before, until we can get you stuck back in this time."

"You make me sound unglued," I said. But I knew what she meant. The apartment didn't seem completely real, as if I was there and not there. It was impossible to describe. Now I knew why Nova talked about being "unmoored in time."

Nova simply nodded. "You said you saw the path and the forest."

"And the beach," I added.

"The beach makes it worse. When did this happen? Do you remember?"

"Ten o'clock, at the start of the 'Jingle Bells' number," I said, retreating across the room to stand near Nova's desk. I hadn't lingered there before, so I thought it was safe.

"Oh," said Nova with a little grimace, "I had such a good idea for the evening."

"You asked Johnny to call me up on stage," I said, looking quickly around the room and relieved to find only one of myself, the one I was, standing there.

"You know about the surprise." Nova looked upset, but then shrugged. "Well of course you do."

I angled back toward my aunt so I could read her lips as well as listen to her words. As I struggled to comprehend her, I prayed the hearing device left in my room would continue to give me some amplification. Apparently, all the hearing in my right ear was completely gone now, and my left was much worse. I'd been warned by several doctors that my hearing would naturally worsen over the years. It seemed time travel accelerated the loss.

"Why did I become unmoored?" I said. "Why here in Kingsport? Why now?" Questions I should have asked days ago, but I'd been so enamored with escaping my unwanted future and rectifying my past.

"Why you?" Nova mused. "Probably because you're a Malone. And you tried to change something, didn't you?"

"I had to do something," I finally admitted. "I don't want my future. I wanted what I had in the past."

"We can't mend the past, but we can always change the future," Nova said, and it was a phrase my mother often repeated to us children. I felt ashamed that I'd forgotten her advice.

"But you went through time," I said to Nova. "You even said you tried to use it for bootlegging."

My aunt grimaced and fiddled with the belt on her robe, an uncharacteristic sign of nervousness or perhaps her own embarrassment. "I made a mistake," she said finally. "I thought we could use the old pathway with new technology, that cars or airplanes could go through it toward the future or escape into the past, just not too far ahead or too far behind. It was a complete disaster for anyone who is not a Malone."

"But why is the path appearing when we sing…" I paused, almost afraid to name the song, "Jingle Bells?"

Nova sighed. "My fault again. After I fell into that place, I needed a pattern to keep my mind from wandering. If you sing, you don't notice other things. Which makes it much easier to direct your steps where you want to go. Even then, it took me several tries to get out again. The tune was the first one I remembered."

Blood under my shoes, the howling of hounds, and the gnashing teeth of the trees, I thought, all summoned or dispelled by a sleighing song. "Everyone sings that silly tune. Why does it cause the world to wobble?"

"Wobble?" said Nova. "That's a good word for it. My father – your grandfather – used to call it rough seas. Those ripples flow into the past, present, and future in unexpected ways. When I started down the path, I fell off into many wrong times before I found the right time. It causes problems."

"So I now exist in two places at the same time? Or do I exist in two times but in the same place?"

"It would take a college professor to explain! But I know it makes you feel like flotsam in a whirlpool," Nova continued. "Best to stay off the path completely and never go there."

"But what or where is the path?" I asked. Paul called it a nightmare in one of his journal entries. I remembered my own brief experiences, the strange dreamlike sensation mixed with best forgotten memories.

Nova shrugged. "Who knows? The grimoire hinted the forest grew in more than one world. Beatrice once told me her equations show it exists both inside and outside of time, whatever that means!"

I checked the clock and it was still early. A look around the room confirmed no ghost of myself had appeared again. Nova's advice of going in the opposite direction of where I'd been before (or was it after?) seemed to be working.

"We'll cancel the 'Jingle Bells' bit," said Nova. "Just to be safe."

I started to agree. But then I thought of Paul. If I failed to open the gate or path or whatever it was which led him in and out of the world, he'd be trapped in a nightmare forever. I couldn't abandon him.

But if I opened the path the same way again, then Agent Tawney would grab Paul. The scaled hounds would leap through. There would be gunfire and mayhem. The Diamond Dog would be destroyed again.

But, I thought, I could sing "Jingle Bells" someplace else. Someplace safe and rescue Paul without ever having to admit to Nova how much I had done wrong in the past few days.

"Cancel the song," I said to her. "Tell the band that I found out about the surprise and decided not to play in public." It was an easy excuse that anyone would believe.

With Nova's agreement to change the evening's entertainment, I went back to my room to dress, thinking all the time about how I could slip away to rescue Paul.

I tried to ignore any worries about more damage to my hearing. What was done was done, as my mother would say. I could only try not to repeat my mistakes in what was now my future.

Once I settled the hearing device on my head with the earpiece over my better left ear, I hummed a few bars of "Jingle Bells."

Almost immediately, I heard Paul's voice, "Il était une fois."

I never heard him speak in anything other than English and a few scattered words that I thought were German or Dutch.

"Paul?" I said. "Paul, can you hear me?"

"I have lost so much," he replied in English. "I can't hold on to the memories. It's all slipping away."

"Paul!" I exclaimed. "It's Raquel! I am coming for you. I promise!"

"It's a terrible way to spend a Christmas Eve," he answered.

"Paul, do you understand me? I am going to save you. Only I can't sing at the Diamond Dog tonight. We'll do it later, when it's safe."

"It's never safe unless Jim plays his horn. Tell them, no matter how often they try, they fail. Tell them that they will die."

"Paul!" I practically wailed, clutching the dresser in front of me, staring into the mirror with wild eyes. "What do you mean?"

"Tell her, tell Raquel, that Jim Culver must play or it goes wrong every time," he said in a fading whisper.

In my desperation, I began to sing full out, the words for "Jingle Bells" tumbling from my lips, trying to force Paul into the room. The mirror in front of me shimmered. I swear I saw the trees, the beach, and the terrible, still water of the ocean which never moved. Then, like a bubble popping, it was gone.

Spinning on my heel, I headed for the door, intent on going down to the ballroom and trying again on the piano. Lying on the table beside my bed, I spotted Paul's journal. Like me, it had changed. Now it was twice as ragged around the edges and dark stains spread across its cover along with something like claw marks. When I picked it up, it smelled like smoke, horrible oily smoke like burned garbage. Or a burned building.

I opened it and rifled through the pages. At the very end of the journal, just filling the final pages, I read an entry that I had never read before. One that I swear just appeared. Yet judging by the stains and blotches on the page, it was as old as all the rest. But it was different too. It was as if Paul was beginning his story again.

LAST INTERLUDE

"Il était une fois," say the French. Once upon... once on... it was once... all the tales begin the same. With time. With an unknown place in an unknown time. What time am I in? Where is the place I am now? I kneel on the beach with the ocean lacking waves at my back. I scratch dates and places in the grit with my hands as the thoughts run out of my mind. If I can write it down, perhaps I will remember. Already the memory of a snowy world is disappearing. Why snow? Isn't it June? No, it's Christmas Eve, I remember people celebrating, but the kind words and wishes of those I have met are fading, fading too quickly.

How could I have met anyone? There is nothing here. Just me on a beach which makes no sense at all.

I have lost so much. I can't hold on to the memories. It's all slipping away.

The purple sand cuts my fingers and fills in the lines I carve into the ground. When did the sand become purple? I don't remember. I continue to scratch until the scrabbling of my fingers is the only sound in the place.

I dug graves in Paris. The thud of the shovel hitting the dirt reverberates through my body and through my memories. A wet sucking sound when it rained or a bone-jarring dry bang when the sun burned the backs of our shoulders. But rain or burning sun, the stink of a city in despair always rose around us as we dug the graves for the hundreds who died during the fever sweeping the city.

This sand smells of nothing. But I remember the stink of sorrow; it's the stench I carry with me always.

I scratch in the dirt as my hands bleed. Perhaps I am digging my own grave. Perhaps I am already dead. Such thoughts wail in my mind as I see the letters and numbers written in the sand: Arkham 1929, Innsmouth 1917, Kingsport 1925, Kingsport 1946, and all the rest.

My mind is a cemetery full of dead memories, and I do not understand.

Then as the world shifts and wobbles around me, snow fills the names and obscures the dates. I tip my head to the sky and I see clouds. Ordinary clouds, a simple gray blanket of clouds, as the snow falls on my tears. And I begin a new story for you.

I found myself in a graveyard.

The monument before me had an inscription on the top: "They will be remembered in our hearts today and forever." Below was carved: "Victims of the Diamond Dog Fire" and a long list of names, all alphabetical. At the end of the list was a single date: December 24, 1926.

"It's a terrible way to spend Christmas Eve," said a voice behind me. "I hate this place. I come here every year. But I hate it."

I turned around. The man behind me was old, withered,

and bent. He leaned upon an ebony cane with a carved silver handle. Watery eyes peered at me though large glasses sliding down to the end of his nose. I had never seen eyeglasses like his. The heavy square frames around the lens covered the entire top of his face, from eyebrow to cheekbone. But the eyeglasses did not hide the tears leaking from his eyes and running down the wrinkled cheeks.

"You're here," he said. "Finally. I'm nearly a hundred. Do you know what I've had to survive to be in this graveyard today? No, of course, you don't. But you will."

I had no words for him. All my languages ran together and the sounds I made with my mouth were like a baby's mewling.

"Take this." He thrust a package into my hands. "Write it down. Write everything you remember, everything you see. If you write it now, after all that has happened, it will change what came before."

I clutched the package to my chest, feeling under the brown paper the outline of a book.

"What?" I finally stammered, the word tumbling out of my mouth like pearls and toads tumbled from the mouths of those bewitched.

"Write your memories on these pages. Pray she reads this in time," the old man whispered to me. "Tell her, tell Raquel, Jim must play, or it goes wrong every time."

When he said Raquel, I heard a voice calling my name. A memory slipped sideways into my head.

"I know who she is," I said to him, joy replacing my sorrow. "I know who Raquel is."

"Change her future and my past." The old man slapped

the package in my hand. "Tell Raquel to ask Nova Malone for help or the Diamond Dog burns. It burns every time."

I remembered the fire. I remembered the smoke. I remembered a woman's hand reaching out for mine and then slipping away. "I want to save her," I said. "No, I tried to save her. Didn't I?"

"Stop talking. Just listen. Tell them, no matter how often they try, they fail. Tell Raquel that they will die," he shouted at me. "It's never safe unless Jim plays his horn."

I tore open the package to see a volume bound in leather and a bundle of pens.

"Blank journal, ballpoint pens, you're supposed to be able to write on the moon with those pens. Damn, they say they'll walk on the moon this summer. I wanted to see that. But I want this more. Write it down and maybe history will change. No, that's not right. It won't be history if you go back. If you go back, you can change the future." He stumbled a few steps away and fell on his side, one hand pressed to his heart. I nearly dropped the book as I moved to help him.

"Don't touch me!" he yelled even louder, arms waving wildly so he created circles in the snow. Great sweeps in the snow like crooked wings sprouting from his shoulders. "Get away from me! Don't lose the journal! Not yet. Later, lose it later so Leo will find it and give it to her. This is all I can do. Please, please let me die in peace. I don't want to dream of their screams one more night. Tell Raquel that I was wrong. Tell all of them that I was sorry." He began to cry even harder as I dropped to my knees to comfort him.

Then the old man sang, a wavering tenor choked with

sobs, and the words wrapped around me as he faded away. "Jingle bells, jingle bells, jingle all the way."

Once again, I am on the beach now filled with blue sand. I sit down and I begin to write. I write about how I became lost, and I write about the first time that I heard your voice.

I fill the pages with words untied from time, words which tell about everything that happened, everything that will happen, so it becomes again the story that you are reading.

A long time ago, and yet just moments ago, I began this book. Now the cover changes as I write, the words appear inside, and outside it grows old, older than me, older than us. But I remember again. I scratch down these words. I must try again. I know why the old man cries in such pain. My tears are falling on the page now.

While I write, I pray. I pray like the old man that you will believe.

Because I have seen your name on the monument, Raquel. I have seen so many names that I know because of you. Nova, Harlean, Billy, Ginger, Cozy, and all the rest. Those names are carved into the stone and an old man is weeping next to your grave.

You will all die on Christmas Eve, 1926, unless we can change your story.

CHAPTER TWENTY-ONE

I flew down the hallway looking for my aunt. She wasn't in the apartment, but then I remembered the basket of gifts by the door. I ran down the stairs and into the ballroom. Nova had just handed out the last present and made her little speech. This time, instead of making my way to the door to find Agent Tawney outside, I ran toward Nova.

"You have to help me," I said, thrusting the journal into her hands. "You have to help me save everyone."

The others gawked at me. Nova simply shooed them away, saying we needed to talk. Being Nova, nobody questioned her and everyone did as she asked. Then Nova directed me to a small table at the edge of the room. She propped the book open and read it cover to cover. Whenever I tried to talk or point out a particular passage, she waved me off.

It was agonizing. But this was my aunt who literally could do anything, even travel through time. If anyone understood, if anyone could help, it would be Nova. I finally understood.

After far too long a wait, Nova snapped the book closed.

"I need to see Leo," she said. Raising her voice, she called, "Otis, get the Rolls. We're going out to Cuffe's farm."

"I never went there today," I said. "Not last time."

"Good. Then we're setting a new pattern. Less duplication of you, as it were. Come along."

She swept upstairs for coats and down again, all the time rattling off directions to the others for the setup of the night's dance.

"You can't go forward with the dance," I said as she bundled us both into the backseat of the Rolls. "Didn't you read what Paul said?"

"I read it," snapped Nova. "Now I want to know how Leo found this book. And in the meantime, you can tell me exactly who this Paul is."

So I told her everything that I told Tawney and Brewster, and even more. All the times that I had heard Paul's voice. I even confessed how the world wobbled in the basement last Saturday, and again when I tried to pull Paul out by playing the piano by myself.

Nova just shook her head and muttered a couple of times. I felt very small and miserable by the time we arrived at the farmhouse. Then, as always, my aunt surprised me. "I guess I should have spent less time trying to impress you with fancy gifts and more time talking to you," she said. "I felt those wobbles, but I never thought about how it could be you causing time to shift. I should have looked closer and listened better."

Which made me feel so much worse and so much better

at the same time. All I could think to say was. "I do love you, Aunt Nova."

She smiled. "Same, Raquel, same to you. Let's see if we can fix this."

Both Cuffe and Leo greeted us when we arrived at the farmhouse. If they were surprised by Nova's arrival, they gave no sign of it.

She pulled the battered journal out of her bag and waved it at Leo. "How did you get this book?" she said.

Captain Leo looked at her like an old friend. It occurred to me that they probably were. "Come inside and let me explain."

We climbed the porch stairs and entered the living room. "We'll need coffee for this," Cuffe said, bustling toward the back of the house. "I'll put the pot on."

"Don't forget the rum," said Nova. "I smuggled enough of it out here for you to spare me a tot."

Cuffe waved at her as he disappeared into the kitchen.

"I went for a sleigh ride on Christmas Eve with Cuffe," Captain Leo said. "Just after I retired the *Molly Gee* in 1921. It was probably the first time we'd taken the sleigh out. Cuffe had just finished fixing it up and wanted to show it off to me."

Cuffe came bustling into the room with steaming mugs of coffee which smelled more like spiced rum. Nova took a long appreciative drink of hers. I swallowed mine without tasting a thing, so intent I was on listening to Captain Leo's story.

"The sled just flew along, and Cuffe began to sing," Captain Leo said. "It felt like it was all part of the tune, the horses' hooves striking the snow, the ringing of the harness bells, and the whisper of the sleigh's runners. Then the world began to ripple."

"Ripple?" I asked.

"Like looking at a reflection in the water. When you're out at sea and the weather is calm, but then a ship so far out that you can't see it starts the waves and you know something is happening but can't see the cause. Just waves passing on the way to somewhere else, but it changes your perception," he said, his voice very calm in a way that reminded me of Nova. But I could see the tension in his shoulders and his face. Whatever memories were stirred by this description still bothered him. "The woods, the snow, and all the rest. It was the same, but it was changing. A mist came up. Sometimes the mist was in front of us, and sometimes beside us. When I turned my head and looked straight at it, it wasn't mist, or fog, or smoke."

"What was it?" I said, but I thought I knew. I remembered the creature in their woods and Mab's whines when it appeared.

"It looked like a dog. A gaunt, starving dog. I thought we were being chased by a rabid dog. It looked so strange – no fur and the skin seemed almost covered in scales. And a tongue as long as its snout. I gave a shout. Cuffe pulled the reins and stopped the sleigh. The dog was running so fast behind us, and the snow was so icy, it couldn't stop. It crashed right into the sleigh. I'm sure it did. Only then there wasn't anything there. We climbed out to look but couldn't find any tracks. Just that." He pointed at the book.

"It was lying in the snow," Cuffe said. "Anyone could have dropped it."

"I think that dog dropped it. The book had been in its mouth, and it ran into the sleigh and dropped it," responded Captain Leo in a way that made me think this was an old dispute between them. He reached out his hand and traced a semicircle of marks on the back and front that looked something like a dog's bite.

"If a rabid dog dropped the book," said Cuffe, "it certainly didn't stop you from reading it on the way home." He smiled at Captain Leo and tipped his cup to him.

"Of course! A mysterious book appearing on Christmas Eve," said Captain Leo. "I read it from cover to cover. I remembered a man helping me when I put into Innsmouth during the last war. He loaded a few boxes and then disappeared. When I read the journal, I wondered if he was the writer. Perhaps another Jack London, sailing around the world and mixing his stories out of fact and legend. The whole incident was strange, but strange does happen around here. Eventually I stuffed the journal away on a shelf and forgot it. Until you put up the sign for the Diamond Dog. The name rang a bell in my head, so I went looking again for the book. There it was, all the mentions of the Diamond Dog in Kingsport. But I noticed something the next time I read it."

"The stories changed," said Nova, pushing the book across the table to Captain Leo. She looked concerned. "Patterns changed and the thing has changed with them."

Captain Leo flipped open the covers and rifled through the pages just as I had a few hours earlier. Then he paused, reading the final entry in the journal.

"It changed all right," said Captain Leo. "I always

remember what I read. Oh, not word for word. I can forget a scene or a chapter and be surprised by it in a new reading. That's half the pleasure of reading old favorites again. But this–" he tapped his finger again on the cover of the book "–was very different the second time I read it. More about the Diamond Dog. More about Raquel." Then he flipped to the final entry. "But there was nothing about the old man dying in the graveyard. I've never read that before. I'll bet my soul on it."

Nova tapped her diamond covered fingers against the tabletop.

"I probably shouldn't have used 'Jingle Bells' for my pattern," she said to us as the clock ticked through my second Christmas Eve of 1926. "But I was in a hurry to make it home and needed something easy to remember. Who can't sing a verse or chorus of that song? But it evokes memories too. Makes you think of Christmas. I was trying for August and kept landing on Christmas Eve. It took a lot of concentration to finally make it to October 1926. I completely lost September this year." She shook her head at the journal. "I did see Paul behind me in Kingsport, but then he disappeared. I should have paid closer attention, but Chilton distracted me."

I wasn't sure if Chilton would call the commandeering of his coat a distraction, but I didn't contradict Nova.

"Paul kept moving around," I said instead, pulling back the book and reading out all the places and people that Paul met. Nova frowned and then smiled through many of the encounters.

"I know them," she said. "I know them all, but not in

the times and places he describes. I wonder how the poor man got there in the first place. It's unusual to find anyone on that beach. Although it does happen. There are some mighty thin spots in Innsmouth, even a few in Arkham and Kingsport."

"But why does he keep reappearing on Christmas Eve?" I asked. "That must mean something, mustn't it?"

"It seems I stuck your Paul in the start of my pattern," said Nova, "without taking him all the way out. I went through Arkham, its downtown and the university, too, and Dunwich, which was horrible, the wrong time in Innsmouth, which was worse in some ways, and then back again to Kingsport. By then time would have been unraveling in my wake, so Paul could have been tossed in various directions, even to places and times that I missed."

"Like the wake of a boat?" Captain Leo said. I noticed that neither Captain Leo or Cuffe seemed perturbed by Nova's maritime explanations of time travel and magic.

"I should have guessed you were Baba Yaga. That entry was in there the first time that I read the book," Captain Leo said.

"I've been called much worse," Nova chuckled.

"So how do we save Paul?" I asked her. "How do we save ourselves?"

"We go forward with the dance," Nova declared suddenly.

"But the dance was a disaster," I said, trying to hold on to the memories which were already fading like a nightmare. "We burned down the Diamond Dog. Well, Tawney caused it to burn, bringing out the hounds and trying to hang on to Paul. The whole town wobbled."

"This last entry implies we can change what happens tonight," said Nova, her brow furrowed as she once again read the final passages. "But the suggestion of Jim Culver is troubling. He's bound to stir up something very dangerous."

Captain Leo looked equally troubled. "Jim is a good man, but his daddy's horn has a terrible hold on him."

"Perhaps we just close this book and hide it," I said very slowly, my heart almost breaking as I thought of Paul lost forever in the strange twilight world where the stars never shone. "If Tawney doesn't see Paul tonight, he won't start shooting and the tree won't fall, the hounds won't appear, and everyone will survive."

Nova shook her head. "I never liked the idea of doing nothing as the solution to a problem. Leo is right. Jim is a good man, however wicked his trumpet is." Her eyes narrowed and her fingers continued to tap on the journal's battered, blood soaked, and now charred cover. "Your Paul appears when the music plays, he disappears when the music stops. So how to haul him into this time and place and keep him from slipping away?" She frowned down at the table.

"I almost had him," I said, fighting to recall what happened on the night that hadn't happened yet. Everything had been so clear in my mind only hours before, but now I struggled to remember. "I did hold on to him. I know I did. He didn't disappear immediately, even after the band fled."

"Drag him to the present and hold on? That might work if we reset the pattern. Send a wave to cancel a wave?" Nova sounded as if she was thinking out loud.

Cuffe scratched one ear. "Sounds complicated."

Nova shook her head. "We keep the song playing until it drowns out all the wobbles." Then she gave a very Nova smile. "And we have a town full of the best gadget to do that! I'll send out the word. Every radio in Kingsport tuned to the Diamond Dog's broadcast at ten o'clock. That's when we have Billy and the band play 'Jingle Bells' for all that they are worth."

"But will that be enough?" I asked, thinking of all the times the song snatched Paul away. "Can it anchor Paul to the present?" I added, picking up the maritime analogies from Nova.

"If the old man was right, it will work if we add Jim Culver," said my aunt. "If anyone can make a song behave the way that he wants, it's Jim."

"When Jim is playing, even the dead dance to his tune," said Captain Leo.

"What about the hounds?" I said. While other incidents faded, those terrifying monsters remained clear in my memories.

"We'll start a great circle of dance through the streets of Kingsport, and dance those creatures into corners, into diminishing triangles as Beatrice advised, until everything disappears except Paul," replied Nova as if she planned the confusion of supernatural creatures every day. Given all that I had learned, perhaps she did.

"And Chilton Brewster and Agent Tawney?" I asked.

Nova's smile broadened and it was a dangerous smile. "I can handle a banker and a Fed."

"Dear lady," said Cuffe, "how can we help tonight?"

"We'll need your sleigh to lead the dance through the town," said Nova and Cuffe cheered.

"Oh, he's going to be insufferable about the sleigh," said Captain Leo to me. "He's always claimed it should be the symbol of the farm. By this time next year, he'll have organized sleigh rides for the whole town and probably be advertising Christmas trees on the side."

"Be outside the Diamond Dog at ten and ready to lead the way," Nova told Cuffe. "A great circle of the town, Cuffe, as round as you can make it with every bell ringing on the harness. We'll jingle this town back into time and confound those government agents."

CHAPTER TWENTY-TWO

Avoiding Agent Tawney and Chilton Brewster proved harder than I expected. When I missed our meeting due to our trip to Cuffe's farm, Tawney came to the Diamond Dog and asked for me in the afternoon.

"Bold," said Nova when the message was relayed down to me. We were in the basement office going over the possible permutations of the evening, including re-reading the passages in Paul's journal that outlined the ferocity of the hounds as well as Beatrice Sharpe's calculations to baffle the pursuit of the creatures.

"I wish I could reach Sharpe and speak to her about this," Nova was telling me when the message came that Tawney was upstairs. "But the woman never stays home. She's on one of her expeditions, according to her friend Judy."

"What should I do about Tawney?" I asked my aunt.

"Ignore him," replied Nova. Then to Lily, who had brought the message, "Does Tawney have anyone with him?"

"No," said Lily. "He's alone."

"Tell him Raquel is out," decided Nova. "I don't suppose we can take back the tickets you gave him for the dance."

"Oh, he's sent his thanks for those and bought some more," said Lily. "He said something about bringing friends to see Kingsport's most famous attraction."

"That's more flattering," said Nova, "but will only get him in the door. Well, we know when he planned to arrive last time and must assume it stays the same this time. We'll see him after nine and before ten."

Lily looked a little baffled by this speech, as well she might. So far, Nova had only discussed the repeat of the day with Leo and Cuffe, whom she said she could trust not to spread it around town. "Those men have their own secrets," she said to me and, probably in response to my look of surprise, added, "and it's not up to me to tell their story."

"But I thought they were both retired gentlemen who did a little farming and book collecting," I said.

"You'll find in this town, and several nearby, that there's a number of old men and women who only seem to be retired from their professions. When help is needed, they give it," said Nova.

To distract myself, I flipped through the pages of the journal, noting again the number of new stains and other marks. I worried about what had happened to Paul since I lost hold of his hand. "What about Mandy Thompson and Dr William Maleson?" I said, reading that passage again. "They encountered the hounds very recently."

Like the other entries in the book, it seemed longer and

more detailed now, not at all as I remembered. One name popped out at me immediately upon this reading.

"Agent Tawney was with them," I said to Nova. "Look, read this." I thrust the book at her, pointing to Tawney's name scrawled in Paul's account of the attack of the hounds in the laboratory.

"Hmm," said Nova. "I missed that. No wonder he was so quick to respond to Brewster's letter. See if you can find other mentions of him or anyone who sounds like him."

I found one other. At least the man was called Ralph, and I remembered Tawney's frequent insistence that people call him by his first name. "Withers?" said Nova. "I looked at some of his research when I was thinking of using our family grimoire for transportation purposes."

"Smuggling," I said.

Nova shrugged and smiled. "I'm not used to being quite so blunt around you. But yes, for smuggling. Withers, Maleson, and Thompson work at Miskatonic University and the research there can be a bit… well, let's just say esoteric is the polite word for it. Tawney must have tracked down anyone with even the slightest interest in time travel. I wonder if he talked to Harvey Walters. Probably not. Harvey has always been more of an occultist than a scientist."

"Your cleaners seem very well informed," I said, remembering how my aunt said she paid them to keep an eye on the university's activities.

"You never know when they might discover something useful." Nova shrugged. "I'm sure the O'Bannions do the same."

The clicking of Lily's heels on the stairs announced another message delivery. "Chilton Brewster sent a note," she said, handing the envelope to Nova.

"Of course he did," said Nova, slitting it open with a wicked looking knife she kept on her desk. She called it a "gutting knife" and I hoped she was talking about fish. "Full of compliments on our work in civic entertainment and how we've helped to elevate – he always uses such fancy words! – the town's reputation. That's a change of tone! Oh, and he's asking to dance with you, Raquel, tonight. Presumably to tell you what to expect at ten. Quite the Victorian gentleman, asking me for permission to ask you."

"Decorum," I said, "is important to Chilton. But it's 1926 and he should ask me directly if he wants to dance. Frankly, I think Johnny has better manners. And he's a bootlegger!"

"Some of the best gentlemen are," said Nova. "Bootleggers, that is. And even the O'Bannions never burned down my ballroom."

Lily looked completely bewildered at this announcement, but Nova waved her away with the words, "Business analogy. Nothing will burn tonight." To me, she added, "I hope. But I've had the men bring down the extra fire extinguishers from my apartment. They'll be standing by the tree when the time comes."

We spent the rest of the afternoon trying not to do what we'd done before, setting a new pattern as Nova called it.

This new pattern included being honest with each other. I promised my aunt to finally write to my family and make plans to go home. If we survived the night.

By the time the dance started, I felt the same as I had before – a complete bundle of frightened nerves, only even worse. Because everywhere I glanced, it triggered a memory of terrible destruction.

I also faded in and out according to Nova, who kept moving me around the ballroom hoping to counteract the effect. Apparently nobody else noticed, but the tree was capturing a lot of attention.

"Perhaps I should just send you upstairs to my apartment," Nova said at one point when I felt as if there were three of me, all shattering like one of the crystal glasses containing the very innocent fruit punch that Nova was serving to the guests.

"All my strong stuff went to the Clover Club as promised," she said, naming Arkham's most infamous night club as I remarked on the punch. "They're having their own party tonight. Which is best. I hate to think what would happen if Marie Lambeau or Finn Edwards came dancing here tonight."

A waiter dropped a glass. The sound of it breaking ricocheted through the room. I couldn't remember anything breaking the last time and told Nova so. "Good," she said, giving me a close look. "The timeline is changing. You do look more present. I can't see through you at all."

When Johnny came to collect me for our last dance before ten o'clock, I turned away from him and walked straight into the arms of Chilton Brewster, something I definitely had not done before. "You told my aunt that you wanted to dance," I said to the surprised banker. I know he was surprised because he let me lead through the first bars of music.

"I expected her to refuse. Or for you to avoid me," he admitted. Then, coming to his senses, he took over the dance, whirling me in a quick step around a kissing couple. His dance moves surprised me. Who would have thought the staid banker had such a good foxtrot?

"I am not running away from you," I said. Then hearing my own words echo in my head, I said more firmly, "I am not running away from anything. Not now."

Brewster gave me one of his blank-faced looks. The lights above reflected off his glasses but dancing nearly cheek to cheek, I finally got a close look at his face. Great shadows marked the skin under his eyes. He looked as if he hadn't slept in a week.

Or perhaps in a year.

I could feel myself being tugged in all directions, the reverberations of Nova's journey on her path twisting around all of us. What if the same had happened to Brewster? What if he had suffered through more than one day of duplicated time?

"You tried to get the coat back from Nova!" I suddenly remembered how he described the incident in his journal. "You ran after her down the path!"

"I regretted it the moment that I handed my coat to her," Brewster admitted. "So I followed her."

"How far did you go after Nova?" I asked Brewster. "How far forward on the path?"

Two journals in his office for the same year. What else had changed for him? What else did he know? Suddenly Brewster's frustration with the world, the constant letters, and his obsession with driving Nova out of Kingsport made so much more sense. I was surprised I hadn't guessed he was a time traveler too.

Brewster faltered and almost stumbled before he recovered the rhythm of the dance. He swept me off to one side. With a strangely old-fashioned bow, he ushered me into a chair. Then he sat himself in the opposite chair.

"Too far," he said in response to my question. "I knew the minute I stepped on the path what it was. I grew up here in Kingsport, but there were Innsmouth and Arkham relatives on both sides of my family. The Fitzmaurice family, all gone now, but we're related to Saturnin Fitzmaurice's daughter. There's even a Malone back a few generations." He must have noticed my start of surprise because he responded with a small smile, "Something your aunt doesn't know. Innsmouth never liked it when one of theirs married outside of town boundaries. A clannish, almost cultish group, you could say."

"How far did you go?" I asked again, not about to be sidetracked by these claims of kinship.

"Too far," he admitted. "A year ahead, all the way to Christmas Eve, 1926. Then back again to where I started, like an elastic snapping. I lived this year feeling as if I was splitting into two."

I knew the feeling and after less than twelve hours with the same problem, I couldn't imagine days like that. I really would have shattered.

"I haven't slept a full night since it happened," Brewster went on. "Since Nova Malone stole my coat from me. And Kingsport continues to shake. I go forward again and again on the path to this place and this time."

"You feel it too. The world shifting."

"It is getting worse," said Brewster. Then he balled up his hand and banged it down on the table. "I cannot explain. Not in any way that anyone will believe. So I make petty complaints about petty people. But it's not enough! Kingsport could be the perfect place, if only I could correct my mistake."

"But Kingsport is lovely," I said. "Nova opening the Diamond Dog isn't hurting anyone."

Brewster shook his head. "You're wrong. This place will kill everyone here. I know it. We must stop it. I have tried to stop it. I failed." He looked around and then pulled an old-fashioned gold pocket watch out of his vest pocket. He visibly blanched when he saw the time. "I have to leave. If I leave, maybe I can change something next time."

He stood up, obviously meaning to skirt the table and head out the door. I glanced at the doors, seeing Ralph Tawney and his men entering the ballroom. Looking at my own watch, I saw it was ten minutes to ten. Almost time for the band to play "Jingle Bells" and Reggie's broadcast to be heard throughout Kingsport.

Brewster was hurrying across the ballroom, dodging dancers as he made for the exit. I didn't remember him running the last time.

Suddenly I realized what Brewster had said. He had gone forward, more than once! I sprang up out of my chair and chased after him, bumping into a few surprised couples. Closing the gap between us, I grabbed Brewster's arm and swung him around to face me.

"You went forward more than once," I said to him as he blinked down at me. "You saw the fire."

"Every time," he whispered, so low that I couldn't hear what he was saying, but I could read his lips. "Every time they all die in a fire. The building burns to the ground. I hear their screams in my nightmares."

Visibly shaking, he tried to pull away from me.

"Why didn't you write that in your letters?" I said, hanging on to him and being almost pulled over by his eagerness to get to the door. "Why didn't you tell Nova the truth?"

We were now off the dance floor, nearer the lobby doors, almost exactly where I remembered Brewster standing the last time I attended this dance, the time that didn't exist yet but would in just a few minutes. "Why didn't you help instead of just complaining?" I said to Brewster.

He tore his arm free from my grasp and practically yelled, "I tried! I used her song and tried. I failed. I have a great future. I will be a great man. I cannot die tonight." Then Brewster whipped around, straight into the arms of Ralph Tawney, who had come up behind him.

"What are you saying?" said Tawney, with an even harder grip on Brewster than I had managed. "What do you know?"

"There are monsters tonight," said Brewster, trying to shake loose. "The place burns to the ground and releases monsters onto the street. Creatures like hounds. They rip men apart."

Tawney blanched. "You miserable man. You are the time traveler, too, aren't you? You know how to get back to the forest!"

"No, no," protested Brewster as Tawney shoved him into

the arms of another agent with curt orders to "hold on to him." Brewster yelped in protest.

"As for you," Tawney said, turning on me, but Johnny was there, having practically sprinted across the ballroom floor.

"Oh, Raquel, here you are," he said in as casual a tone as he could while panting. "Your aunt wants you on the bandstand. We have a surprise for you." The words almost ran together as he tugged me away. However, I guessed immediately what he was saying and followed him as fast as I could.

As we neared the stage, my aunt hugged me and said directly into the microphone of my hearing aid, "What happened?"

"It's Brewster," I told her. "He travels too. Tawney thinks he can find the forest. Does any of that make any sense?"

"More than might be expected," said Nova, still speaking slowly and clearly so I could catch every word. "Four of us traveling the path, all through this point and time. Brewster, Paul, you, and me. No wonder the world wobbles. We need to dance ourselves into midnight and end all this."

Lined up behind the bandstand, I saw Otis and Tim stationed near the fire extinguishers and hose. Other burly men were near the Christmas tree, including Chuck Fergus, trying to look casual with extinguishers propped near their feet. "O'Bannions came through," said Nova with a nod. "All rivalries put aside among bootleggers tonight. I'll owe them in the morning."

All those phone calls by Nova, and everyone answered. I'd never been so proud of my aunt.

Another line of young men and women stood on

the other side, directly under the mistletoe. They were armed with what looked like yardsticks and chalk. "The Miskatonic University Math Club," said Nova. "I promised more than sherry for their next party."

"But don't we need…" I started to say as a tall thin Black man carrying a battered trumpet case emerged from the crowd.

"Mr Culver," said Nova, striding forward and shaking his hand. "Delighted you could play tonight."

"Jim," he said with a shy smile. "Just call me Jim. It's an honor to perform here. I cannot wait to play this dance. I do admire Billy Oliver's style."

Billy waved from his piano stool. Jim hopped up on the stage and pulled his horn out of his case.

"Well," Nova said to me. "Are you ready?"

"Yes," I said as firmly as possible. "And Aunt Nova, this time I'm staying for the dance, all the way past midnight. No more trying to run away." This time I would save Paul, I thought, and suddenly there was only one of me there in the hall. All the fractured feeling had disappeared. I knew where I was, when I was. And I knew I was enough.

"That's my niece," said Nova.

I grabbed a string of bells from the basket by Cozy's drums. Ginger gave a little tootle on her saxophone. Harlean pulled me to stand beside her at the microphone. Across the room, I saw Johnny at the broadcast booth's door. He waved at us. Reggie must be ready to broadcast to all the radios in Kingsport. I hoped that all sets were tuned to our station tonight.

"Places, people, places," said Harlean into the microphone. "Grab your bells and get ready to dance!" Waiters circulated among the dancers, handing out the bells for everyone to ring. "Remember, once we start the song, it's out the doors and follow the sleigh. All around the town tonight. This is one dance everyone will remember!"

Harlean turned to me with eyes sparkling with excitement. Behind her, I could almost see my memories of fire, smoke, and creatures dripping with blood. The tree toppling and taking the Diamond Dog with it.

"Not now, not here," I said to myself.

"Ready," I said to Harlean and the world.

"Ladies and gentlemen, grab your partner," Harlean called into the microphone. "And dance!"

Billy's hands crashed down onto the keyboard of the piano. Jim lifted his horn and played right alongside him as Ginger found her own place in the song and Cozy kept the beat.

Harlean began to sing. I sang with her.

The dancers danced in circles, streaming toward the double doors thrown open wide by Nova's employees. Tawney, Brewster, and the other federal agents were shoved off into a corner by the movement of the crowd.

As "Jingle Bells" rang out through the hall, as I rang the bells and sang, the world wobbled and changed. Trees appeared in the center of the ballroom with a path winding under their swaying branches. I saw Paul sprinting toward us, pursued by the scaled hounds.

CHAPTER TWENTY-THREE

I leapt from the stage, grabbing Paul's hands, and they were warm, solid, and so blessedly real. He almost stumbled as he tightened his hands on mine, but his feet found the rhythm. I swung him into the dance. "Circle, circle," I shouted over all the noise, as we waltzed after the last of the dancers streaming out of the double doors.

Behind us the path, the forest, and the hounds wobbled and wavered, one moment there and one moment gone. The band played on, Jim's horn sending notes floating in and above the music, somehow more distinct, as if I was hearing them through my soul rather than my damaged ears. In my earpiece, I heard another world, a howling rising with frustration as the hounds diminished and disappeared before chalked lines and triangles drawn by an enthusiastic group of mathematicians.

Paul and I danced across the lobby. The radio speakers set earlier by Reggie blared the music after us. Out the doors of the Diamond Dog and into the street we followed the dancers.

Ahead of us, the harness bells on Cuffe's horses rang out

as the sleigh took its position at the front of the parade. Singers crowded on the back bench of the sleigh caroled with the broadcast floating through the air. Looking up the street, I saw windows open in buildings with radios balanced on the sills. From all rose the song, "Jingle all the way!" as Billy and the band kept the broadcast going from the Diamond Dog.

Then Jim Culver danced down the steps past us, weaving amid the throng. Following close behind him were more slavering scaly hounds, slinking low, crawling on their bellies like snakes, as they flowed into the street. Jim led them all away from the dance, toward the opposite end of the street, and close behind ran the Mathematics Club, chalking straight lines and triangles all around the entrances of buildings and drawing the same symbols in the snow wherever they could.

Every now and then a hound would throw back its head and howl, and I heard it clearly in my earpiece. But on the street, all the music, all the ringing of the bells, drowned the beasts out. The dancers flowed after Cuffe's sleigh, apparently unaware of the beasts being drawn away in the opposite direction.

As we danced, the feeling of being split in two, split in three, split into a multitude of possibilities returned to me. This feeling, I now knew, was time unraveling and then coming back together. It was a wobble but it was more than that; the reality of Kingsport flying away in different directions and nearly overwhelming me. The only thing anchoring me to the here and the now was the feeling of Paul dancing with me and the ringing of the bells.

Settling my grip more firmly on Paul, I followed Jim, remembering Nova saying that Jim could make the music do what was wanted.

I looped my left arm around Paul's waist and rang my string of bells in my right hand. Paul rang a single silver bell clutched in his left hand. Side by side in our strange dance, we followed the wild music of Jim's trumpet.

But the more we danced, the more Paul seemed to be slipping away from me. From the corner of my eye, I could see him fade and reappear and fade away again. The bells grew more and more muffled as if the last of my hearing was also flickering out.

Still we danced. And I held on. Because nothing else mattered but that I hold on.

I gripped Paul tightly and danced, ignoring pains shooting up my legs, ignoring the dizzying sight of two pairs of legs becoming four, eight, or a hundred. Gritting my teeth, I danced. Snow and ice slushed into our shoes. Bright spots of blood marked where we stepped.

And I danced with Paul.

We stumbled through the steps, both of us dragging on the other. Holding tight to Paul, my arm felt like it was on fire. Against my other hand, the string of bells absorbed all the cold of the night, striking like frozen little hammers against my wrist or forearm with every shake. I felt each jarring note, every bruise, as the music blared from every window with a radio.

We danced.

"Here's the spot!" called Nova, who jogged out of the doorway of the garage where she stored her liquor. I realized she must have run through her bootlegging tunnels to beat us there. I was dizzy from dancing, and tired of dancing, and determined never to stop dancing.

"Here's where Chilton, Paul, and I all crossed paths," said Nova. "Hold on to Paul. We're almost done." I heard that. I don't know how, but I heard her when all the world's sound was fading away. Her voice came clear through my earpiece. I heard pride, and love, and fierce determination to never let go of all the future could offer.

"Hold on to me," I said to Paul and though he was shattering into three men, all of them looked at me. All of them saw me. And all kept dancing.

Jim nodded to Nova, never stopping his playing, but his variation on Billy's version of "Jingle Bells" began to change. It became even more compelling, more strident. The hounds twisted and leapt, trying to get away from the music. Paul pulled against my grip as if he felt compelled to dash into the alley's opening. I wound my arm as tightly as possible around him and pulled back, digging my heels into the snow and slush. He nearly pulled me off my feet, and two long drag marks, two straight lines, appeared behind me.

"Stay here!" I yelled at Paul.

With an agonized cry, he started to pull away. "I don't want to go!" he said, the very first words he'd spoken to me that night. "But I must. The dance must continue."

"Not you, not now," I said, toppling against him and clapping my hands over his ears. "Your dance is done."

We fell in a heap in the very same spot where Paul knocked Chilton Brewster off his feet a year ago.

Nova strode to us and without any hesitation sat on Paul's legs. "Hang on!" she said to me. "Almost midnight! We've done enough."

A terrible blue glow shading into horrible purple and green, a sickening light, grew at the end of the alleyway. I shifted my position, so I was kneeling across Paul's shoulders and one of his arms, my hands still muffling his ears. The ice and snow soaked through my skirt and stockings. But all I felt was the fetid warm air which blew from the forest appearing before us, a long path snaking between the grotesque trees.

With a cry, the hounds jumped over us onto the path. They sped away from Jim's playing. They ran away from Kingsport.

"Nearly time," panted Nova.

"It can't be midnight yet," I said. "We only started the dance."

"Time's been playing tricks," said Nova, "but my watch is accurate." She thrust out her hand to display her platinum and diamond watch encircling her sturdy wrist.

"Hold him down until the path closes," Nova instructed me, never budging from where she sat on Paul's legs. "Hold him tight."

I leaned into Paul with a whispered apology for any bruises. His eyes were staring into nothing, and I don't know if he heard me. I wasn't even sure if he was still alive, he lay so still under my hands, but I held on.

Shouts erupted behind us, breaking through the music. One of the hounds twisted its head, looking back over its shoulder at us.

"Stop, stop," yelled Tawney as he raced down the street, his men following him and dragging Brewster with them. "What are you doing?"

"Closing this path for good," Nova yelled back.

Tawney skidded to a halt beside her, looking longingly at the strange road leading through the monstrous forest. "You can't!" he said. "Think what we could do if we could alter the past!"

Brewster was dragged beside him. The once tidy banker twisted in his captor's arms, looking back at the Diamond Dog. "There's no flames," he said in wonder. "It's not burning."

"You can't mend the past," said Nova to both men. "But you can change the future." She checked her watch again. "One minute to midnight. This day will be over. The path closes forever."

"No!" shouted Tawney. "I must return to the night in the laboratory. I need Maleson's machine!" He had his pistol out and waved it wildly at all of us. "Get in there," he said, prodding at Brewster, "show me the way back!"

"I can't!" wailed Brewster. "I can't go there again!"

But Tawney dragged him forward onto the path. Both men appeared to be locked in a strange waltz, a series of steps which I realized matched the haunting rhythm played by Jim. The hound still watching us began to snarl.

"Stop!" I screamed, watching Tawney plunging under those strange trees, taking Brewster with him. But there was nothing and no one to hold them back. I couldn't let go of Paul. I could only watch as they disappeared onto a path that I hoped to never see again.

"Midnight!" declared Nova.

Without a wobble, without any sign at all, the alley was just an alley, cold and empty on a snowy December night.

Nova rose off Paul's legs. I gave him a hand to pull him into a sitting position and then hugged him hard. And, with delight, felt him hug me back.

"Merry Christmas!" Nova yelled at all of us.

"Baba Yaga," said Paul, scrambling to his feet and then shaking Nova's hand. He dropped her hand and threw his arms around her, hugging her hard. "Baba Yaga!" he said again in his husky voice.

Nova patted him on the shoulder once or twice, and then shoved him toward me.

"Go hug Raquel," she told him. "She's the one who saved you."

Paul stood in front of me, his clothing covered with bits of snow and ice where we'd pressed him to the ground. He was such an ordinary looking man. He looked wonderful.

"Oh," I said, not knowing what else to say. "Oh, you're here." I pulled him around, using both hands on the back of his jacket, trying to knock some of the snow away, trying not to cry with relief.

Paul turned impatiently and grabbed my hands. Then he pulled me into a tight embrace. "Raquel, Raquel," he murmured in my ear. I didn't have to hear him to know what he was saying.

Then he pulled back a little, freeing one hand to wipe the tears from his face. "My voice of hope," he said to me.

The sleigh went flashing by us, dancers still whirling in its wake. From all the windows, Billy and the band still played on the radio, loud enough for even me to hear.

"Let's get inside," said Nova, grabbing at us both. "I told the cooks to have pots of chowder ready for everyone."

Pulling me into a one-armed embrace, she whispered in a voice that could have been heard in Arkham, "And if there's sherry in the soup tonight, don't tell the government boys. Not that they seem all that interested in us."

I glanced behind her and saw the remaining brown-suited men searching the empty alleyway, calling for Tawney and Brewster. I linked arms with Paul and turned away.

"Come along," Nova said to us, "it's time to go home."

"But is it over? Truly over?" I said as we all walked up the steps into the Diamond Dog. "Is Paul here to stay?"

He smiled down at us both. "I cannot feel the path any longer."

"It's done," said Nova, not even looking back at the alley where the path had appeared and disappeared. "As I told Tawney, you cannot correct the past. But you can always change someone's future. There were enough people here, enough good intentions, that we shifted time into a new pattern."

The ballroom doors stood wide open. The tree glowed in its corner. Not a single decoration was harmed, not a smidgeon of smoke or ash could be seen.

As we strode through the ballroom doors, Billy gave a shout and brought his hands down on a final crash upon the keys. Poor Harlean, who had been singing straight for apparently two hours, was barely whispering into the microphone, but she saw us and smiled. Cozy banged his sticks upon the cymbals while Ginger played us in on her saxophone.

Back on the street, Jim Culver blew one last note on his horn and tipped his hat to the dancers streaming back into the hall.

"Chowder for everyone!" yelled Nova. "Soup is on!"

I pulled Paul into the line for the buffet table. "Nova says her soup is good for everything that ails you," I told him.

He stared in amazement at the tree and decorations, at the people chatting and laughing all around us, and then, finally, very warmly, he was smiling down at me.

"Then chowder we shall eat," he said.

Such a silly little sentence, and I could barely hear him, but it made me so happy. I adjusted the volume on my hearing aid and held his warm, living hand. I had found the phantom who had whispered in my ear, the lonely writer behind the fairytales in the journal, and he was real. I knew then the future would be worth living, no matter what it held.

Sometime later, we sat at a small table with bellies full of hot soup. Around us the music swelled until it shook the very walls. I could feel it although I would never hear it again as I had in the past. The distortion of the hearing aid gave the tune a hiss and a crackle. But there were no uncanny whispers or howls beneath the electric noise. Although I concentrated, I could hear no shouts from Chilton Brewster or Ralph Tawney. Wherever they were, their voices were silent to me.

I wrestled a battered little book out of my bag, where it had been crammed next to the battery for the hearing aid, and handed it to Paul. "This is yours," I said.

"This is ours," he replied, his hand covering mine on the cover. I turned my hand over and tangled my fingers in his.

"Merry Christmas," I said.

"Happy New Year," Paul said, and his fingers tightened around mine. "Year after year of new years." His voice broke and his hand trembled. "I survived," he said after a pause. "I am here, now, with you. The rest can be forgotten."

I examined the journal with its tattered cover. "I wonder who he was. The old man in the graveyard."

"An angel or a saint. He saved my mind. Without this book, that place would have eaten all my thoughts and left me an empty man."

"I wish we could thank him," I said. "But I think you met him too far in the future to find him now."

Paul nodded. "I don't know how we could thank him. He was dying when I saw him and so sad. I wish I could tell him that we succeeded."

With my free hand, because I was not yet ready to let go of Paul, I ran my fingers over the journal and for the first time noticed a pair of regular indentations different from the other scrapes and scratches. "Look," I said, "there's something here. Initials, I think, stamped on the cover."

Paul looked closer. "There was," he said slowly. "Two letters, in gold, but they wore away."

I traced the outlines of those initials. "CB," I said and then remembered the row of diaries behind the man's desk, all bound in leather and stamped on the corners with his initials in gold. His memoirs in the making, he told me. Every journal carefully preserved, except for this one.

"Chilton Brewster," I told Paul. "This journal belonged to

Chilton Brewster. Did he know when he gave you the journal that it would destroy his future even as it saved ours?"

"He was an old man dying full of regret. I do not think he cared what happened as long as the Diamond Dog was saved."

I would never like Chilton Brewster but, in that moment, I found enough mercy in my heart to hope that he would find his own way out of the woods, wherever and whenever that terrible place existed.

Billy ran his hands up and down on the piano keys. He called to the room, "Last dance! Pick your partner! Merry Christmas, everyone!"

I grabbed my headband and took it off, dropping it on top of the journal. Shrugging off the purse and disentangling the microphone's cord from around my neck, I freed myself from the hearing aid. I left the entire contraption on the table and stepped into Paul's arms.

He pulled me close. We danced to the music that I could no longer hear as clearly as I wished but I would always feel in my heart.

With every movement of Paul's body pressed so close to mine, the music reverberated through my own. Every breath we took, every step, formed its own music. Perhaps I would lose all ability to hear, but I would never lose my ability to feel. It was enough. It was more than enough on this Christmas Day.

Tugging my hand away from his waist, Paul pressed a single silver jingle bell into my palm. I curled my fingers around it and shook it, feeling the vibration against my flesh.

Paul leaned closer and kissed me. Like the bell in my hand, the kiss sounded through me.

When Paul broke off the kiss, he spoke directly into my left ear: "Snip, snap, snout, the tale is out."

I shook the jingle bell one last time and quoted my favorite ending back to him: "With the ring of a bell, they lived happily ever after."

1926 DECEMBER 1926

SUN.	MON.	TUE.	WED.	THU.	FRI.	SAT.
			1 *Chapters One to Three*	2	3 *Chapter Four*	4
5	6 *Chapter Five*	7 *Chapter Six*	8	9	10	11 *Chapter Seven*
12	13	14	15 *Chapters Eight to Ten*	16 *Chapters Eleven & Twelve*	17	18
19	20 *Chapters Thirteen to Fifteen*	21 *Chapter Sixteen*	22 *Chapters Seventeen & Eighteen* WINTER SOLSTICE	23	24* *Chapters Nineteen to Twenty-Three. Interlude. End.*	25 CHRISTMAS DAY
				30	31	

*Paul's interludes always occur on December 24:
1929 – "Ashcan" Pete and his dog Duke (Arkham)
1917 – Captain Leo (Innsmouth)
1944 – Agent Adams (Kingsport)
1919 – Carson Sinclair (Arkham)
1924 – Mandy Thompson and Dr William T Maleson (Arkham)
1933 – Preston Fairmont (Arkham)
1936 – Jim Culver (Dunwich)
1939 – Zoey Samaras (Kingsport)
1913 – Beatrice Sharpe (Arkham)
1908 – Agatha Crane (Arkham)
1925 – Nova Malone and Chilton Brewster (Kingsport)
1922 – Norman Withers (Arkham)
1946 – Young couple (Kingsport)
1890 – Sydney Fitzmaurice (Arkham)
1968 – Old man (Kingsport graveyard)

ACKNOWLEDGMENTS

Once again, this book could not have happened without my wonderful editor Lottie at Aconyte, who responded to my initial outline about an *Arkham Horror* novel set at Christmas with, "As long as you don't put Cthulhu in a paper hat." Thank you to the equally fabulous folks at Fantasy Flight Games who said, "This sort of thing would happen in Kingsport."

Special homage must be paid to the artist Dan Strange, who has now drawn three covers for my *Arkham Horror* books. He made Jeany, Betsy, and Raquel look exactly as I pictured, and the settings even better than I could describe. Nick continues to be the best art director ever, discovering an old photo which showed what must have been the exterior of the Diamond Dog, and making the insides of each book look as fabulous as the outside.

Finally, this one's dedicated to a lady long gone, a great-aunt who left home to attend music college and returned to become a bookkeeper. According to family legend, she never spoke of why she left college so abruptly and it wasn't until much later that she used a hearing aid in daily life. Her sisters often speculated that her deafness resulted from an illness while away from the family. One of my grandfathers also suffered severe hearing loss after freezing his ears while painting boxcars during the Midwest winters.

Another inspiring ancestor on the family tree was a cabin boy who walked off a ship in nineteenth century New York and kept going until he landed in Chicago. Upon entering a German neighborhood and hearing a language spoken that he understood, he stayed. Where he came from originally remains a mystery and why he left there is also unknown. However, anyone who has studied the history of the thousands who fled poverty, war, and religious persecution in the early twentieth century can find people like Paul.

A source of stories which sparked some ideas was David Armstrong's wonderful podcast *Broadway Nation* and his two-part episode on the writing of "White Christmas" by the Jewish immigrant Israel Beilin, better known as Irving Berlin. Still the bestselling record in history, the song created the notion of the desirability of a snowy Christmas in American culture, to the point that it is rare to hear a weather forecast in December that doesn't speculate about whether or not there will be a white Christmas. The song's most popular recording was done by Bing Crosby, a singer who quickly caught on to the importance of the new microphone technology when he started out in the late 1920s. Although Crosby didn't like being called a crooner, he definitely used the new mikes to make his singing more intimate and immediate for the listener.

David's podcast also reminded me of the incredible contributions of James Hubert "Eubie" Blake to American music. The Black pianist and composer and his collaborator Noble Sissle wrote "Shuffle Along," long credited as the first Broadway musical to not only feature an all-Black cast, but also be created and directed by Black artists. A huge hit in 1921, the musical was performed in New York and toured across the country, launching the careers of such stars as Josephine Baker and Paul Robeson. In 1923, Blake and Sissle performed their popular music in three short films with sound using the Phonofilm process, years before Al Jolson and *The Jazz Singer* heralded the end of the silent movie era.

Radio in the 1920s was as wild and wacky as the early days of the movies. At the beginning of the decade, stations were generally run from homebuilt transmitters and shared the same frequency with each other. Almost anyone with a little technical knowledge or willingness to learn could become a broadcaster.

Competition and the public appetite for content led to bigger live programs and variety entertainment on the radio. The heyday of scripted serials like *The Shadow* would come in the 1930s and 1940s. The 1939 Christmas Eve broadcast of *The Shadow* heard by Paul can be found on YouTube for your listening pleasure.

By the end of the 1920s, stations in larger cities were broadcasting live fourteen hours or more a day and "coast to coast" networks like NBC (National Broadcasting Company) were in place. But American radio still was, and would remain for decades, very flavored by the individuals who ran the stations and the community businesses who paid for the sponsorship of programs.

But what about bootleggers and bankers running radio stations? In 1920s Seattle, a couple ran a popular radio station out of their home. Raided by federal agents, Elise was accused of broadcasting coded information to Roy's rumrunners during her children's story hour. She was not convicted but Roy, who was also the chief of police at the time, did serve five years for his smuggling activity. According to some accounts, he ordered his bootleggers to not carry guns to prevent shootouts and smuggled "good" liquor out of Canada to stop alcohol poisoning from homebrew operations.

Across town a pair of Seattle bankers started a large scale radio operation, bringing in the best musicians from other cities for live programming. In the mess of the stock market crash of 1929, their frequent "borrowing" from their savings and loans to support the station and other business ventures led to fifteen years of incarceration for defrauding their customers and stockholders of $2 million. The station was sold to another banker who also eventually served time for inappropriate use of bank funds to support his radio venture.

The advances in sound technology also led to increasingly smaller and more portable hearing aids. Raquel's device is similar to those that I've been able to find online for the period with some adjustments for plot purposes. All the wonderful gadgets that Nova brought into her home can be found in the magazine advertisements of 1926. Kodak's Vest Pocket Autographic was a real and very popular camera which allowed photographers to jot notes directly on the paper backing of film. According to Kodak histories, 1.75 million were sold between 1915 and 1926.

As mentioned at the end of *The Deadly Grimoire*, female bootleggers operated throughout Prohibition. Many were, at the time, as famous as their male counterparts.

I'm profoundly grateful to my local public library system for access to the newspapers and publications of the era as well as the many enthusiasts who share their love for this history online.

With love and gratitude for all her support, many thanks to my mother for her reminiscences about her family and her own brief career as a teenage radio host (long after the 1920s! she asks me to clarify for you).

Most of all, to everyone who has read this far, thank you for coming on this adventure with me.

ABOUT THE AUTHOR

ROSEMARY JONES is an ardent collector of children's books, and a fan of talkies and silent movies. She is the author of bestselling novels in *Dungeons & Dragons'* *Forgotten Realms* setting, numerous novellas, short stories, and collaborations.

rosemaryjones.com // twitter.com/rosemaryjones

ARKHAM HORROR™

Countess Alessandra Zorzi returns!

*An occult thief takes on a sinister society
threatening to tear the fabric of this world
apart, in this daring noir-thriller set in
the crooked heart of Venice!*